Seduced
by
Sunday

Also by Catherine Bybee

Contemporary Romance

Weekday Brides Series

Wife by Wednesday
Married by Monday
Fiancé by Friday
Single by Saturday
Taken by Tuesday

Not Quite Series

Not Quite Dating
Not Quite Mine
Not Quite Enough
Not Quite Forever

Paranormal Romance

MacCoinnich Time Travels

Binding Vows
Silent Vows
Redeeming Vows
Highland Shifter
Highland Protector

The Ritter Werewolves Series

Before the Moon Rises
Embracing the Wolf

Novellas

Soul Mate
Possessive

Erotica

Kilt Worthy
Kilt-A-Licious

CATHERINE BYBEE

Seduced by Sunday

BOOK SIX IN THE WEEKDAY BRIDES SERIES

 Montlake
Romance

Published by Montlake Romance, Seattle

www.apub.com

Amazon, the Amazon logo, and Montlake Romance are trademarks of Amazon. com, Inc., or its affiliates.

ISBN-13: 9781477827772
ISBN-10: 1477827773

Cover design by Crystal Posey

Library of Congress Control Number: 2014952559

Printed in the United States of America

For Meg . . .
because why the hell not?

Chapter One

"If I ever decide to leave the matchmaking business, I'll have to consider taking up being a wedding coordinator." Meg Rosenthal lifted her flute glass and smiled at the passing bride.

"If you planned this little party, you wouldn't be standing beside me sipping champagne." Eliza Billings, first lady of the state of California, rested a hand on her six-months-and-counting baby bump. She wore her pregnancy with the grace and elegance of a woman due her title. Long, sleek black hair trailed down her back in dark contrast to Meg's short blonde bob and amber eyes. "You'd be running behind Shannon reminding her of the cake cutting and bouquet toss."

Shannon Redding, now Shannon Wentworth, was the bride du jour. She had married Paul Wentworth, the Republican candidate for the governor seat. Eliza's husband, Carter Billings, would vacate said post in a little over a year and a half. Paul and Shannon Wentworth had a wedding arrangement due to last two years, less if Paul didn't obtain the popular vote. The voting public wanted their politicians married and stable. Since Paul was ready to run for office, but not marriage, he hired Alliance to find him a suitable bride. With any luck, after Paul spends four years in office, the people of California would have faith in the man's ability to hold the governor's office as a divorced man.

Eliza was right. Meg would rather set up temporary marriages such as Paul and Shannon's than pick wedding colors and venues. Her job was much easier and much more lucrative.

Paul came from a long lineage of political families. He had money, influence, and charm. Unfortunately, his taste in women often left him on the front page of the tabloids instead of the *Wall Street Journal*.

Shannon also happened to come from a family of lawyers and wannabe politicians. Much to the dismay of her family, law wasn't something she was willing to study. Photography was her passion. Pictures didn't pay the bills, however, and her family wasn't willing to give her a trust fund if she squandered away her life taking snapshots.

Shannon was the exact client profile Alliance loved to recruit. Intelligent, lovely with a certain poise one was born to, and determined to live by her own set of rules. A prenuptial agreement, along with a private contract that only Alliance and Paul's lawyers knew about, linked the happy couple long before the wedding day. Paul would set Shannon up as his wife, take care of her every need during their marriage, and when they walked away after two years, Shannon would have six million dollars in her bank.

She wouldn't need her family's trust fund.

Meg stepped aside when Carter swept up to his wife's side and slid an arm around her waist. "Loveliest woman in the place," he said loud enough for Meg to hear.

Eliza snuggled closer to her husband as color filled her cheeks. You'd think after over six years of marriage, with a baby on the way, a woman wouldn't blush with a compliment from her husband, but apparently Meg was wrong.

The sound of someone ringing the side of a glass filled the reception hall. The attention of the guests moved to the couple, who were obliged to kiss every time someone started ringing.

Meg watched with interest as Paul set his glass down and reached for his bride. With the exception of herself and the Billings, everyone here thought the couple had married for love and forever. The kiss in the church had been brief. Sweet, but brief. What would it be now?

Paul removed the glass from Shannon's hand and offered a playful smile before he lowered his lips to hers.

Meg started to count. *One one thousand, two one thousand, three one thousand . . .* Shannon's palm gripped his lapel *. . . four one thousand . . .*

"Interesting," Eliza whispered when they broke off at six one thousand.

Shannon carried a rose-colored blush, and Paul stood back regarding her with a whole lotta heat in his eyes.

Meg leaned toward Carter. "You might wanna remind your friend of the rules."

Carter shook his head and lifted both hands in the air. "Not my job."

The rules were simple. Alliance arranged marriages, not sex. If the temporary contract resulted in true feelings or even temporary feelings, Alliance didn't deal with child custody. Period. As Samantha, or Sam as her friends called her, the owner of Alliance, had put it . . . if the couple decided to live married life past the time the contracts were set up, they should enjoy their happily-ever-after and name the first child after her. Or in this case, Meg . . . since she'd been the one who had arranged the marriage.

Carter pulled Eliza onto the dance floor and Meg made her way over to the bride. She knew that as the night wore on, their time in the same room would be limited.

"That looked very cozy," Meg whispered once she pulled Shannon away from listening ears.

Shannon fanned herself; the smile she'd worn all day didn't fall. "He was a player before becoming a politician."

Meg tapped her shoulder. "You remember that."

"You don't have to tell me. Certain things are expected here. Our honeymoon will be easier."

"Where are you going?"

"There's a private resort in the Keys, very posh. Plenty of celebs and people who want their private life private choose the destination as a getaway. Security is top-notch, and all the clients are pre-screened."

"Prescreened for what?" And who would pay to go on a vacation where you had someone checking your background?

"Reporters, those who might leak information to the public on who is there and who they might be with . . . that kind of thing. We have a freestanding two-bedroom bungalow on the beach. Very private. There won't be any press there to catch . . . or *not catch* anything."

Interesting.

"Why is it I don't know about this place?" It sounded exactly like the kind of resort to find private clients, or to ensure her current clients could vacation without the watchful eyes of the press.

"Not sure. Seems like a given in your line of work," Shannon said.

It was a given, wasn't it? Alliance needed places like this all around the globe.

Paul found the ladies. His tie hung over his collar, his easy smile and charm that turned many women's heads fell on Shannon. "I thought you'd left me already."

Shannon rolled her eyes and didn't flinch when he placed a hand on her back.

Paul glanced at Meg and winked.

He laughed when she narrowed her eyes and frowned.

"They need us for cake cutting," he told his temporary bride.

Before they could leave Meg's side, she shook her finger at Paul. "Behave."

He winked a second time.

Meg knew that *behave* wasn't a word in Paul Wentworth's vocabulary.

———

Sapore di Amore Villa and Suites was a hell of a lot more than a hotel.

It was an island. A private island sandwiched between two of the larger keys. Getting there required a private plane, or a charter off the mainland. Helicopters were a favorite form of transportation for those wanting to bask in the Caribbean sun without the flash of the paparazzi cameras.

From the pictures Shannon had sent her after she and Paul returned from the resort, Meg made it a daily task to arrange her trip to Sapore di Amore.

She secured the finances to visit the island through Sam, and then procured Sam and Blake's private jet to fly her there.

Now all she needed was a date.

The date was the kicker.

Until she remembered that Michael Wolfe, Hollywood hotshot movie star, was the big brother of her best friend, Judy.

Every uterus in the free world sought after Michael. Problem was, he didn't play for that team, a fact that Meg had realized after joining Alliance.

The shock had come to Meg shortly after her BFF Judy married the love of her life, Rick Evans.

Meg and Judy had gone to college together and then moved to Southern California. Both were headed in different employment directions. Judy was destined to rise in the ranks of professional architecture, where Meg had no idea what she would do with her business degree. Luck and timing placed her with Samantha Harrison and Alliance. The matchmaking service for the elite wasn't anything Meg thought she'd studied for. Yet the job suited her perfectly.

OK, maybe not with perfection.

Having grown up with very little, it was often hard to blend with the rich and famous. But in the last couple of years, she'd managed to do just that. She'd found a handful of clients, both paying men and willing women, to fill the client base of Alliance.

Once Meg proved herself to Sam, she learned the secrets of Alliance. She discovered that Michael had married a woman through Alliance simply to fend off any media or bad press due to his personal life.

Michael's career was lucrative to the degree of thirty to forty million per film, and Hollywood liked their heartthrobs heterosexual.

Michael had opened up to a few family members and those within Alliance about his sexuality. His parents and the rest of the world had no idea.

In her opinion, Michael would probably keep his personal desires hidden for years to come.

So when she'd asked him if he would be game to a little cat and mouse in the Keys, he'd been more than happy to jump.

When she'd told him about how the resort was a paparazzi-free zone, and she was there on a recon mission to determine if the place actually kept secrets . . . secret, he was even more intrigued.

One tiny problem.

Meg wasn't passing Sapore's background check.

Or at least that's how she translated the letter from the desk of Valentino Masini.

Valentino had some nerve.

Madam,

While we have accepted the application of Michael Wolfe, we've yet to secure the credentials of Margaret Rosenthal. While we respect the references of the past eighteen months, we're concerned about the previous timeline. Please accept our apologies while we search further.

Please understand that every guest at Sapore di Amore is highly respected and their privacy is of utmost importance . . . as is yours if you join us.

We shall have an answer to your request within the coming weeks.

Sincerely,
Valentino Masini

Meg knew a form letter when she saw it. Place a name here, omit a name there . . . bottom line, before Alliance, Meg was a nobody.

In reality, she still was. She just knew some seriously loaded and influential people.

Meg's own people were on the *nobody* side of life.

Letters like this drove home her biggest insecurity. She stood beside the elite, wore clothing from the same boutiques they did . . . rode in private planes for crying out loud . . . but she wasn't one of them.

Still.

Rejection ate at the pit of her stomach and made her skin crawl.

How dare Valentino reject her. Valentino! What the hell kind of name was that anyway?

Made up, she decided. A name formed by ambition and not given by his mother.

Besides, Valentino's secretary probably wrote the letter.

Valentino was probably a balding old man sitting in some musty brick building in Italy where the sun made him thick with musk that would choke anyone standing by.

"*If I join you* my ass," Meg said to herself while she responded to the e-mail.

Dear Mr. Masini,

While I completely understand your concern and I respect your need for privacy, you'll see by my references and my traveling companion, security and secrecy are just as important to me as they are you. More so.

I despise name-dropping, however, it seems necessary for me to encourage you to expedite our reservations.

Perhaps you're familiar with Carter and Eliza Billings. I'd suggest you call the governor's mansion, but the staff there would never let you through.

Enclosed is a personal number for Eliza and Carter. I'm sure you understand the need for their private number to remain private.

I expect to hear from you shortly.

Sincerely,
Miss Rosenthal

"Asshole," Meg mumbled to herself before she called Eliza.

Once she hung up the phone with Eliza, she turned off her computer and walked into the kitchen.

Her boss and the first lady once occupied the Tarzana town house. Seemed Alliance had a steady home, but those in the day-to-day running of the business changed every few years. Early on, Meg had been told that those who slept in the master bedroom of the house found their spouse within a few short years of sleeping there. The evidence was in the vows exchanged by the employees of Alliance through the years.

Needless to say, Meg didn't sleep in the master bedroom.

She'd always found herself attracted to men who couldn't provide anything . . . emotional or financial. The thought of marriage and forever made her break out in hives.

She did not intend to find a mate. Living where she worked, however, made perfect sense.

When she'd first started working for Sam, she'd thought . . . maybe . . . maybe she could do the temp-hubby thing. What was wrong with finding a temporary spouse who would pay her off at the end of a year?

Then she realized she could make some serious money setting up said marriages and live her life as she saw fit.

Call it superstition . . . or maybe it was the scent of the pot her parents loved to smoke seeping in . . . but Meg wasn't sleeping in the master bedroom for fear the room was cursed.

She banked the money she made, took a couple of trips to see her parents . . . paid off her student loans, loans she didn't think she'd ever pay back. She'd always assumed those loans would be a part of a chapter, *something* in her future. Did anyone ever pay back their student loans these days?

As it stood, Meg made decent money and lived virtually free.

Trips to places like Sapore di Amore were on Alliance, and Alliance had deep pockets.

At the end of the day, however, when Meg tossed off her designer heels and slipped out of the evening gown, she sat in sweatpants with a big bowl of popcorn watching the latest action flick on TV. There were the nights she'd spend with her friends, shooting pool, or in her case, watching them shoot pool . . . or the occasional karaoke night where she'd dream.

Tonight was popcorn night.

Karaoke wasn't in the cards without her best friend, and the other people she knew were all either married or busy.

Popcorn it was.

Taking a beer from the fridge, Meg walked over to the upright she'd purchased with her first paycheck.

The piano sat in the living room and did more than house family photographs.

After plucking a few notes, Meg found herself playing a classic.

Only the words she used for "My Funny Valentine" weren't as the original composer intended.

No . . . *her* funny valentine had a few choice names and descriptions that fit her mood.

Valentino was an assable. And every day was *not* Valentine's Day.

Chapter Two

"I can't believe you're pretending to date my brother just to check out a hotel." Judy, Meg's best friend, flopped on the bed and leaned on her arm.

Meg moved through the room while she packed.

"What better way to determine if this resort is everything the brochure says it is than to have Mr. Famous walking around the place? If it's überprivate, then very few people will know he's actually there. He won't end up in a tabloid, and no one will think I'm dating him. Well, except for those at the actual hotel."

"Why bother then? Might as well take me." Judy grinned and batted her lashes several times.

"Neither of us are famous. No one will be looking for a beautiful blonde"—Meg flipped her short hair and winked—"and her sidekick friend. Michael, on the other hand . . ."

Judy shook her head and laughed. "I know. We can't go to lunch without a camera lurking. How long are you going to stay?"

"A week."

"Why so long? Seems like a lot for a recon mission."

Meg rolled her eyes. "Recon mission? You're starting to sound like Rick." Judy's husband was a Marine . . . well, former, retired, or whatever it was he called it. He said things like *recon mission* all the time.

"Isn't that what it is?"

Meg packed the side pockets of her suitcase with a couple of bathing suits.

"I suggested four days, Michael wanted a week. Between him and Samantha, they're buying. Who am I to say no?"

Judy pushed off the bed and moved to the closet. "You need more summer dresses. It's going to be hot and humid."

Having grown up in Washington State, where moss grew on every side of a stone, owning a pair of sandals, as in one pair, was more than enough for the summer. Adjusting to the California sun had been a pleasure, but Meg still hadn't embraced summer dresses to the extent Judy had.

"Michael and I are going shopping during the layover in Dallas. If we don't find everything I need, then I'll have Michael take me to Key West."

"Won't that compromise your privacy?"

Meg wiggled her eyebrows, did her best *I'm devious* impression. "It will. I'll be interested to see how the resort will handle an onslaught of lookie-loos boating up the Keys to catch a glimpse of Michael. If they can keep the cameras offshore, then I might have found the right place to recommend that our clients honeymoon."

"What keeps you from texting pictures or hooking up with social media?"

"You hand over your cells when you arrive. If you want to make a call, there are phones in your room and around the resort. You're not completely unplugged, but as close as you can be and still live in this century."

"No cell phones? That's crazy."

"I know."

"You'll have to charter something and head to Key West. I think you'll go nuts on a private island without the Internet."

Meg shoved several pairs of shorts next to her bathing suits. "The lack of Internet isn't my concern. It's the week with stuffy people that I find troubling."

"How do you know they're stuffy?"

"They're hiding. Chances are they'll either be holed up in their bungalows banging someone they shouldn't be, or holding their chins high and flaunting their wealth or fame. The place is stupid expensive."

"Not everyone with money is stuck-up."

"Did we ever meet any of Michael's neighbors when we were living in his house?"

Judy wrinkled her nose.

"Exactly." They'd lived in the Beverly Hills estate for eight months when they'd both moved to the state. Meg remembered talking with the hired help in the neighborhood, but not the owners.

Of course, many of them were like Michael . . . not home very often.

"Michael knows how to party. He doesn't know how to hide in the background. I'm sure you'll have a great time."

Meg shrugged. She wasn't going there for the ultimate vacation. She planned on finding the resort's flaws. After waiting nearly two months for an approval from Valentino Masini, the man, and his hotel, deserved a microscopic test.

She planned on delivering it.

⎯⎯•⎯⎯

Val Masini tapped the edges of the last e-mail he'd printed out from Miss Rosenthal against his palm before checking his watch. He didn't always meet his guests on the tarmac, but for Miss Rosenthal and Mr. Wolfe, he'd make an exception.

He'd personally made the phone call to the first lady of California, half expecting a fraud to answer his call.

He'd been wrong.

In fact, Eliza Billings not only told him that Margaret Rosenthal was everything she claimed to be, but that if Valentino Masini knew what was good for him, he'd be on his best behavior during Margaret's stay.

Miss Rosenthal alone had the power to bring him a client base that would prove lucrative for years to come. Since word of mouth was how Val made Sapore di Amore thrive, he needed voices singing his praises. Even if that voice belonged to the snarky woman who delivered stinging letters.

"Gabi?" Val knocked on the door to his sister's suite.

"Just a minute."

Less than two seconds passed and he knocked again. "Check your makeup in the cart, Gabi. We can't be late."

He was about to knock a third time when the door swung open. "I just need to gather my purse."

Before Gabi could turn away, Val grabbed her hand and pulled her out into the sunshine. "There's no need for a purse."

"Val!"

"The plane will land in ten minutes. There's no time."

Gabriella pushed out her bottom lip in a full pout. His sister's beauty would make the *Mona Lisa* cry with envy. Lush black hair, dark watchful eyes, and olive skin that many women worked their entire lives to achieve. Gabi was born to it. They both were.

"I don't understand why you're in such a rush. You've had other, more important guests come to the island."

"Michael Wolfe is in a class by himself. The paparazzi will search him out en masse if they learn he's here."

"Your guests never tell the media where they're vacationing."

"Yet the press always hunts for them." Sometimes they found them. But not on Sapore.

They stepped into the open bench seat of one of the villa's golf carts.

The driver took off the moment they were secure.

Sapore di Amore was Val's pride. In five years, he'd taken a simple island getaway and turned it into one of the most exclusive resorts in the world.

Screening all of his clients to ensure their privacy was of utmost importance.

Some clients, like the one arriving today, weren't on his top list of wanted guests. Well, he was intrigued with Margaret's tenacity and thinly veiled jabs. Val looked through them and expected to dismiss her. Yet he couldn't, and since he'd had no choice but to accept her presence, he was determined to learn as much as he could about her in a few short hours and decide for himself if she was a security risk. Keeping his temper in check if her demeanor was the same in person as it was in an e-mail would prove challenging.

Between the wind blowing off the sea and the speed that their driver managed on the narrow road, Gabi's hair blew in every possible direction. "I don't know why I bother with anything other than a tie in my hair," she said.

A long cascade of trees lined the road. It opened to a small airstrip where only private jets and the occasional helicopter would land. "If you didn't primp, I'd know something fatal was on the horizon."

Gabi clicked her tongue. "Such drama, Val."

He lifted the left corner of his mouth and glanced to the sky.

The private jet carrying his guests descended on the island on a rapid approach. The runway was short, not giving the pilot much time to bring the plane down.

The landing gear hit the tarmac, the engines screamed as the pilot reversed the engine thrust.

Gabi smoothed back her hair once the golf cart came to a complete stop.

Val offered his hand to his sister and led her to the welcome cabana as the plane taxied into position and an attendant secured the wheels. The airport employees scrambled to assist the onboard flight crew as they opened the hatch and lowered the stairway.

Val tapped his index finger along his thigh and lifted his chin.

His sister laid a hand on his, stopped his tapping. "They're just people," she reminded him.

Yet as his gaze fell on the heeled foot of the female passenger and slowly made its way up, he knew this woman was much more than *just* anything.

Her sundress, all polka-dotted red and cut in the style of the twenties, was anything but understated.

He swallowed, hard.

Val decided the slim-fitting dress wasn't a sundress after all . . . it was something that belonged on Hollywood's glamour queens from days past.

He liked it . . . all the way from the tops of her shapely knees— since when did he notice the shape of a woman's knees?—to the slim belt at her waist. The cut of the dress emphasized her breasts . . . happy, healthy specimens that overflowed the bounds of cloth with just enough skin to make him a happy heterosexual male.

When he finally looked at her face, he noticed she wore her hair in a manicured style that matched the twenties, with big curls and lots of hairspray. Her lips were ruby red. Her sunglasses hid the color of her eyes.

He liked the look of the whole package. Why she had to be so sexy when he really wanted her to be this side of a troll, ticked him off.

His body responded even when his head was telling it to shut up.

Only then did he look past the woman to the man who placed his hand on her waist and helped her from the plane.

The movie star wore clothes complementing his girlfriend's, his sunglasses just as large . . . but he couldn't hide who he was.

Val pulled his thoughts back into focus and took a few steps toward his arriving party.

He lifted his hand to Margaret first. "*Signorina*, welcome to my island."

She brought her hand up on instinct, and hesitated when Val lifted it to his lips for a kiss.

"Mr. Masini."

The taste of his name, albeit his surname, on her lips had him holding her hand a tad too long.

"I feel as though I know you," she told him.

He couldn't see her eyes, furthering his irritation. He couldn't tell if her comment was a continuation of the jabs or a statement of fact. "I hope that's a good thing."

She said nothing, only smiled.

Jabs.

"Michael, Mr. Masini." Margaret introduced them as if it were her job, and he finally let her hand go.

"Mr. Wolfe needs no introduction."

Michael Wolfe glanced beyond him to his sister. "And who is this starlet?"

"You're so kind," Gabi said, her smile beaming.

"*Signorina* Rosenthal, *Signor* Wolfe, my sister, Gabriella. Whatever we may do for you during your stay, you need only ask."

Margaret sighed. "Is Sapore di Amore a family affair?"

"Not at all. This is my brother's brainchild. I'm simply window dressing."

"*Cara!*" The endearment was anything but.

Yet Margaret's smile blossomed. What color were her eyes, he mused. Blue, green? A mixture of both? The pictures he'd seen did her no justice.

"My sister spends much of her time on the island. I'm lost without her."

Although he meant for his statement to remain on the surface, he felt it down to his bones.

"Ah, behind every good man is a woman, eh, Gabriella?" Michael's charm filled any awkward space.

"I think I like you, Mr. Wolfe."

Michael Wolfe smiled, moved closer to Margaret.

She hesitated and moved closer toward her companion.

"We'll be taking a short drive to the villa. We use battery-operated carts on the island. Your luggage will follow."

She tilted her sunglasses to take a good look at the cart, then returned them to the bridge of her nose.

He smiled, seeing her eyes for the first time.

"How very *green* of you, Mr. Masini." Margaret's short tone sounded like a cut and reminded him of her e-mails.

Her eyes forgotten, he swallowed his desire to snap at Margaret's words, and he revealed the facts about his island in the same short tone she'd used. "The golf carts have more to do with space than my desire to reduce my carbon footprint. The island has limited resources, fuel being one of them. Not to mention my guests come here to relax, get away . . . they don't want the noise of oiled-fueled engines interrupting that."

"Meg told me all about your island," Michael said, changing the subject. "I'm looking forward to a little R & R."

Meg . . . she went by Meg.

That suited her better, Val decided. Margaret fit a work persona. Meg fit the woman standing in the flirty dress and sexy smile.

"Then R & R you shall have." Gabi always knew exactly what to say. "My brother's resort will offer you everything you could possibly want."

"Meg tells me your island is free of random photography. How do you control that with all the cell phones in this world?"

Val led his guests to the golf cart, encouraged them to take the backseat, and lifted a hand to Gabi as she climbed in.

"It's not that complicated. The use of smartphones on the island isn't allowed."

Michael Wolfe appeared mildly amused. "Not allowed?"

Val twisted in his seat as the driver pulled away from the airstrip.

"When we arrive at your private villa, I'll ask that you surrender your phones. Your accommodations will have telephone access; you'll be given digital cameras for on-island use. The images will be checked before you return home for the protection of our other guests."

"And if I give permission for some of your other guests to take my picture?"

Val grinned. "Release forms will be signed by all parties. You'll find that most of my guests like to remain anonymous while they're here. Celebrities such as you visit us often, but my team generally takes the only images of them here. We will be happy to take professional shots throughout your stay if you like."

"I might feel naked without my phone," Michael said.

"You'll feel liberated," Gabi told him. "It's difficult to relax when your phone is buzzing every few minutes."

Michael glanced at Meg. "Did you tell me about the phone thing?"

"I told Tony. He said he hated the idea but you'd taken to phone silence at least once before and returned from that vacation ready to work."

The cart slowed to a stop in front of a private villa. "Here we are," Val said.

Massive hibiscus plants of all colors bloomed along the path leading to the front door. Palms and ferns filled the space between the larger trees. Val knew the landscape well, he'd picked nearly every plant species himself when he'd first commissioned their planting. He wanted to inspire tranquility, give the air fragrance, and camouflage the other villas nearby.

"The pictures don't do this justice," Meg said under her breath.

"Thank you, Miss Rosenthal."

The slight smile on her lips fell. Val couldn't help but think her compliment wasn't meant for his ears.

Gabi opened both doors and crossed into the open great room.

The vaulted ceiling held several rotating fans and had a white pine finish. Muted colors of the Caribbean complemented the space. Overstuffed sofas and love seats, an open kitchen with marble countertops, and a dining room for four . . . tile floors and, of course, wall-to-wall windows that opened to the deck beyond. The ocean view and walk-out beach were nothing short of perfect.

Michael whistled as he walked into the space and opened the disappearing glass doors. The sound of the lapping sea filled the room. "I think I can give up my cell phone for this." He reached into his pocket and tossed said phone on a nearby chair before stepping outside.

Gabi stepped outside with him while Meg stayed back.

"What about you, Miss Rosenthal? Have I fulfilled your needs?"

She met his gaze and removed her sunglasses. Her eyes were a honey amber . . . not brown, but not quite hazel. Her driver's license probably categorized them as a normal light brown. They were anything but normal.

"It takes more than a view to ensure my needs are met, Mr. Masini. It took some convincing to get here. I hope the rest of our stay will be easier."

"Whatever you and Mr. Wolfe need," he said with a slight bow. "You need only ask."

She reached into her small clutch, removed her phone, and extended her hand.

Val's fingertips grazed hers with the exchange and she pulled back.

Her cheeks flushed and she looked away.

Gabi's and Michael's voices carried into the room. They laughed at something, shaking Val out of Margaret Rosenthal's amber-eyed trance. "You'll find maps of the island, our chef's specials, spa hours . . . everything you need in your welcome packet."

"I've had clients swear by your chef's specials. I look forward to sampling them." She licked her red lips and Val had an instant desire to sample her.

He was staring and had to stop.

Val pushed away from the counter and stepped toward the open veranda. "Gabi. We should let our guests settle."

Gabi offered a practiced smile and reentered the villa, while Val said good-byes. "Enjoy your visit, Miss Rosenthal."

"I plan on it."

Chapter Three

"Good Lord, Meg, you didn't say the man who owned this joint was hot."

If there was one thing she loved about Michael, it was his ability to open up about his sexuality when it was just the two of them.

"I honestly didn't know. Pictures of Valentino Masini don't exist." The fact probably had something to do with the irritating rules about taking pictures while on the island. Lord knows she wouldn't have been able to refrain from taking a shot of him to show Judy when she returned home.

When she'd stepped off the plane, the weight of Valentino's eyes had fallen on her like a restraint on a rollercoaster. She knew, given the snappy, short conversations via e-mail, that he hadn't expected her professionalism, or her appearance. She sure as hell hadn't imagined him to fill out his suit like a man who lived in the gym . . . well, maybe not lived, but Masini didn't dip into the dessert menu from the looks of his taut chest, which slimmed to a tight waist and perfect ass.

She really hoped he hadn't seen through her dark sunglasses. Getting caught checking out his butt would have completely shattered the image she was trying to portray.

Masini's face looked like it belonged to a man who lived on an island. His clothes, however, were a different story. She wondered if he wore the uptight suit all the time. A farmer's tan on that body would be a crime.

He's still an ass, she reminded herself.

Meg smoothed a hand over her waist, happy she and Michael had a little shopping spree during the necessary layover in Dallas.

"No girlfriend of mine would walk around in ordinary shorts and flip-flops," Michael had told her.

The 1920s vintage look was a last-minute decision. Surprisingly, Meg liked it. The dress made her feel like finding a dark, smoky bar with an open mic. She wondered, briefly, if there was such a nightclub on the island. Or maybe Key West.

"Well, he's sexy. Love the accent."

Meg hated that she'd noticed. Valentino was a good six one, his hair was coal black, his face clean-shaven. He'd be hard to resist with a little stubble on his chin. Then there was the way he stared with his dark, smoldering eyes. Meg found herself sucking in a frustrated breath.

"Maybe you two can hook up," she told Michael.

"Oh, hon . . . he's straight. Guaran-ass-teed. His eyes were on you, not me."

"He wasn't looking at me."

"Ha!" Michael's laugh filled the room.

A knock on the door interrupted their conversation.

An attendant placed their luggage in one of the bedrooms, and after Michael attempted to tip the man, he shook his head and promptly left.

"He didn't even blink. Do you think he recognized you?" Meg asked.

"I couldn't tell."

Meg moved to take her suitcase off the folding stand. "I'll set up in the other bedroom."

"This one's larger, you take it."

"Don't be ridiculous."

Michael hoisted his case and moved toward the second bedroom.

"Won't the maid become suspicious?"

"Isn't that the point of being here? Find the possible breach in their system so your clients know what they're walking into?" Michael said.

He had a point.

"Fine." She unzipped her suitcase. "The closet in here is bigger anyway. I need it for all the crap you bought me."

Michael offered his Hollywood smile and walked away.

Secretly, Meg hoped Sapore di Amore was everything Masini boasted it was. Truth was, if Michael managed to keep his lifestyle hidden on the island, Meg saw him returning with a lover. Even in this century, Hollywood liked their ladies' men straight. Since Michael earned a small fortune with every action film he shot, he wasn't about to reveal his lifestyle anytime soon. Then there was Alliance. Meg and Samantha had both jumped at the idea of a private island that could house their clients after their weddings.

"What do you want to do first?" she asked through the open doors while she hung up her clothes.

"I say we check the place out, see for ourselves just how secluded Sapore di Amore is."

Meg moved into the adjoining bathroom and placed her toiletries on the counter. The medication she took to control her asthma came next; she placed an inhaler inside her small clutch and zipped it closed.

She took in her reflection in the mirror. Her makeup was heavier than she normally wore. She made kissy lips and marveled at how well the lipstick stayed on. They'd taken a private charter from Miami to the island, but she'd applied the lipstick in Texas. That had been hours ago. "I can use a drink."

"Me, too."

She turned around and attempted to reach the zipper of her dress behind her back. After three attempts, she gave up and walked to Michael's room. She presented her back. "You talked me into this thing but a girl needs to breathe."

The zipper went down and Michael gave her a little shove. "You look great in it."

"I'm not a girlie girl, but I have to admit, I like it, too."

After changing into one of her new sundresses, a simple orange number, and sandals instead of flip-flops, she grabbed her clutch and met Michael in the living room. He'd changed into a short-sleeved silk shirt and cotton shorts. Even with the big-rimmed glasses, there was no hiding his identity.

She placed her sunglasses on her nose and stepped beside him. "Ready?"

There were still a couple of hours until dinner and the high sun was starting to ease its way down.

They followed the walking paths instead of the beach route. Each of the private villas hid behind a beautifully landscaped greenbelt.

The main building was a sprawling two-story structure with open balconies with both vacationing patrons and employees milling about. The swimming pool meandered around makeshift islands, complete with water falling into it from what appeared to be a man-made stream.

Island music spilled from hidden speakers. Like with any high-end resort, waiters walked around the pool, filling drink orders and bringing fresh towels.

A few heads turned their way when they found a high table close to the outside bar.

Meg noticed at least one woman lounging by the pool point their way. It wasn't possible to go unnoticed, the question was how people would react.

A waiter, probably in his midtwenties, and extremely cute in a boyish kind of way, placed two napkins in front of them within seconds. "Welcome to Sapore di Amore," he greeted them. "My name is Ben and I'll be serving you while you're by the pool."

"How do you know we've just arrived?" Meg asked, already quizzing the staff to find flaws. She noticed her tone sounded bitchy and tried to smile to cover for it.

"Mr. Masini assigns staff to his guests, Miss Rosenthal." Ben stood back, placed his hands behind his back.

"And how does Mr. Masini determine who takes care of whom?" She knew she was interrogating the man, but understanding the system would pave the way to finding the weakness.

Ben offered a quick smile to Michael before he continued. "I might have been the only one on the poolside staff that didn't squeal when we heard Mr. Wolfe was joining us."

That had Michael smiling.

"You don't watch my movies?"

"Oh, I watch them. I'm not starstruck. I hope that's OK with you."

Michael smiled. "Perfectly."

"Before I take your order, how would you like the staff to address you? Do you use an alias?"

Meg couldn't hold in a laugh. "Maybe we should call you Harvey."

Michael removed his sunglasses and offered a pointed stare. "Let's stick with Michael."

"But Harvey—"

"Margaret!" Oh, that burned.

"You can call me Meg and Michael, Michael."

Ben offered a quick nod. "What are you drinking?"

Ben walked away after taking their order and she took another look around. "Am I the only one who feels like we've taken a plane ride to Fantasy Island and Mini-Masini is going to pop out at any moment?"

Michael tossed his head back and laughed.

———

Val sipped his bourbon and watched the activity by the pool from his office perch. His eyes were drawn to his new guests the moment they walked into view. Margaret Rosenthal's vintage hairstyle and natural beauty gave her the movie star appearance, Michael, *her* arm dressing.

His gaze moved beyond the couple to the other guests.

Mrs. Clayton, wife of billionaire Ron Clayton, Internet gaming mogul, kept eyeing Michael and laughing with her guest, Cynthia Hernandez. Though the women were here on a *girls' weekend*, in truth, they were both sleeping with men who were not their husbands, who had taken another villa next door to theirs. The fact that Mrs. Clayton kept staring made Val take note. About half of his guests were at his resort for clandestine rendezvous. The others didn't want to be bothered during their vacations.

The question was . . . where did Michael and Margaret fall?

Clandestine?

Or don't screw with me?

Val couldn't help but think they weren't on a simple vacation.

"You worked hard to obtain access to my island, Margaret . . . why?" he whispered to the closed window.

The phone on his desk buzzed, he pressed the speaker to answer. "Yes, Carol?"

"Mr. Picano is pulling into the loading dock."

"Is Gabi there?"

"She's on her way."

"Thank you." Val disconnected the call from his secretary and took his sunglasses from his desk before heading out the door. Spying on the movie star and his companion would have to wait.

He jogged down the stairway instead of taking the elevator to the ground floor.

The mouthwatering scents from the kitchen told him the staff there was already baking the evening's desserts and the roasts were in the ovens. There would be fresh fish selections plucked right from the sea surrounding them and organic vegetables brought in daily from the mainland.

When he thought of the word *organic*, he pictured Margaret making her comment about *being green*.

Words like *fresh* and *organic* were all over his chef's menu. That's what happened when you employed only the finest in the culinary arts. Would she poke fun at his menu? Would she find fault? And why was he spending any time wondering what the woman thought?

Val sat behind the wheel of his personal golf cart and sped toward the docks.

He found Gabi and Alonzo Picano standing beside each other. Alonzo's personal yacht was a buzz of activity as several crates were removed and stacked on the pier.

"Picano?" Val called to acquire his attention.

The man turned and presented a full-wattage smile. "There you are."

Val offered a strong handshake, felt the confidence inside the other man with the simple gesture. "What have you brought us?"

"Wine, of course. What else?"

"Isn't it lovely, Val?" Gabi asked. She moved closer to Alonzo and pushed her hair behind her shoulder.

"I can't have my future brother-in-law's cellars run dry, now can I?"

Alonzo placed a possessive arm around Gabi and kissed the top of her head.

His sister glowed.

Val spoke at a charity dinner in Miami where Gabi and Alonzo first met. Alonzo, much like many men in the room, sought out his sister, only he stuck. From there, the man made it his primary goal to snag her.

They'd been dating for four months when he pulled Val aside and asked permission to marry her. The tradition might have been ancient, but since Val and Gabi had lost their father early in life, it seemed only fitting that Alonzo respect his family in this way.

Even for Val, the courtship had been fast. He welcomed Alonzo into the family, but honored his mother's request that they have a long engagement. Longer than Alonzo wanted, in any event. If it were up to the groom, the couple would already be honeymooning. As it stood, the wedding was going to take place in the fall. Since spring was just now sizzling into summer, there was some time to plan and make damn certain Gabi was making the right choice.

"I have many wine vendors, Alonzo. I doubt my guests will drink me dry."

"But my wine is free. That must count for something."

"And it's lovely," Gabi chimed in.

Alonzo owned a winery in Italy, and was in the process of obtaining property in Napa Valley to extend his production. According to Val's research on the man, he'd been in the wine business just shy of five years. The wine was working for the man, but it wasn't making him rich. No, his family had made him a wealthy man before grapes became part of his life. The Picano portfolio was packed with investments in shipping, property in major ports, and a handful of banks in South America. Diversifying to wine made sense.

"You're biased, my love."

"No other wine shall pass my lips."

The lovebirds were making Val roll his eyes. And he never rolled his eyes.

The wind blew off the sea and pushed Alonzo's yacht against the dock.

"When do you expect your next shipment, Val?" Alonzo asked.

"In the morning. You can tell your captain to tie up overnight."

Alonzo boarded his ship and disappeared.

"How long is he here this time?" Val asked his sister.

"Only tonight, but he'll be back at the end of the week for a longer visit."

Alonzo's visits were becoming briefer with each one. The man had a business to run, but it seemed he didn't have a lot of time for his future bride. Perhaps it was time Val asked exactly how Gabi was going to fit into the entrepreneur's life. Truth was, while he was a little concerned about the man, he liked Alonzo and wanted to make sure his sister was happy in her choice for a husband.

Several of Val's staff wheeled the crates of wine back toward the villa. One of Alonzo's men called after them, reminding them which bottles were the champagne and to go slowly. They all disappeared before Alonzo returned.

"Gabi tells me you're leaving tomorrow." Val directed them to his cart and pulled away from the docks.

"Can't be avoided," Alonzo said. "I need to fly to California to finish the paperwork on the new vineyard."

"I can't wait to see it," Gabi said from the backseat.

"My wedding gift to you, m'dear. It needs to be perfect before you walk through the doors."

"Isn't that wonderful, Val?"

Almost too much, he mused.

"You'll never guess who is visiting the island."

If Alonzo were anyone but Gabi's fiancé, Val would shush her. "I can't imagine."

"Michael Wolfe."

"The actor?"

"Is there another?" Gabi asked. "He's such a nice man."

Val glanced in the mirror to see his sister smiling. "You could tell that with your brief visit?"

"You can tell a lot about a person in a few minutes," she defended. "His girlfriend is just as pleasant. I'm not sure why they worried you so much."

"I'm not worried."

Gabi shook her head, not buying his denial for a second.

"Val hasn't been right since they arrived," she told her fiancé.

Val felt his jaw tighten, knew his nose flared. He forced a deep breath and stretched his neck. "I can't be too careful, Gabi. You know that."

"How long is he going to be here?" Alonzo asked.

"A week."

Val's future brother-in-law managed a smile. "You'll know his character long before he leaves, I'm sure."

Yes, but if he, or more to the point, Margaret, couldn't be trusted, by the time they left it could be too late . . .

———

"I don't like him," Simona Masini spit from her perch overlooking the sea.

"You don't know him," Val insisted.

"It's in the eyes, Valentino. The truth is in the eyes."

"He loves Gabi."

His mother huffed out a laugh. "He wants you to believe he loves your sister."

Val ran a frustrated hand through his hair. The last thing he needed on this day was his mother contradicting everything he said. "The invitations have already been sent. The wedding will take place in just under five months."

Simona pointed her chin toward the window. "Sometimes you're so much like your father it scares me."

Val felt his back teeth grind together.

"Speaking ill of the dead, Mama?"

"Speaking the truth. He seldom saw the truth when something more pleasant filtered his view."

He had no idea what his mother was saying . . . didn't want to ask what she meant. His sister met and fell in love with a man. Who was Val to step in and say she was making the wrong decision? He was her brother . . . not her father. He laughed at his own thoughts.

"We're having dinner in an hour. Gabi invited our new guests to the table."

Simona sighed, tired with the entire conversation.

"Join us."

"Very well."

Val turned to leave the room. His mother's words stopped him. "What of you, Val? When will you find a woman, settle down? Give me bambinos?"

"Leave that to Gabi."

"You should marry first. That is the tradition."

His mother would be the death of him. "We're not in Italy."

Simona blew out a long-suffering sigh. "Tradition holds no borders."

Without furthering the frustrating conversation with his mother, Val left her suite, dismissing her concerns.

He made his way into his office, past Carol, who should have left for her on-island room long before.

"I need you to extend an invitation to my table this evening," he told her.

"Our new guests?"

Val hesitated. "How did you know?"

"Gabriella already asked. She thought an actor would appease your mother."

A rare smile met Val's lips. He loved his sister, would miss her when she moved away. "Word the invitation with color, Carol. Plain text won't woo our guests."

"Of course, Mr. Masini."

Val stepped into his office, exhaustion nipping at his eyelids.

The sting in Meg's tongue reminded her to keep biting her words. She should have guessed Valentino Masini would *highly encourage* them to join him and his party for dinner. The man was still checking up on her, and ticking her off.

What would he do if she refused?

Michael didn't give her a chance to find out.

"The invitation says his mother is a huge fan. How can I say no to a mom?" Michael had asked her.

"I say no to mine all the time."

"If my mother received word of me refusing, I'd never hear the end of it."

"The man is still screening me," Meg insisted.

"Your insecurity is showing, Meg."

"I'm not insecure." She tried to control the lift in her voice and failed.

They now stood beside the head table, where Gabriella sat beside an older woman Meg assumed was Mrs. Masini. Valentino, of course, was absent.

"You made it." Gabriella stood when they approached the table.

Semiformal dinner attire put Meg in her third outfit for the day. Talk about excessive. Gabriella wore a cream linen dress that stopped at her knees. The rhinestone heels highlighted her olive skin. The dress wasn't overly flashy, just stylish and fitted.

"How could we say no?" Michael asked.

"Oh, you could have, but I'm happy you didn't. Mama, this is Michael Wolfe and his companion, Margaret Rosenthal."

Mrs. Masini offered the same smile her daughter owned. "You're just as handsome in person as you are on the big screen, Mr. Wolfe."

Michael flashed a smile and winked at Meg. "I think I need to sit beside you, Mrs. Masini."

The older woman patted the seat at her side. "Wonderful idea."

Michael pulled out the chair beside him for Meg.

"Are we early?" Meg asked, looking at the two vacant seats at the round table.

"Val and my fiancé will be along shortly."

Meg glanced at Gabriella's ring finger, noticed the engagement ring for the first time. "When is the big day?"

Something close to a grunt sounded from Mrs. Masini.

Gabriella placed a hand over her mother's and answered, "Four and a half months."

"Congratulations," Michael said.

"You must be excited," Meg said to the future mother of the bride.

Mrs. Masini's smile fell when talking about her daughter's wedding. "I should be, shouldn't I?"

Interesting.

"Mother!"

"What?"

"Please."

Michael lifted a brow.

Before any further questions, comments, or otherwise tension-building conversation could continue, Valentino and Gabriella's fiancé arrived.

Now the tension could really begin.

Michael stood, shaking the other man's hand. "Sorry we're late," Valentino said. "I see you've met our mother."

Alonzo Picano was pleasant to look at, but not the stunning bookend Meg thought should be sitting beside Gabriella, or Gabi as the others referred to her. The man smiled easy enough, attempting to convince Mrs. Masini to grin, too, only to have the older woman look past him.

As everyone took their seats, Meg realized she had the privilege of sitting beside the man determined to find fault with her. On the surface, she'd have a hard time saying she didn't like the look, or the spicy scent, of him.

He wore a solid black tux, crisp white shirt, and bow tie. Normally, the look did nothing for her. But Valentino owned the classy threads as if born to it. The other men at the table were dressed well, but didn't compare to their host.

Mrs. Masini pulled Michael into a quiet conversation, while Gabriella whispered something to her fiancé.

Beside her, Valentino sighed. "Thank you for joining us, Miss Rosenthal."

Meg lifted her ice water to her lips. "I didn't realize I had the choice to refuse."

"You're a guest. You have the right to decline."

Even though she felt the weight of his stare, Meg refused to look directly at him. "I'll remember that."

For the first time, she heard him chuckle, and the sound made her grin.

The dining room was filling with guests, while a man wearing a tuxedo played a baby grand in the corner of the room.

Linen covered every table; hurricane glasses covered flickering candles surrounded by fresh floral sprays.

The Masini table sat on an elevated platform along with several others. The space between the tables was vast enough to avoid anyone overhearing conversations. Though the ceilings soared a good twenty feet, the room was relatively quiet with the exception of the piano and chatter. Huge windows took in the azure blue sea.

"Mr. Wolfe . . . tell us, what new film are you working on?"

"I'm in between projects right now or I wouldn't be here. And please, call me Michael."

Mrs. Masini beamed. "I liked that car movie."

Michael laughed. "So did I. Nothing quite like driving someone else's expensive cars fast."

"You do your own stunts?" Gabi asked.

"Some."

"Mr. Masini loved to drive fast, rest his soul. It would kill him to be here on an island with only golf carts."

"Papa would have found a way to make the cart do ninety."

"You're right about that, *cara*," Valentino told his sister. His occasional words in Italian made Meg's belly warm.

"Do you like fast cars, too, Mrs. Masini?" Meg asked, doing her level best to ignore the tingle spreading through her limbs.

"I do."

The waiter arrived and presented Valentino with a bottle of wine.

With a nod from Valentino, the waiter proceeded to open it.

"You're welcome to order whatever you like," Gabi told them, "but Alonzo owns Grotto di Picano. His wines are wonderful."

Michael sat forward, his interest focused. "This is your label?" he asked.

"It is."

The waiter poured Michael a small amount of wine and stood

back. With a swirl, sniff, and sip, he swallowed and nodded. "Your winery is in the Umbria region?"

Gabi smiled and Alonzo blinked. "It's in Campania, actually."

Michael took another sip and shrugged. "It's good."

"Thank you."

"You know wine, Michael?"

Meg preferred a shot of whiskey or a nice cold beer over wine. She'd learned to drink wine, knew what went with what, and didn't mind some of the heavier reds, but knowing what region a wine grape came from . . . no, not her thing.

"A little."

Meg shook her head. "Michael's wine cellar is full."

Michael bumped her knee under the table.

"You'll have to add Alonzo's to your collection."

Alonzo shifted in his seat and tapped Gabi's hand on the table.

"I might do that," Michael said.

Wine was served and the chef's specials were presented.

"What is it you do for a living, Miss Rosenthal?"

The question was common, the answer always vague. "Acquisitions and client relations," she said, pushing her salad plate aside.

Alonzo seemed disinterested, where Mrs. Masini narrowed her eyes. "Is that in the movie business?"

"No."

"What exactly do you acquire?" It was the first direct question Valentino had asked.

"You don't know? Seems you make it your business to learn every possible thing about your guests before they arrive on the island."

Michael leaned in. "Meg is a little sore on the subject, Valentino. Seems your delay in approving our stay left a bad taste in her mouth."

It was Meg's turn to hit Michael under the table.

"Is that right?"

The nerve of the man. He knew damn well she wasn't happy with his snail-paced delivery of their approval.

She found him staring at her, his steely-eyed expression and lack of a smile unreadable.

Why couldn't he be bald and unappealing? Why did her pulse beat like a drum on the African plain anytime she looked at the man?

"Women dislike being told no, Val. How many times must I tell you that?" Gabi, bless the woman, offered a valid argument.

"I grew up in a home with three sisters. I can verify that statement." Michael went on to talk about his family, directing the conversation far away from Alliance and its true service. It would never be public knowledge just who Meg, Sam, and anyone who worked with Alliance set up.

While Michael engaged the others, Val leaned close. "I couldn't help but notice that you avoided my question."

"Question about what?" she asked, even though she knew what Val was asking.

"What the company you work for acquires."

She picked up her wine, took her time tasting it. Over the rim she said, "Rejection bites, doesn't it?"

He chuckled, then mumbled under his breath. "Touché."

When their meal arrived, Meg took her first bite of the sea bass and moaned.

"That good?" Michael asked with a teasing grin.

Instead of answering him, she broke off a piece with the edge of her fork and fed him a bite.

"Oh my God."

"Right?" she said between mouthwatering bites.

"My chef will be delighted you're pleased." Val sat back and watched her as she swallowed her fish.

After blotting her lips, she managed, "It's amazing." Considering some of the places and people she'd managed to dine with since landing the job with Alliance—a Duchess, fake dating a Hollywood icon, and otherwise schmoozing with the überrich—the fish was damn good. The company didn't suck either.

She dug into another piece, waved the fish in the air. "There's a place in San Diego . . . Market Fish, or something like that—"

"On the wharf?" Michael asked.

"Yes. They come close, but this is so much better."

Gabi leaned across the table. "My brother prides himself on the fresh selections."

Meg managed a peek from the corner of her eye. Val still had yet to bite into his food. "Do you cook?"

"I don't have time to cook."

Which didn't answer her question.

"I suppose you never have a need to cook with all this at your disposal."

"I've taught both my children to cook. Not that they practice their skills often." Mrs. Masini nibbled the chicken on her plate.

"Do all of you live on the island?" Michael asked.

Mrs. Masini shrugged. "If I want to see my children, this is where I must be."

"Paradise is at your feet," Michael told her. "Never-ending sunshine."

"I like the rain."

"We're tropical, Mama, it rains every day," Gabi said with a smile.

"Not the same."

Maybe it was the wine, or the amazing food, but Meg found herself relaxing even with the reserved man beside her.

———

They'd been on the island just shy of twenty-four hours. Michael ran in from the warm ocean, water splattering in his wake. He pushed into the lounge chair beside Meg, and grabbed the ice water at her side.

She looked up from the book in her hand. "I think you were a fish in a former life."

"I can't get over how quiet it is out there."

"You make it sound like I'm talking your ear off."

He leaned his head back and closed his eyes. "I've come to the conclusion I have a loud life."

"You're a movie star. Comes with the territory."

He sighed. "I know . . . but this doesn't suck."

No, it didn't. Considering Michael's fame, there were few people who approached them. Even the night before at their "required dinner" with Valentino and his family, not one other guest snapped a picture, gawked, or asked for an autograph.

Meg had known Michael for nearly three years now, and that never happened in the real world.

Maybe Sapore di Amore was all it claimed to be.

"There is only one thing this island is missing," Michael said.

Something was missing? "What's that?"

"Sex."

He could say that again. "From the looks of some of the poolside guests, you're not the only one who thinks that."

Michael rubbed a towel over his face. "I haven't really noticed."

She had, if only to keep an eye on the tabloids once they left the island. How much leaked from Sapore di Amore? Was it possible the papers didn't see a senator's wife hooking up with a kid half her age? Did said wife recognize Meg? They'd met a year before in Sacramento.

Even now, Meg and Michael were outside their villa and precious few guests were milling about on the beach. This wasn't a place people brought young children. Maybe because children had a way of telling everyone the things they saw.

41

CATHERINE BYBEE

Meg reminded herself to ask the question to Valentino about kids. Did they flat-out refuse young people to come? Or was there a place on the island exclusively for families?

Instead of talking about children and families, Meg asked, "Is there someone you would want to bring here?"

Michael's gaze left hers and met the sea. "I-I don't . . . yeah."

Meg liked to think there wasn't an insecure bone in the movie star's body. But when it came to intimacy—real intimacy—he wasn't the confident movie icon at all.

"And would this person want to be here with you?"

"Lotta good that would do. Our lives are too different."

"He's not married is he?"

Michael shook his head. "God no. We're just . . . it's complicated."

"He's not in the movie business?"

"He's a teacher."

She wasn't expecting that. Instead of asking more questions, she watched the gentle waves hitting the shore. "Have you ever just wanted to say fuck it? Screw Hollywood and live your life the way you want to?"

"Millions of dollars a film, Meg."

"I know . . ." Lord knew she had grown up without money. Her parents still had next to nothing. In reality Meg had managed to put some away after paying off her student loans, but it would be a long time before she'd be able to afford a vacation at Sapore di Amore on her dime.

"But when will you have enough?"

"Is it too much to want money and a life?"

No, she mused. It wasn't.

Michael rolled over onto his stomach, stretched his arms over his head. "What do you think of our hosts?"

Meg gave up on her book and pushed her lounge chair back into the shade. No use burning up this early in the week. "Mrs. Masini is a kick. She adored you."

"Nothing says *I haven't lost it* like charming the old ladies."

"Gabi is sweet, but that guy she's going to marry seems out of place."

Michael turned his head her way, looked at her between squinted eyelids. "Something about him didn't seem right to me."

"Too much listening, not enough talking."

Michael leaned up on his forearms. "Did you notice when I asked him about his vineyard he tried to change the subject?"

"Yeah, why was that? I'd think if I owned my own label, I'd shout it to the world. He seemed excited enough to share his wine when we first sat down."

Michael shook his head. "I don't get it. Decent wine, too. I can see him avoiding the conversation if his wine sucked."

Meg tapped a finger against the chair. If she had her cell phone, she'd be looking up Alonzo Picano's name on the Internet to learn more about the man. Then again, she could make a phone call home and have Judy check out the name.

"You're tapping."

Meg stopped the rapid pace of her fingers. "I'm going through online withdrawal."

Michael laughed. "I'll be joining you there tomorrow."

"We're pathetic."

"I noticed you said nothing about Val."

She started tapping again. "The man is annoying."

"You can tell that with the few words he managed at dinner?"

"He studied us the whole night."

Michael closed his eyes. "You have half that right. He studied you."

"Which was rude. I'm with you."

"The man isn't blind."

"It didn't help that when Mrs. Masini asked why we weren't married you nixed any possible monogamy questions."

His chest rumbled.

"It wasn't funny. *Friends with benefits.* Seriously, does anyone say that anymore?"

He continued to laugh.

Meg found the ice water at her side and didn't think twice.

Michael sprang from the lounge chair like a cat avoiding a bath.

Meg had the good sense to put her chair between them, but didn't get far before Michael picked her up and ran toward the ocean.

Chapter Five

Resorts such as Sapore di Amore always housed gyms that rivaled any paid membership fitness center, but unlike the clubs in LA, these were empty. While Michael slept in, taking full advantage of his vacation, Meg pushed herself out of bed. The chef on the island was sure to put an extra five pounds on her if she didn't at least make an effort to burn some of the delicious calories off.

She'd considered a swim, but without a spotter who knew her lungs didn't always play well, she'd be risking more than she'd gain.

The twentysomething attendant at the gym handed her a bottle of water and a workout towel and greeted her by name, even though Meg hadn't yet set foot inside the gym.

She couldn't help but be a little impressed with the attention of Val's staff.

Once inside, upbeat music pumped through hidden speakers, the views outside the glass panels presented a lush garden view.

Meg managed a long stretch and moved to one of the ellipticals to warm up. She took her time and paced herself.

"Good morning, Miss Rosenthal."

So much for a peaceful workout.

Without stopping, Meg turned her head toward his voice and paused.

Why couldn't Valentino Masini be tucked into a Dri-FIT short-sleeved shirt and shorts? Then she could see for herself if the man sported a farmer's tan.

The fact that he was perfectly polished in a suit and tie shouldn't have surprised her. "Working out in a tie must really suck."

His gaze dropped, briefly, then met hers. "The ocean is my gym."

The instant image of him trying to swim in a business suit made her smile. "I didn't know they made suits to swim in." She realized, after the words were out of her mouth, how they sounded.

"The island is private, but I usually wear something while swimming."

The image of him butt naked and facedown in the water had her cheeks heating up. "Skinny dipping on your own island seems like a rite of passage," she said, hoping he didn't notice her blush.

When he was silent, Meg glanced over and noticed his grin. He smiled so rarely, she couldn't help but enjoy the tingle up her spine when he did.

The brat. Now she'd be searching for private spots where he dipped his ass naked.

"Now I know the real reason pictures are discouraged."

"You've figured me out, Miss Rosenthal."

"Ha! I doubt that." She took a swig of her water and felt the burn in her legs as the elevation on the machine changed automatically. When he didn't say anything to that, she added, "So, you hang out in the gym wearing a three-piece suit often?"

"I make an appearance to many parts of my island daily."

"Ah. A workaholic." Which might sound like stability to some, but to her, it sounded like an early heart attack.

"Perhaps." The smile on his face faded, leaving her disappointed with the direction of their conversation. "You appear to be a woman who likes order and routine."

"Why do you say that?" she asked.

"You're working out on vacation, which tells me you either vacation a lot and therefore feel the need to exercise while away from home, or you crave routine."

She thought about that for a minute. "Or maybe I just want an excuse to indulge on your menu choices and I don't want to get fat."

The lazy sweep of his eyes heated the room. "I doubt you have to worry about that."

"Every woman worries about that. They might not say it aloud, but they worry."

One side of his lips lifted in amusement . . . not a smile, she decided, but very close. "Thank you for the lesson on the female psyche."

"You're welcome."

Val stared briefly, before he pushed away from the treadmill he leaned against and tilted his head. "Enjoy your I-don't-want-to-get-fat workout, Miss Rosenthal."

The man made her smile. "Try not to work too hard."

He'd avoided them all day and into the evening. Made a point to stay far from the private villas . . . but on the third morning he found an e-mail in his in-box with a picture.

Margaret Rosenthal laughing in the arms of Michael Wolfe as he tossed her into the ocean. The picture wasn't intimate or suggestive, but it had been taken.

And it had been taken on his island.

He released a string of obscenities in Italian and pressed the intercom. "Carol. I need security in my office in five minutes."

"Is everything all right, Mr. Masini?"

"Five minutes." He disconnected the call and printed out the photograph.

Lou Myong stood before him four minutes later, the photograph in his hand.

"This was taken from the island, not the ocean, not above in a plane."

Val could see that.

"Can you tell who sent it?"

Val shook his head. "I expect an Internet team on this. I want to know the IP address, the origin. I need to know who sent the photograph."

Lou folded the copy of the picture and tucked it in the inside pocket of his suit jacket. A second-generation Korean American, Lou stood a few inches shorter than Val, but the man had a good thirty pounds over him. Lou had been the head of his security on the island since before the first guest arrived. He understood the need for secrecy and made damn sure pictures like the one in his pocket weren't taken.

"The question is why send it to you? Why not just print it? Pictures of movie stars on vacation fetch thousands of dollars."

"Someone wants me to know they can do it."

"Or someone is placing focus on these two."

Val didn't like the sound of either scenario. He flicked the switch on his desk. "Carol, can you come in here please?"

"Right away."

Once Carol stood before him, he started spouting off orders. "I need a list of every employee assigned to the Wolfe party."

Carol tossed a nervous glance to Lou and back to Val.

"I want everyone interviewed, the interviews recorded. I need to know what they've seen, who they've seen. I need to know if the security breach is internal."

His private secretary's eyes grew wide. "Breach, Mr. Masini?"

"Someone is watching our guests, Carol. I need eyes on the eyes and a moment-by-moment account of our guests."

A blank stare fell across Carol's face. "That might be difficult, Mr. Masini."

His back stiffened and his gaze narrowed. "And why is that?"

"Mr. Wolfe and his companion took a charter to Key West after breakfast."

Damn it. It was one thing to contain security on his island, not possible when his guests joined the party in the south.

Val met Lou's dark eyes. "Put your most trusted man on the employees. I need you in Key West. Find them, follow them, and see if anyone of interest is watching."

"Yes, sir."

"Carol, not one word. Right now there are three people who know there's a breach."

"Yes, Mr. Masini."

The two left the office in silence.

"Key fucking West."

Michael Wolfe and Margaret Rosenthal's photographs will be in every rag magazine available by morning.

Where Sapore di Amore was silence and solitude, Key West was the exact opposite.

Meg was surprised they lasted two nights and almost forty-eight hours before looking for excitement off island.

The charter off the island was exclusive to Sapore di Amore. Only guests of the island used the charter. They were given a cell phone and were asked to return to the dock by ten that evening.

With so many shops and restaurants and otherwise touristy spots to spend their time, Meg wasn't sure ten o'clock would be long enough.

They hid behind massive sunglasses, told passersby that Michael wasn't Michael, but yeah, he could be a stunt double for the man.

Still, Meg noticed a few cell phones swinging their way. She made sure she pushed in close to give the vibe they were together.

Halfway through lunch on an outside patio, Meg felt the need to look over her shoulder. "I don't know how you do this," she told him.

"You ignore it."

"But someone is watching us."

He shrugged, sipped his margarita. "Isn't that the idea? See if we're followed back to the island? See if it's as secure as Val says it is?"

She glanced over her shoulder, didn't see the eyes she felt. "Yeah."

"Then that's what we do. We play tourist and return to the island at dark. If nothing hits the papers by the morning, we step it up."

"And how do we step it up?"

Michael looked over the rim of his sunglasses and wiggled his eyebrows. "I'm more than a pretty face on the big screen."

Meg grabbed her purse and stood. "I'm in need of the little girls' room and am going to make a quick call to your sister."

Michael reached for the borrowed cell phone.

"I don't trust that. I'll use a house phone."

"Do they have those anymore?"

Meg laughed, but wondered if there was a house phone once she walked away. She stepped around the bar and found her path cut off by three bikini-clad women. "Is that Michael Wolfe you're with?" they asked.

Meg glanced at an Asian man watching from across the bar.

"If I had a dime for every time someone asked us that," Meg said. "We'd be as rich as Michael Wolfe."

The youngest of the beach-bound women offered a full pout. "We thought for sure."

"Sorry to disappoint you." She walked away with a tiny smile.

Meg found a house phone, which was really a cell phone from the manager, and she made a quick call to Judy.

"Hey, chica."

"Don't tell me you're back already?"

"No, we just got started. Snuck away to Key West."

"I didn't think my brother would last a week in seclusion."

"The island is amazing. We just wanted to test the bounds early. Listen, I need you to look something up for me."

"Find a new client?"

"Nothing like that. We haven't even really talked to many people outside of the owner of the resort and his family." Meg went on to tell Judy about Gabi and her fiancé. Asked her best friend to look up the winery and see if she could learn anything about the man.

"If he's not a prospective client, why bother looking him up?"

Once again, Meg felt eyes watching her. Only she wasn't beside Michael. *I must be paranoid.*

Music from the outside steel band filled the bar and made the conversation on the phone difficult.

"Something about him bugs me. Call it a byproduct of screening men for Alliance. It was obvious that Gabi's mother didn't like the man, and yet Masini and Gabi were both oblivious."

"Was he an ass?"

"No . . . just . . . blah. I can't put my finger on it. And Gabi is so sweet and sheltered. I'd hate to have a gut feeling and not follow up on it."

"Sounds like Gabi is competing for BFF status."

Meg tossed her head back and laughed. "Jealous?"

Judy giggled. "I was always your first. She can't take that away."

As an only child, Meg relished her friendship with Judy, missed some of the day-to-day stuff now that she was married. "So, can you look him up?"

"Of course. Consider it done."

"If anything looks crazy, give the information to Sam, see if she can dig more."

They spoke for another minute before Meg returned the phone to the manager.

"Miss me?" she asked when she sat back down beside Michael.

———

They arrived back on the island before the last charter and Val was still seething.

There were times when his sister was a teen that he'd sat waiting for her to return home after a date . . . but he'd never felt this stressed.

The employee interrogation turned up next to nothing. He tucked away a few tidbits the housekeeper offered, but none of the information would lay a finger on why, or who took a photograph of Margaret and Michael.

Did Margaret have someone snap the shot and send it to him? The woman he met online, maybe . . . the woman he met in person . . . he wasn't sure.

He found no fault in her genuine response to some of the simplest of things. Her reaction to his mother, the way she engaged his sister in conversation, held a sincerity he thought was real.

As for Michael Wolfe, the man was an actor. Much like politicians, Val knew better than to record anything he said as scripture. Besides, if what the housekeeper said about the sleeping arrangements was true, the lies were stacking up.

As tidbits went, that one left a smile on his face.

Margaret Rosenthal and Michael Wolfe might be *friends with benefits*, but those benefits didn't start *or* end in a bedroom.

The titillating information thrilled him, and also made him question why they were there. Why Sapore di Amore? Why together? Why now?

Why did the idea of his guests sleeping in two different bedrooms delight him?

Maybe because it had been some time since he felt himself taken by a woman. Margaret Rosenthal was a colorful package with many layers to unwrap to determine what made her tick. Outside of the hotel, there weren't many things that intrigued him. He'd dedicated every minute of his life to the island. Assuring his sister and mother were taken care of was paramount. He'd had the occasional brief affair. Most were physical and lacked any real emotion.

Funny how Margaret was all emotion.

"You need therapy, Val."

Now he was talking to himself. He pushed his mind away from women and continued his Internet search for recent sightings of Michael Wolfe.

Lou walked into his office thirty minutes after the Wolfe party had returned to their accommodations. It was late, the man was working past his designated hours . . . he never complained.

"What can you tell me?"

Lou started detailing every move from the moment he found them.

"They didn't call attention to themselves?"

"They did the tourist thing, hid behind sunglasses. I even overheard Miss Rosenthal tell some of his fans that she'd be rich if she earned money off every time Mr. Wolfe was mistaken for Michael Wolfe."

"Did they meet anyone?"

Lou shook his head. "No long conversations."

"Pictures?"

"A few on the cell phone they took of themselves. Nothing more. The phone was checked in per protocol. None of the shots included any of our other guests. Nothing suggestive."

"Vacation pictures." Val rubbed the bridge of his nose.

"Exactly."

"Keep eyes on them."

"Already done, Boss."

"Thanks, Lou. Get some sleep. I have a feeling it's going to be a long week."

Val drove his golf cart past his guest villas and decided to walk along the beach back to his office. Normally the walk, the sea . . . the moon shining on the water would calm him.

Not on this night. This night he wished for the counsel of his father and could only hope he was somewhere silently guiding him.

He'd been a young man when his father had passed. He had been finishing up his last year in high school and remembered in vivid color the last look his father had given him.

Val wanted to spend time with his friends, celebrate life as any seventeen-year-old would. His father understood, but didn't completely approve. Some of Val's friends at the time went on to do a little time. Not that he fell into the crowd, but growing up in a big city like New York, it was hard not to know kids from all walks of life. His parents had provided well for him and Gabi, but they certainly didn't live on Park Avenue.

Still, there had been one look between Val and his father, the night Masini senior had died of a heart attack, that stayed with Val his entire life. Val was running out the door with his friends and his father stopped him with an out-of-place hug. When he pulled away, he stared into Val's eyes. His look said two things: *I trust you. I depend on you.* Now, years later, the feeling inside his veins matched that of one so many years before. He longed to trust and depend. On someone.

He walked past the Rosenthal/Wolfe villa and tried hard not to stare. Lights were on in the back of the house, but those in the front were dark.

Cameras wouldn't catch anything tonight.

Tomorrow, however, was an entirely different story.

The next morning, long before the sun rose, Val sipped his first cup of coffee for the day and opened his e-mail.

A picture of himself popped up. Val saw himself staring into the darkened Wolfe villa, the sea at his back.

———

A shadow fell over her, drawing Meg's attention from the nap she was trying to take. It might have been unfortunate that she opened her eyes to find a pair of dress pants with a rather impressive bulge hiding the sun, but Meg found herself tearing her gaze away to follow the overdressed path to broad shoulders, partially shaven face . . . dark eyes. "Mr. Masini."

"Miss Rosenthal."

"You're a little overdressed for the pool, don't you think?"

The weight of his eyes traveled over her exposed skin. The bikini hid the important parts, but didn't leave a ton to the imagination. She couldn't tell if Val's lips twitched with admiration for what he saw, or disapproval. Either way, she felt a little like a Catholic schoolgirl who'd shown up for the first day of school with the wrong uniform . . . which had actually happened to her before her parents decided to ignore her grandparents' suggestion and that public school might prove best.

His gaze lingered on her thighs and Meg felt the need to squirm. Instead, she simply called the man out. "You're staring, Mr. Masini."

He jolted as if his own personal earthquake woke him. "Please, call me Val."

"We're on a first-name basis now?"

Val rocked back, placed his hands into his pockets as if he didn't know what to do with them.

He'd been nothing short of cocky since before she'd arrived . . . this new look suited *her* just fine.

"I welcome all my guests to use my name."

"Yet you don't go by Valentino. I'd think you'd prefer only friends call you Val."

"Are we not friends?"

Meg couldn't help it, she laughed. "Sure, Val, let's be friends . . . you can call me Margaret. Miss Rosenthal reminds me of my great-aunt who never married."

His eyes laughed even though his lips didn't. "Don't you use Meg?"

"Let's not push it, *Val*."

The man laughed.

And damn, it was a sexy, throaty laugh that brought some of her girlie parts to life.

"Now that we have the name thing figured out, why are you standing over me wearing a three-piece suit while I'm in next to nothing?"

Val's laugh dried up and he licked his lips. Poor guy really didn't stand a chance with her. He had to be politically correct while she could dig and dig.

Meg loved digging.

"I wanted to extend an invitation for you and Mr. Wolfe for lunch."

She lifted her knee, noticed his eyes travel. "Lunch?"

"Yes, that would be the meal between breakfast and dinner."

Maybe she wasn't the only one who could dig.

"I can't speak for Michael. He's sleeping off yesterday's tequila from Key West."

"Ah, yes . . . how was your trip off island?"

"Fun, actually. I'd never been."

Some of the humor left Val's face. "About lunch?"

"Is this a formal meal?" She purposely let her eyes travel over his suit. "I have to tell you, midday dress-up while on vacation holds little appeal for me."

"Casual."

"You mean you own clothes without starch?"

He tugged on his collar. "I live on an island, Margaret, of course."

He really was fun to get a rise out of. "Lunch it is then. If only to see what you consider island clothing."

Val grinned. His eyes swept up her frame, and she felt her cheeks warm. "Though I wouldn't complain, a bikini might be a bit underdressed."

Holy crap, was that a compliment? "Why Mr. Masini, are you flirting with me?"

His deep gaze found hers. "Just seeing what it takes to make you blush, *Margaret*."

He turned and walked his very fine ass away.

Chapter Six

Michael used the morning alone to sleep and consider his options. For a few brief moments the day before, he and Meg had blended with the world . . . yeah, he felt the eyes, the stares, but there were brief moments when no one approached them, no one questioned them.

Something else he saw, which he did whenever he hid in the crash of people . . . couples. Real couples. Not all of them matched the way society still felt was necessary. The image of those couples brought a wave of envy he hadn't expected. It wasn't like he hadn't noticed lovers before.

He didn't regret his life . . . how could he? He'd been sought after since before he was twenty years old. Hollywood, movie producers, and his fans made him a common name on the big screen. He loved his Hollywood life a good 95 percent of the time.

When he'd told Meg he wanted Hollywood and a love life, he'd done so without much thought. Since then he'd thought of nothing else. Here he was in arguably one of the most beautiful, peaceful places he'd been in years, and all he could do was want more.

Michael reached for the bedside phone and dialed in to his assistant. Tony answered on the third ring.

"Tony!"

"Damn, Michael . . . I thought you were shitting me about your cell phone being off."

Michael might have been alarmed by Tony's intensity, but that was a normal operating tone for the man. "Meg warned you."

"Who takes away your cell phone? That's terrorism, dude."

Oh, the drama. "Tell me all the tabloids are free of my image."

Tony laughed. "The price of no cell phone might work for you, but not for me. I've got nothing showing up. I've been watching, too."

Meg had laid out instructions to Tony as if she were his client and not Michael. "We were in Key West all day yesterday . . . anything from there?"

"There were a few tweets, but nothing concrete."

Michael felt a smile pulling at his lips. "You call the island if that changes."

"I will. When will you be back?"

"I'm not coming back early." Not if his plans worked the way he wanted them to.

"Enjoy, Michael. Let me know if you need anything on this end."

"I will."

Michael hung up and dialed another number. "Hey, Ryder, it's Mike."

Val half expected Meg to show up in a bikini, high heels, and red lipstick. As it was, she managed a sundress and simple sandals.

The red lipstick was a bonus.

She was alone.

Gabi greeted her at the gate; from the instant pout from his sister, Val knew Michael wouldn't be joining them.

Wind kicked off the ocean, spraying the smoke from the barbeque right into his face. Val waved it away and managed his grill. He lowered the heat and closed the lid. When he glanced up, he noticed Margaret's eyes on him.

She did the sweeping thing he'd done to her earlier in the day and offered a slight nod. Short-sleeved silk and cotton pants might seem overkill for a lunch barbeque, but it was cool and unstarched. He'd have to ask Carol how much starch was used in his suits and if it was really needed.

A hand slapped his back, snapping him out of the Margaret Rosenthal thrall. "You didn't tell me you'd have so many beautiful guests."

Val looked into the eyes of an old friend. "All my guests are beautiful."

"And young . . . too young for my old ass."

Val smiled. He'd met Jim the first six months after he'd opened the resort. Rest and relaxation were a tall order for the man who had said *I don't* to his fifth wife. Problem was, the man didn't know how to be single . . . didn't know how to wait for the right woman. He was only in his early sixties, he'd raised a few kids, not all of them his, and had more experience in life than Val had in his big toe.

"Not all my guests are in their twenties," Val told him.

Jim nodded toward Meg. "That one is."

Yeah, Val knew . . . Margaret Rosenthal was a few months away from her twenty-seventh birthday. She looked it, too. The memory of her in a bikini staring up at him wouldn't leave his brain anytime soon. How he'd managed to string two coherent sentences together by the pool, he'd never know. Still, he'd invited her, wondered if she'd bring her roommate, and planned on getting to know her a little better. He needed to know if she was behind the pictures, or if someone else was watching her.

Val heard the meat on his grill sizzle and lifted the lid to make sure he wasn't charring their lunch.

"Oh my God, you're Jim Lewis."

Margaret had managed to cross the room in a breath. Only she wasn't looking at Val, she was looking at Jim with star-filled eyes.

"And you're my future wife."

Margaret Rosenthal blushed. Her cheeks grew crimson in a flash, her smile more radiant than Val had yet seen. The green-eyed monster known as jealousy smacked him upside the head.

"Holy crap. Seriously? I meet Jim fucking Lewis on Fantasy Island and I can't even take a picture?"

Jim let loose a belly laugh . . . and the man had a serious belly to offer a baritone that would rock Carnegie Hall.

"Those are the rules, Miss . . . ?"

"Meg. Holy shit."

She extended her hand, blushed even further when Jim kissed the back of it.

"Meg? You just met him and he's allowed to call you Meg?" Val couldn't come up with anything else.

"I'm having a fan moment here, Masini. Let it go."

Val watched her fan moment and realized he was seeing the real Margaret Rosenthal. This woman, the one with the unfiltered tongue and wide eyes, was the woman determined to make her way onto his island.

This woman Val wanted to know . . . thoroughly.

"You're too young to know about *Fantasy Island*."

"My parents had tapes. I keep looking for the Mini-Masini, but he's not here."

Jim tapped his chest and roared with laughter. "That hurt. I'm so old."

Meg giggled . . . looked around and lost part of her grin. "Sorry. Of all people, I should know not to jump on a celeb."

"Of all people?"

It was Val's turn to step in. "Margaret is here with Michael Wolfe."

"The actor?"

"Yeah," she offered. "Wow . . . I've listened to you since . . . forever."

Val noticed that Jim hadn't let go of Meg's hand. His back teeth ground together.

"You're a blues fan?"

"I grew up with all kinds of music. Blues stuck. Soulful, music with purpose . . . worthy of singing."

Val found himself pushing between them, felt a smile when Jim let loose Meg's hand.

"You're a singer?"

"Yes. No . . ." Meg glanced at Val, quickly looked away. "I work in an office."

Jim tilted his head. "But you sing."

"Not like you."

Jim smiled.

Something popped, and all three of them looked at the grill. "Mini-me isn't here, Masini . . . you might want to get that."

Jim shoved him, laughed.

Val pulled the meat from the grill in record time to save their lunch.

"Cooking skills?" Meg asked.

Val shoveled lunch on a ready platter. "And I'm not wearing a tie."

Meg lifted the plate full of food and grinned. "When you're in shorts and barefoot, we'll talk."

Jim let loose a laugh. "This one has your number, Val."

"Jim freaking Lewis," Meg mumbled as she walked away. "What are the odds?"

Meg got it . . . really got what it was to have crazy fans meet their icons. Jim Lewis had been a part of her life since she played the first notes on the piano. Sure, he was shorter, rounder, and a whole lot grittier than she'd pictured him to be, but it was Jim Lewis.

And he knew Val.

She licked her lips. Val might not be in serious island casual, but the flowing silk shirt and relaxed pants were a far cry from the stuffy shirt and tie she'd seen him in from day one. He'd even managed to skip a shave, and damn if that wasn't sexy as all get-out.

"Bring that over here." Mrs. Masini waved her to a table laden with food.

Meg placed the platter of barbecued ribs and chicken onto the center of the table.

"*Perfetto.* Gabi, tell Luna to bring the fruit and we can eat."

"Yes, Mama." Gabi winked at Meg and disappeared into the private villa.

The far north side of the island held Val Masini's private space. Meg couldn't help but wonder if the vast ocean in front of his home was where clothing-optional swimming took place.

Only a handful of guests milled about the tropical, lush garden where the invitation-only lunch was taking place. The space could have taken on a hundred guests without feeling crowded.

"It's beautiful, yes?" Mrs. Masini asked.

"I haven't seen a space on this island that isn't," Meg told her.

The older woman smiled. "Valentino works hard to make that magic."

Meg found her gaze moving to Val, he caught her eyes for a nanosecond before she turned away. "Does he ever take a break?"

Mrs. Masini shrugged. "This is his break. He cooks a meal instead of depending on his chef once a week."

Meg noticed a table full of side dishes and carbonated beverages and a few bottles of wine chilling in a bucket. "Something tells me Val didn't make all this."

Val's mom laughed. "He grills." She dipped her finger into the side of the ribs, licked it off. "A master at the grill, my boy."

"Bragging on your son?" Jim moved beside Meg and placed an instant smile on her face.

"I'm just expressing his culinary skills." Mrs. Masini met Meg's eyes and held them. "Do you cook?"

Meg thought of the microwave at home, the freezer full of instant meals. "Depends on what you consider cooking."

Jim laughed and Val joined them.

"Any wife of mine doesn't need to cook," Jim offered.

Mrs. Masini frowned.

Jim laughed.

Meg felt her cheeks fill with heat and Val said, "Maybe if you found a wife that cooked, you'd still be married to one of them."

Jim slapped a meaty palm to Val's back. "I might have to try that."

"What's all this talk of wives? Is there another Mrs. Lewis close at hand?" Mrs. Masini asked.

Meg's personal icon draped a hand over her shoulders and pulled her close. "You didn't hear? Meg loves me, and she sings. It's meant to be."

The man flirted with style; Meg had to give him that.

"Is that right?" Mrs. Masini had an actual twinkle at the corner of her eye. "What is Meg's last name?"

Jim glanced at the sky, leaned in close. "What's your last name?"

"Rosenthal."

Jim retreated with a playful smile. "Jewish? That might not work."

"Said the black kettle to the Jewish pot."

Jim pulled her against him again. "We can piss off all kinds of people with the union." The man was joking, but damn if it wasn't fun to be a part of a joke with Jim freaking Lewis.

"My mother is Catholic."

That had Jim pulling away only to laugh. "Our children would be so messed up."

"You're too old to give her children," Val said with a frown.

"I'm told that a healthy man can have sperm produce children until death." Meg found Val's eyes and held them.

Gabi made her way back to the party and asked, "What's this about children and death?"

"Nothing, *tesoro*. Jim is just a shameless flirt and found an audience with poor Miss Rosenthal," Mrs. Masini said.

"Call me Meg."

Mrs. Masini patted her hand and Meg noticed Val frown.

"Did he call you his future wife?" Gabi asked.

"He did."

Gabi rolled her eyes. "You need a new line."

Val pulled away and encouraged all his guests to eat.

Meg found herself sitting beside Gabi and Mrs. Masini.

Jim and Val spoke with several guests, their laughter carrying over the courtyard.

"You really don't cook?" Mrs. Masini asked halfway through their meal.

"Is a microwave considered cooking?"

Gabi winced. "You didn't just say that."

Mrs. Masini dropped her fork. "How will you find a husband if you don't cook?"

Meg thought of her database full of prospective husbands. "Well . . ."

"You must know how to cook something."

"Spaghetti."

Mrs. Masini's face lit up.

"As in jar sauce and boiled bag pasta."

Mrs. Masini's face fell.

Gabi groaned. "Let me say this now . . . run, Meg."

"Pasta isn't something that comes from a bag." Mrs. Masini's voice took on the quality of a Mom-Demon. Her low voice wasn't something a mere mortal could ignore.

"In my house—"

"Jewish father, Catholic mother . . . I heard." Mrs. Masini waved a hand in the air. "To find the right man, you must know how to cook at least one meal properly."

"I'm really not looking for the right—"

"Enough!"

Some people might say they felt the weight of the world coming down, but never had Meg felt it before. The determination in Mrs. Masini's voice, her words, and the sheer distress hovering over Gabi's face made Meg squirm.

"Tomorrow you will meet me here, in Val's kitchen."

Meg started to shake her head.

Mrs. Masini narrowed her eyes and waved a hand in the air. "Jimmy!"

Meg glanced at Gabi, who looked across the lawn. Jim Lewis nodded and moved toward them, Val at his side. Once the men were at Mrs. Masini's side, she relaxed in her chair and offered a casual smile.

"Yes, ma'am?"

"You're singing tonight, yes?"

"Val asked if I would."

Mrs. Masini waved a hand in the air. Her eyes never left Meg's. "You will sing something with Miss Rosenthal."

Meg's mouth dropped.

"You said you sing," Mrs. Masini reminded Meg.

There were no words. "But . . ."

"You sing with Mr. Lewis, and tomorrow you will return here so I can teach you how to cook one meal properly."

Having grown up with a combination of Jewish guilt and a hefty dose of Hail Marys, Meg knew when a parent was going to win.

"Mama, if Margaret doesn't want to—" Val started.

Meg lifted her hand. "Zip it, Masini." The opportunity to sing with Jim Lewis was simply too great to pass up. Only Meg wanted one tiny change in the contract. "On one condition."

All eyes were on her.

"Someone records it."

Jim lifted a brow.

"Just us," Meg said. "If we suck, you take the video. If not, I keep it for my grandchildren."

"Don't you mean *our* grandchildren?" Jim asked, laughing.

Val rolled his eyes, Gabi laughed, and Mrs. Masini waited.

"Deal?" Meg asked.

Chapter Seven

Who was the woman who'd taken over Margaret's body? The fun-loving, laughing, flirting woman was nothing like the person Val painted when he'd read her first letter of request to come to the island. She had his mother and sister rapt before the lunch plates were taken away.

Then there was Jim. If the man weren't thirty years older than Margaret, Val might be worried.

The sun was pushing past noon and most of his guests had left when Val felt his phone vibrate.

Carol knew not to disturb him during his afternoon off. Not that Val ever felt as if he were truly off. Owning the island resort had always been a full-time job. Even when he left the Keys, he never truly left his job.

Val checked caller ID and excused himself to answer Carol's call.

"Sorry to disturb you, Mr. Masini."

"My guess is you would have avoided it if you could. What can I do for you?"

"We have a little situation."

Val instantly thought of the pictures in his e-mail the last two days and held his breath.

"Which is?"

"It appears Mr. Wolfe is requesting a guest join him and Miss Rosenthal."

"Requesting?"

Carol cleared he throat. "He is returning from Key West with a Mr. Ryder Gerard. The two of them are en route now. Captain Stephan is waiting for your orders."

There had been times when his guests had "unexpected" additions to their party . . . and yes, more than one would pick up a stray in Key West. But Michael Wolfe? And with the pictures showing up daily in his in-box?

Val moved his gaze to Margaret, heard her laugh at something Jim was saying. What did she know about this Ryder Gerard? How could she have eaten lunch with him and his family and say nothing of the new arrival?

"Run a quick check . . . find out where the man lives."

"I'm already working on it."

"Tell Stephan to circle the island until I know this man isn't a plant."

"Yes, sir."

Val hung up the phone and approached his family.

Margaret met his gaze and her laughter faded. Michael wasn't sleeping off an evening of drink. He was wandering off island. Suspicion of the woman and the man made Val's blood boil. So much for trust and depending on her.

"Someone doesn't look very happy."

Val ignored his sister's comment and directed his attention to Margaret. "Can I have a word with you?"

Margaret pushed away from the table and walked to his side.

On instinct, he took hold of Margaret's elbow and led her away from anyone who might overhear them.

"Why do I feel like I'm being led to the principal's office?" she asked.

Val found no humor in her voice. "Who is Ryder Gerard?" he asked without any prompt.

"Excuse me?"

He stopped walking, turned toward her.

Margaret pulled out of his grip, making him realize that he held her a little too tight.

"Seems your *friend with benefits* is requesting another guest join your party."

She blinked a few times until his words sank in. "He is?"

"Don't play coy with me, Margaret. Michael isn't sleeping anything off in your rooms."

She crossed her arms over her chest, her eyes sharp points of accusation. "I don't play, Mr. Masini. Michael was in our villa when I left to join you here. If he left once I was gone, that's news to me. It's not like he can send me a text to tell me where he is."

"I suppose next you're going to tell me that Mr. Wolfe said nothing to you about bringing a friend to join you."

She lifted her chin. "Seems you've already accused me of lying, Mr. Masini. To serve what purpose? I'm the one who arranged our stay here. Michael knows you have a background check for every guest. He understands why better than most of the people here. If he is asking for someone to join us, my guess is he has a good reason and that person is as trustworthy as your mother."

"Don't bring my mother into this conversation."

"You know, Masini, your people skills could use some work. I'm not your enemy."

"The privacy of my guests is paramount."

"As if I don't know that."

"I don't care for surprises."

She glared with her lips in a straight line. "Must be a bitch for your family around your birthday."

"Who is Ryder Gerard?"

"I couldn't tell you."

Val twisted his hands into small knots and shoved them in his pockets.

For a brief moment, Margaret simply stared him down. It was a visual game of chicken and Val had a sneaking suspicion that he was about to lose.

She blew out a long breath. "Listen, Val. I honestly don't know who Michael wants to bring to the island. But I do know Michael. The man seldom has a vacation or even a meal without hordes of fans wanting a piece of him. My guess is he feels safe here. I don't think there has been any media watching us since we've arrived and maybe Michael wanted to have an old friend join us. I'm sure whoever Mr. Gerard is, he's perfectly safe."

Val hated how sincere she sounded. How innocent her eyes were.

"You're not upset someone is interrupting your vacation?" Why had he asked that?

A slight lift to Margaret's lips made him eat his words. "Michael and I are friends."

"With benefits."

She lifted her left brow, paused. "Right."

Was Margaret a better actor than her companion? Was she playing him? Val hated that he didn't know her well enough to trust her.

"All right, Margaret. So long as Mr. Gerard isn't a known felon or working for any media cooperation, I'll honor Michael's request."

She smiled.

Her grin was contagious and he felt his lips smiling back.

"How old was Gabi when your father passed?"

He found the question off his radar and answered without thinking. "Fourteen."

"So all her dates had to go through you?"

"I was the man of the house."

"What a bitch that had to be."

Val shook his head. "It was."

"For her. What a bitch *for her*. No offense, Masini, but you'd be the worst high school principal ever."

"Didn't your brothers look out for you?"

"I'm an only child, Masini. A fact you might have known if you'd actually done your background check a little better. Even I know where you were born, what college you went to, and what your major was."

She turned and started to walk away before her words registered.

Val reached for her, let go when she looked at his hand holding her elbow as if it were made of hot tar.

Margaret silenced him with one sentence. "You were born in New York, spent summers in Italy before your grandparents passed, went to NYU, my guess is to stay close to home to watch over your mother and sister after your dad died of an early heart attack."

"How do you—"

"You weren't the only one doing background checks, Masini."

With that, Margaret turned and walked away.

———

"Holy crap, Michael." Meg walked into the villa cussing.

Michael stood in the kitchen pouring wine into two glasses, the smile on his face just this side of radiant.

"Hey, darlin'. I take it you heard we have company."

Before Meg could utter a word, a man just a tad shorter than Michael, with a build almost as nice, walked into the room.

"Ryder Gerard, I assume."

Michael's guest offered a sheepish smile. "You must be Meg."

Meg offered her hand, mumbled a *nice to meet you*, and turned to Michael. "A little warning, Michael."

"It was a last-minute decision."

"The island isn't that big. You could have found me, told me."

"You weren't here."

Ryder backed away. "Should I leave?"

Both Michael and Meg said, "No."

Without much thought, Meg moved to the windows and started pulling the shades. "Masini cornered me, asked about your unexpected guest. I played dumb, which wasn't difficult since I didn't know what was going on." She tugged the last blind and turned.

Michael handed a glass of wine to Ryder and pulled another glass from the cabinet. Meg took the wine, though she really wanted a stiff shot of something much stronger, and sat across from Michael and his friend.

When Ryder moved to the far side of the couch, Meg laughed. "Please, Ryder. I'm guessing you're Michael's teacher friend."

Ryder had a soft quality to his voice. "We're on spring break."

"That's convenient. Wait . . ." Hadn't Michael suggested this week, a different week than the one she had originally suggested before she set up their vacation? "You planned this . . ."

Michael studied the ceiling. "I wouldn't say planned."

Meg set her wine on the side table and leaned forward. "Michael!"

"Hoped, OK? When yesterday didn't result in anything other than a tweet, I called Ryder."

How could she be mad at the man? "Why didn't you say something?"

"Because I've found that the least amount of information to the fewest number of people is best."

"C'mon, Michael. You can trust me. You know that."

Michael laid a hand on Ryder's thigh and left it there.

The grin on Michael's face was a shade off nirvana. "So what's the plan?" Meg asked. "What do we tell anyone who asks? As much as I might like being a girl in a threesome, I'm not sure that excuse will fly."

Ryder covered Michael's hand with his and spelled out their plan.

The single-bench golf cart at their disposal had been switched up to one that seated four. The cart simply arrived sometime before dinner. Val paid attention to details, Meg had to give him that.

Meg, Michael, and Ryder had dinner in the villa and then dressed for the evening entertainment.

Meg was never more pleased with the closet full of new dresses. She couldn't stop smiling. Of all the people in the world to find on the island, being able to sing with Jim Lewis was a dream she never even realized she'd had. All she had to do was agree to a cooking lesson from Mrs. Masini.

Score!

"Tell me about this Jim Lewis again." Michael zipped up the fitted dress in the back and patted her shoulder.

"I can't believe you don't know who he is."

"I listen to rock and roll."

Meg turned toward the full-length mirror and pulled her "girls" to a respectable position in the dress. Once her cleavage was properly in place, she moved to the edge of the bed to put on her shoes. "Well, prepare your auditory palate for a new sound. Jim Lewis will have you feeling every word he sings unlike anything hard rock can deliver." She loved the hard stuff, too, but she'd take a smoky blues bar over a concert hall any day. Well, the blues, not the smoky bar.

"Are we ready?" Ryder glanced into the room.

"We're waiting on the girl."

"Figures."

Meg stood an extra four inches taller than nature intended and picked up her clutch. "Ready."

Flanked by two attractive men, she walked the short distance to the golf cart and tucked herself into the passenger seat.

It had been a while since she'd had an audience. Karaoke only counted for so much. Truth was she hadn't made time to sing to something other than her piano in close to a year. She missed it.

She knew early on that singing for a living was a long shot she didn't want to pursue. It didn't help that her asthma kept her from smoky bars, venues . . . even concert halls.

"Are you nervous?" Ryder asked from the backseat.

"Excited." Yeah, maybe a little nervous.

"Well, you look great."

She accepted Ryder's compliment with a smile.

"Did Val really give you crap when he heard I wanted to bring a guest?"

Michael rounded the corner onto the path straight to the main villa that housed the nightclub where Jim would be singing.

"The man really doesn't trust me."

Michael frowned. "I don't understand why."

"He doesn't know me," Meg said when they pulled to a stop behind a dozen golf carts. "And he couldn't learn much about me through any regular channels."

"If there isn't any dirt, how can he be so untrusting?"

"I think that might be the problem. Everyone here . . . well, many of those here have some dirt. When someone doesn't have anything to hide, they have nothing to lose."

Michael walked around the cart and helped Meg out. "He couldn't crack Alliance."

"He couldn't smudge Alliance. Sam perfected the barriers around that long before you and I came along."

"I don't think I like this Val guy," Ryder said.

That's what Meg kept saying to herself . . . then she'd see him in person and she'd ask herself what the harm was in flirting with the man.

"There's only one tiny problem," Michael said.

They walked to the door to the nightclub and met the center of their conversation. He was back in a suit, this one black and perfect for the host of the evening. He'd managed a shave, damn shame that, and he wore something that held a sandalwood musky pull.

She licked her lips and denied the desire to move closer to the man to reach the full effect of the scent of his skin.

His eyes swept down and took a slow dance up her frame. "You look positively stunning, Margaret."

"Thank you." Without much thought, she reached forward and straightened his bow tie. "James Bond called, wanted to know when you're returning his suit."

His gaze fell on her lips when he smiled. "Is that right?"

"That's the rumor."

Meg broke free of his gaze. "Valentino Masini, I'd like you to meet Ryder Gerard."

The two men shook hands. "I hope you enjoy your time on my island."

"It's beautiful. I appreciate you accepting me on such short notice."

"Not a problem. If you need anything, please ask."

Meg squelched the need to roll her eyes as another set of guests moved in behind them.

"I have a table for you close to the stage," he told them.

On cue, the maître d' closed in and asked them to follow.

Once the three of them were seated and their drink orders were taken, they moved close to finish their conversation.

"See the problem?" Michael asked Ryder.

"Bright and clear."

Meg watched Val at the door, his easy smile and grace with his other guests made her wonder if he distrusted them, too.

"See what?" Meg asked.

Val must have felt her gaze and he narrowed his eyes on her. She purposely looked to the men she was seated with. "What?"

Ryder broke into a grin and Michael laughed. "He might not trust you, but he has it bad *for* you."

"Keep your enemies closer . . . as they say."

"You keep telling yourself that, Meg. Let me know how that works out."

Chapter Eight

He couldn't stop staring.

She'd stepped out of a 1930s pinup magazine. Her creamy, soft breasts pushed out of the skintight fitted red dress that narrowed at her waist. The hem stopped at her knees and had a slight slit in the back. Tiny black beads ran the back length of her stockings; her feet were tucked into slim high heels with straps that wrapped around her ankles. She was completely polished on the outside with a flippant tongue hiding on the inside. Val wanted the whole package.

Val wasn't the only one looking, either. Men of all sizes, ages, and marital statuses were watching her. Lord help him if she sang as sexy as she looked.

"Is that Meg?" Val heard Gabi's voice on his right. He nodded without looking at his sister.

"My goodness, she takes performing with Jim to quite an extreme."

"It's her fan moment." On *his* Fantasy Island.

From across the crowded room, her eyes lifted to his. Instead of looking away, she hoisted her martini glass in salute before tipping it to the edge of her red lips. When she licked the moisture off the rim of the glass, he had to look away or risk embarrassing himself in front of his guests.

"It looks as if her two companions aren't quite enough to entertain her," Gabi said without malice.

The lights on the stage went up, keeping Val from commenting on his sister's observation.

He zigzagged through the crowd and took the stage to introduce his special guest. "Ladies and gentlemen, thank you for joining me this lovely evening." Val looked over the heads of his guests, found the bright eyes of Margaret watching his every move. "Tonight I've asked a special guest, and an icon I dare call friend, to my stage. Please put your hands together for a man who needs little introduction, Mr. Jim Lewis."

Few people in attendance knew Jim was going to perform, and with the announcing of his name, the audience applauded with enthusiasm that honored his friend.

Jim walked from the back of the club, shaking hands along the way. When he reached the stage, he shook Val's hand and leaned into the mic. "How about a round of applause for your host."

The crowd kept clapping.

Val tilted his head in appreciation and moved offstage.

"It's hard to say no to Val," Jim said. "Especially when he gives me the best villa for nothing."

The audience laughed and Jim took to the stool in the center of the stage. Val's house band moved into place behind his friend. A stagehand produced Jim's guitar and set a glass of water on the table beside him.

Jim ran his fingers over a few chords and the room grew silent.

"I've been singing for my meals for nearly thirty years." He strummed the guitar again, stopped.

The crowd laughed.

"I've performed in concert halls, auditoriums, stadiums . . . but none are better than venues like this . . . where I can play, chat, and feel like I'm in your living room talking crap about the neighbors."

The keyboard player knocked back a few notes and stopped.

"Have you ever had a neighbor, hotter than your girl?"

The keyboard played again, and this time the drummer played with him.

"Oh, baby, it's a bad thing when your girl finds out."

The keyboard, drums, and now a bass prepared for Jim's opening.

"That you have 'The Baby Next Door Blues.'"

Jim leaned into the mic, hit the first note, and wrapped the audience around his chubby little finger.

Val had heard him many times, sometimes in his own living room. But here, onstage and in his element, Jim vibrated.

Val found himself watching Margaret. Her hand tapped the top of the table to the beat of the music; her lips mouthed the words to one of Jim's most famous songs.

The song dipped low, wound its way to a high note, and finished with a round of applause.

Margaret was the first on her feet, and one of the last to sit down before Jim moved to another hit.

Val wound his way through the tables until he found the sweet spot in the back where all the notes could be heard in full stereo. Jim helped design the acoustics, making sure there wasn't a corner missing anything critical. But here, in the center of the room, Val could hear every note as clear as an early morning bird greeting the day.

The second song moved faster than the first, two horn players added flavor to the music.

When the song was over, and the audience calmed down, Jim looked over the crowd. When his eyes landed on Margaret, Val felt his pulse jump.

Was she nervous? Did anything make the woman numb with anxiety?

"Have you ever met someone in your life and said, hot damn . . . if only I was twenty years younger?"

"Try thirty," Michael Wolfe countered from the floor.

Jim tossed his head back and laughed. "I met this sassy, sweet thing only a few hours ago. If her voice is as sexy as her dress, we're in for a treat. Let's hear it for Meg Rosenthal."

Margaret took the stage as if she'd done it so many times before. Val found himself mesmerized. Jim slid a hand around her waist, kissed her cheek. She lifted a leg and batted her lashes at the audience.

"Go girl!"

Val heard the call, but didn't note where the man who yelled it was.

Instead of moving to the microphone, she blew a kiss to Jim before moving behind the keyboard. "Do you mind?" she asked.

Ruben lifted both hands and stepped away, giving her space. One of the stagehands moved forward and tilted the mic to the level of her lips.

"So what are we going to sing, baby girl?" Jim asked.

Margaret placed her fingers to the keys, ran through a couple of familiar chords. "It's baby girl now? What happened to your future wife?"

Jim's grin lit the stage. "Honey, if you were my wife, I'd be dead before morning."

The audience laughed.

Val found himself enjoying the banter.

Margaret found Jim's eyes, danced her fingers over the keyboard, letting everyone know she knew her way around the instrument. "Something fast and sweaty, Jim?"

Jim pulled at his collar, let her run the show.

She slowed the tune, made the room sigh. "Something slow and sensual?"

It was Val's turn to tug at his tie.

"Baby doll, you pick, and I'll just try and keep up."

Margaret lifted her hands, rubbed them together, and started. "I think you might know this one."

It took two chords for the audience to recognize the tune. "Ever been to San Francisco, Jim?" She kept playing.

Jim closed his eyes and waited, as did Val, until Margaret leaned into the mic and took command of the first few lines of "Sittin' on the Dock of the Bay."

Jim let out a whoop of approval and sat on the dock with her. When Margaret left her home in Georgia, the glassware in the room rang with the pitch-perfect tone of her voice.

They bounced between lines in the song like they'd done it before. The rest of the band sat back and listened.

It was Margaret, Jim, and a lone piano. They harmonized with the chorus, let each other take center stage for a line, then gave it up to the other for the next.

Her voice easily bounced over the ending notes to the song, bringing it home with both of them pleasing the audience.

Everyone stood, and Jim offered a hand to Margaret as she stepped down from the platform the keyboard was perched on.

The woman glowed.

Jim kissed her again, squeezed her waist, and walked her off-stage.

"Baby girl, you can sing with me anytime."

———

She'd just belted out one of her favorite songs with Jim Lewis and lost herself in the music. Meg couldn't stop smiling.

Michael kissed both her cheeks when she returned to the table. "You were phenomenal. I had no idea."

Ryder pulled out her chair and they listened to Jim's next song.

When the lights came back up between sets, they ordered another round of drinks and Jim made his way offstage and to their side.

"I don't know what you're doing working in an office with a voice like that," he told her.

She'd probably stop smiling sometime near Christmas. "Does that mean I can keep the video?"

"So long as I have a copy." He shook the men's hands. "I need to pollute my lungs," he said before he turned and left.

Meg accepted the kind words of those around them. But when she looked around, she didn't see Masini anywhere.

When Jim finished singing for the evening, the house band continued to play.

Michael and Ryder were talking in low tones when Gabi sat next to her. "You were amazing."

"Jim's the pro. I'm the window candy."

Gabi continued to deny the claim when Michael interrupted them. "We're going to head back."

Meg took one look at them and decided three was a crowd. "I'm going to stay here a bit longer."

Michael handed her the key to the golf cart. "We'll walk back."

Gabi sat back, nodded at the retreating men. "So what's with the friend?"

"Ryder?"

"Yeah."

"He's an old friend. Just went through a breakup. Since Michael has a crazy schedule, he decided to invite him down to cheer him up."

The excuse worked. "Seems lots of celebrities like to combine friends and family when they can. I don't think I'd want to be so busy I couldn't do both."

"Do you think you're going to be busy once you're married to a winemaker?"

Gabi smiled. "I honestly don't know what my life is going to look like when Alonzo and I marry. He seems to think I'll stay here most of the time while he runs the vineyards."

"You'll live separately?" That sounded like an Alliance marriage. "Until the California property is ready for us."

"Won't that be difficult? It seems you're close to your family."

"It's time I found my own place. Val has had the burden of watching over both of us for years. My mother can always move close to me."

"Alonzo is OK with that?" Meg couldn't imagine having a parent living that close. Then again, Meg visited with her parents on occasion, but didn't pine for their presence.

"Like I said, we haven't really discussed it."

Meg couldn't help but wonder what they had talked about. For a bride-to-be, Gabi had little idea of what married life was going to look like.

"Miss Masini?" One of the waiters interrupted them. "I'm sorry to bother you, but there seems to be a problem and I'm not sure where Mr. Masini is."

Gabi stood. "I'm sorry."

"No, please. I was just about to step outside."

Much of the club had cleared out. Meg stepped out into the warm Caribbean evening and headed in the opposite direction of her villa. The last thing she wanted to do was interrupt Michael and Ryder. Besides, it was too nice a night and she was still riding high from her moment onstage with Jim. She couldn't wait to see the recording.

She itched to pull out a cell phone and text Judy with the evening's events. That would have to wait.

Meg walked along the wide porch of the main building. The outside patio where the restaurant spilled was free of couples.

She stopped long enough to enjoy the gentle waves lapping on the shore, watched the light from the building twinkle on the water.

She understood why Val would live where he worked. The view, the temperature of the air and water, was perfect.

The piano used to entertain guests outside stood covered for the night. Meg approached it, touched the edges of the covering briefly before pulling it back.

There was something about the sound of a baby grand that no other piano could capture. For an instrument that spent many days outside, it was tuned to perfection. Meg looked over the water, let a few chords of the song she'd sang earlier play.

She wondered if Val enjoyed her performance, and wondered even more why she thought about him now.

Meg slowed her fingers and lent her voice to the song of desire and want. It was sultry and a little sad, and fit her mood. When she finished she let the piano fade and heard a lone clap.

Val leaned against the railing, his tie loose on his neck.

The man was too delicious for his own good.

Meg offered a smile and nodded a tiny bow. "Well thank you, kind sir."

"You were brilliant tonight," he said from the shadows.

His approval warmed her. "I enjoyed myself."

"Everyone could tell." He pushed away from the rail and leaned over the piano. "How long have you played?"

Not knowing what to do with his attention honed in on her, Meg plucked at the keys softly. "My parents always had instruments in the house. They were too young for Woodstock, but if they could, they would have run around naked with a guitar covering their goods."

"They taught you?"

"More like I taught myself. Formal education wasn't important to them." She played a few notes of Bach, switched to Pink Floyd.

"Can you read music?"

"I get by. My high school choir teacher said I had a talented ear."

"And voice."

She smiled, caught the scent of Val's skin. "That and an open guitar case might have made me a few bucks on a city corner."

"You weren't willing to risk a roof over your head for the dream of a singing career." His observation was on-target.

"My parents live week by week, Masini. I didn't want that." The music coming from the piano started to sound dark. Meg purposely switched it to something quick and lively. "What about you? Ever want something different in your life that you didn't go for?"

When he didn't answer right away, she glanced up to find him studying her.

"Not yet."

"Sounds like there's something."

He brushed the side of her face with the back of his hand, moved closer.

Meg stopped playing, felt her pulse jump.

"Where's Michael?" Val whispered.

"Michael?" The name didn't register.

Val lifted his left eyebrow. "The man you're here with."

Right. "He's a . . ." Damn, he smelled edible.

Val's palm captured her neck and guided her to her feet. "He's *just* a friend, isn't he, Margaret?"

The way Val's lips moved drew her closer. The need to taste them, feel them on hers was impossible to walk away from. "If I told you we were more than friends . . ."

Val's eyes traveled from her lips to her eyes. "Then I'd have to let you go." He loosened his fingers on her neck, but instead of moving away, Meg leaned in.

"Sounds like you might regret that decision." She laid a hand on his firm chest. The man wasn't soft under his stuffy suits.

"I don't pursue another man's woman."

He wasn't moving away.

"Good to hear, Masini." She lifted her lips close to his, felt his breath mix with hers. "I don't belong to anyone."

Val hesitated for a nanosecond, and then took her lips. His closed-mouth kiss started off soft, like a hesitant man worried about rushing. Yet when Val wrapped his free hand around her waist, and his body fit against hers, Meg opened for him, encouraged him to taste.

When he did, she lost it. He tasted of bourbon and sex. God help her, she wanted to crawl into his kiss and explore it for hours. The man kissed like he was on a mission. And maybe he was. Who knew if Val Masini made it a weekly occurrence to kiss a new woman? Somehow, she didn't think so. He was too reserved most of the time.

Not now . . . not with his tongue exploring hers and his strong hands pressing the small of her back closer. Every hard ridge of the man met with every soft curve of hers.

The kiss went on until she found her chest tightening with a familiar warning. Sexual excitement had to be paced or she might find herself in a full-blown asthma attack. A frustrating fact of her life in the last few years. One that kept her single most of the time, her encounters lukewarm at best.

Val was threatening the air in her lungs with just a kiss.

A heated *knock her on her ass* kiss, but a kiss nonetheless.

She eased away and Val chased her lips.

She tried to slow her breathing, couldn't catch a deep breath. "Wait," she managed, pulling away.

"Too much, *cara*?"

You have no idea.

She reached out, felt her head spin a little. Her inhaler was in her purse. Her next two breaths didn't satisfy the need for air. Instead of trying to fake her way out of his arms, she gave him a tiny shove. "Can't. Breathe."

He smiled, then the smile fell when he realized she wasn't being cute. "Are you OK?"

"Purse."

He guided her to the bench and handed her the clutch.

The rescue inhaler did its job, and she managed a few deep breaths and felt her pace slow.

Val knelt beside her, watching with his hands at her sides. "Are you all right?"

Embarrassed, she nodded. "It doesn't always come on like that."

Concern brought his eyebrows together. "Should I call a medic?"

She placed a hand on his shoulder. "No." The tightness passed, slowly. "I can usually avoid this. I didn't mean to scare you."

Val squeezed her thighs. "I want you breathless, but not like that."

Meg smiled. "You can add lethal kisser to your resume."

He captured her hands, brought them to his lips. "Is it always like that?"

"No. Just when . . ." Admitting she was turned on by a simple kiss didn't feel right, not after a first kiss.

Holy crap . . . she'd just kissed Val Masini. And here she was on an island posing as Michael's girlfriend. What was wrong with her?

She tried to stand up. "I should go."

Val pushed her back down. "Wait."

"I really shouldn't be out here with you . . . like this."

His gaze narrowed. "You said you didn't belong to him."

"I don't. But that isn't the point."

There was knowledge behind his eyes, and a sense of confidence that Meg wasn't used to with the men she'd been with. "OK, Margaret. I'll let you run away . . . for now."

"What's that supposed to mean?"

"It means we're not done."

"Cocky much, Masini?"

He didn't answer, just stood, and helped her to her feet.

"I can make it on my own," she said when he started walking alongside her.

"I'm sure you can. But I'm not leaving your side until you're at the door to your villa."

Arguing took too much effort, and besides, she wasn't stupid. Her lungs were still a little tight, and exerting herself without someone close by was a recipe for disaster. "Fine."

Val laughed, and kept a hand on her back as he walked her to the golf cart to take her home.

Chapter Nine

"Someone came in late last night," Michael started in while he poured a morning cup of coffee.

"Someone turned in early last night," Meg countered.

Michael took the first sip of his coffee and closed his eyes with the pleasure of it. "Damn I feel good."

"Sex will do that to ya."

Michael wiggled his eyebrows and sat at the kitchen counter.

"Where is Ryder?"

"He's an early riser. Decided on a morning jog on the beach. Utah is surprisingly shy of shoreline."

Meg rested her chin on her hands. "I don't think I've seen you glow, Michael."

He snapped up in mock surprise. "Men don't glow."

"Bullshit on that."

Michael stared into his coffee cup for a few seconds. "I wonder, sometimes, what it would be like to live with someone . . ."

"Like Ryder?"

"Like Ryder." The smile on his face faded.

"You know, Michael, the only way you'll ever know how that would work is if you did it."

"My career would be over."

"You don't know that. Hollywood spins things to match their needs all the time. Who says you can't spin what the world knows . . . or what the world thinks it knows."

He was thinking about it. That, Meg could see.

When his eyes started to scowl, Meg changed the subject by confessing her evening's sins. "I kissed Val."

Michael's jaw slacked open.

"He kissed me, actually. Then the oxygen level dropped and damn it . . . but yeah, we kissed."

Michael was smiling, enjoying her unease with her confession. "How was it?"

"Before my lungs seized? Great. I mean, have you looked at the man?"

"Lots of lips, just the right amount of tongue?"

Meg squeezed her eyes shut, started to laugh. "How did you know?"

"Just a guess."

She blew out a sigh. "I shouldn't have."

"Why not? He's sexy, straight. Perfect for you."

"I'm here with you."

"Something tells me you didn't have an audience."

"We were alone."

"So what's the problem? Val would be breaking his own rules by spilling the encounter. He doesn't strike me as a kiss-and-tell kind of guy."

She still didn't feel right about it.

"Listen," Michael said. "Karen and I were married for a year and a half. Neither of us were involved with anyone and no one got hurt. You're here as a date. Last time I looked that didn't amount to jack in this day and age."

"But—"

"But nothing. Kiss him, sleep with him, do whatever you want with the man. I have no claim and wouldn't say otherwise regardless of what might come of this vacation. Besides, it isn't like there are a bunch of cameras snapping pictures and asking questions. This place is off the map. I know I'm coming back."

Some of the tension inside Meg's chest eased. "With Ryder?"

"Maybe."

The bell to the front door of the villa rang with a noise that surprised the both of them.

Michael answered while Meg watched.

"Sorry to disturb you, Mr. Wolfe. Miss Rosenthal has mail."

Mail? On vacation?

Michael took the envelopes from the man and closed the door. "I thought vacations were no-mail zones."

Michael glanced at the three envelopes before handing them over.

"One is from your sister." Judy's handwriting was as familiar as her own. The return address, however, was illegible.

Meg tore into Judy's first.

Hey, Livin' the High Life on Someone Else's Dime,

Two things since I can't pick up a freakin' phone and call like any normal person in this century . . . First, I've heard NOTHING about you or Mike since you left. I'm watching every platform, as is the ball and chain and his partner.

Meg knew that meant Rick and Neil. Both had a background in military intelligence and could be trusted with her life.

Second . . . the man you asked me about. I'm not liking the information I'm finding. Or not finding, as the case may be. Not sure why you're asking about him, but " don't trust him." Those are the ball and chain's words.

Hope you're having a fantastic time.

Can't wait to hear all about it . . . or not hear all about it.

Give my bro a kiss for me.

J

Meg scratched her head.

"What is it?"

"Judy says hi." Meg let the kiss go for now. "Said all is silent in the real world."

"Sounds good to me."

"Yeah."

"Then why the frown?"

"I asked her to check on that Alonzo guy."

Michael frowned. "What did Judy find?"

"She didn't say. Just suggested that Rick and Neil said not to trust the man."

Michael turned, leaned a hip against the counter. "Not a problem since the man isn't here."

"I guess."

The back door to the villa opened, catching both their attention. Ryder stepped into the living room, half-winded. "Utah has nothing on this place," he said.

"Sparkling water and ocean breezes . . . I have to agree." Michael opened a cupboard and removed a cup. "Coffee?"

"Love it. Morning, Meg."

"Good morning."

She opened the second envelope. This one didn't have an off-island address.

My mother is a dictator in the kitchen . . . fair warning.

Val

"Damn."

"What?"

She'd forgotten about the cooking lesson. "I-I have a debt to pay." She glanced at the clock. She still had time for a shower. Makeup and polish would have to wait.

Without thought, she gathered the mail and rushed from the room.

A quick shower, a pair of shorts, and a little mascara, and Meg fled the villa.

Simona Masini wore an apron and already had Val's kitchen brimming with fresh tomatoes, flour, and eggs when Meg arrived.

The scene was out of a horror movie. Well, Meg's idea of macabre, in any event.

"Sorry I'm late," Meg apologized as she walked in through the back door.

Mrs. Masini offered a placating smile. "I have all day." The older woman handed Meg an apron. "Put this on."

"All day?" Meg wrapped the thing around her waist, asked herself if she'd ever worn an apron before. *Nope.*

"Don't look so glum, Margaret. You appear to be a bright woman. I'm sure I can teach you the basics of pasta."

Mrs. Masini opened a huge rubber container and dumped several cups of flour right on the smooth counter. "We start with the pasta so it can dry while we prepare the sauce."

"When you start with dry pasta, you're ahead of the game."

It was hard not to laugh at the older woman's scowl. "I will show you first, and you will follow. Wash your hands."

Meg moved to the sink on autopilot, did as she was told. "I have to warn you, Mrs. Masini. The kitchen and I are sworn enemies. Even my cookies come from a bag."

"Doesn't your mother cook? Make anything from scratch?"

Meg thought of the potted marijuana plants and the drying racks her parents used even before it was legal. "She dried her own herbs."

Mrs. Masini wasn't impressed. She made a fist and stuck it in the middle of her pile of flour and started cracking eggs into the center of her mini flour volcano. "Pasta is the most basic of foods. The recipe easily memorized." Her hands whizzed over the flour, added a dash of salt, and something else. "Why are you standing there watching?" She waved a messy hand to the other side of the counter. "Start with the flour."

Meg tried to mimic her teacher, dipped her hand into the center of her mound a little too much and realized that if she were to add an egg the thing would blow through the side like Mount St. Helens. She repaired the side of her mountain and cracked an egg.

The first egg went in perfectly; the second took part of a shell, which Meg pulled out before reaching for the third egg. Meg glanced over at Mrs. Masini, who silently watched.

"This isn't that hard."

The third egg toppled over the edge of the flour and spilled onto the counter. Meg tried to stop the flow with the palm of her hand only to find the rest of her mountain crumbling. "Oh, no."

The more she tried to stop the lava flow, the bigger the mess became.

Mrs. Masini wiped her hands on her apron and removed a trash barrel. With the help of a paper towel, the entire mountain found its way to the garbage.

"Start again."

The second volcano didn't erupt until after Mrs. Masini showed her how to mix the egg into the flour. The third attempt was next to perfect.

Or at least a passing grade.

Mrs. Masini chatted while they cut the pasta, rolled it into tiny strands, and placed it on a rack to dry.

Mrs. Masini brought out a bottle of cabernet once all the tomatoes were cut, along with onion and fresh garlic, and handed it to Meg. "Open this."

Meg was starting to like Mrs. Masini's idea of cooking. "Where are the glasses?" she asked once the bottle was uncorked.

Mrs. Masini rolled her eyes, took the bottle from Meg's hand, and poured a splash into the sauce they'd mixed from raw ingredients and put into a pot.

"Oh." Meg glanced at the label with disappointment. "This isn't your son-in-law's wine."

"He's not my son-in-law!"

"Yet."

Mrs. Masini grunted.

"I take it you don't approve of your daughter's choice."

She hesitated. "The man won't look at me, doesn't meet my eyes."

"You think he's hiding something?"

Mrs. Masini didn't agree or disagree. "What man presumes to fall madly in love, then leaves his intended for weeks at a time? He has yet to introduce Gabi to his family. Who are his people?"

Meg thought of her own family. "Not all families define their children."

"True, but marriage is more than simply two people coming together. How can I approve his family if I've not met them? I don't trust him."

The venom in the woman's words rang inside Meg's head. It was her turn to watch in silence as Mrs. Masini moved about the kitchen. She found a cupboard and removed two glasses. She poured wine for the both of them and took a big sip. "Know the man you marry, Margaret. Know his family."

"Marriage isn't in my plans."

"Why is that?"

Meg had been giving that some thought since she went to work for Alliance. "I find myself smiling and happiest when I'm beside an artistic type."

"Like Jim?"

Meg nodded. "Albeit a few decades younger," she said with a laugh. "But guys like Jim don't stick around and can't manage rent, let alone a power bill."

Mrs. Masini weighed her words, sipped her wine. "Then you find someone with more stability."

Meg knew a lot of suits. She'd been hooking them up for a couple of years. They might be stable, but the inability to laugh and enjoy life was a serious killjoy. "I decided some time ago that I didn't want to settle for half the package . . . I also learned that the perfect man doesn't exist, and Lord knows I'm nowhere near perfect."

"None of us are, dear."

"It would be easier if my expectations weren't so high. My parents are happy being dirt-poor together. If either of them wanted something different, one of them would be miserable." She'd rather be single and happy than married and miserable.

"So you're looking for the stable artistic man."

"I'm not looking for anyone."

"What about your *friends with benefits*?" Mrs. Masini delivered a snarky grin, one that told Meg that there had been a time when Mrs. Masini was in her twenties.

"Friends for fun aren't the same as friends forever."

Something told Meg that she would hear Mrs. Masini's grunt well into the future. "Every woman marries eventually."

Meg opened her mouth to deny the claim only to have Mrs. Masini talk over her. "Eventually you'll want children."

"I'm a—"

"When you hold your baby for the first time. All the pain in your life disappears. You'll sacrifice many things for your children, your family. It's hard to watch them make the wrong decisions."

"Like marrying the wrong person."

Mrs. Masini tilted her wineglass in Meg's direction. "Like marrying the wrong person."

"What worries you the most about Mr. Picano? Do you think he'll be cruel?" They'd switched to the subject of Gabi in a nanosecond and Mrs. Masini didn't miss a beat.

"I've seen very little emotion from the man. How can an Italian man have so little emotion?" Mrs. Masini was waving her hand in the air now, her voice up at least an octave. "Mr. Masini, rest his soul, lived life with passion. He loved with his whole heart. He would want nothing less for his baby girl. A man who can't voice his anger bottles it up inside until it bursts. Then I fear for my daughter."

"Some men don't get all that excited about life's stresses."

Mrs. Masini shook her head. "Alonzo Picano holds it in. I see it in his eyes."

Wow, she really didn't like this guy.

"Maybe you just don't know him very well."

She growled. "Now you sound like my son. I know him well enough. He's not good enough for Gabriella. He will be back on island tomorrow. You'll see what I see if you look."

Mrs. Masini moved from her perch and stirred the marinara sauce before replacing the lid and turning the temperature down.

"I thought Gabi said he wasn't coming back for a week."

"He changed his mind. Like a woman. A man of business doesn't have the luxury of changing his mind."

Meg couldn't argue with that. "Something came up?"

Mrs. Masini groaned.

———

Michael reached the peak of the cliff before Ryder. They'd started the day off with wakeboarding and then decided on a hike and picnic lunch on the northern point of the small island. Seemed most of Sapore di Amore's guests enjoyed the pool or the beach, because they hadn't passed one person since they set out.

The breeze was stronger a few hundred feet above sea level, the view breathtaking.

Ryder reached the top and turned to take it in. "Wow."

"Views like this never get old," Michael told him.

"Makes me wonder why I'm living in Utah."

"It's where we grew up. It's safe." At least that's how Michael thought of things when he'd lived there. He enjoyed going back now that things with his parents, or more importantly, his father, were on better terms. Not that he would ever return to live there. In the past few years, he had revealed his sexuality to his older sister and brother, and just recently one of his younger sisters. It was only a matter of time before he had a conversation with his parents. Distance helped keep his secrets. Still, revealing his sexuality to his father was a pinnacle in his life he had yet to cross.

Ryder leaned back on his forearms, drawing Michael's attention. The two of them had shared more together than anyone else in Michael's life. When they stole time together, it was as if they were kids again, or at least a decade younger. Life felt full and packed with the promise of a bright future. "You know, they have high schools everywhere. You don't have to stay in Hilton."

"Trying to lure me away to the big city, Mike?" Ryder's teasing grin sprayed two mirrored dimples.

Was he? "Why does our life have to be so damn complicated?"

"Because we're gay."

Michael let out a short laugh. "Is that it? I didn't realize."

Ryder rolled onto his side, smiled up at him. "If I left Utah, where would I go? Beverly Hills with you, become a kept man?"

No one could keep Ryder. He was too strong, too pigheaded. "You'd work."

"And when people asked why I was living with you?"

"People have roommates all the time." Saying the words aloud gave Michael room in his brain to consider the possibility. "Aren't you tired of a small town filled with narrow-minded people?"

Ryder reached out, laid a hand on his thigh. "We could jeopardize everything you've worked for."

His heart jumped. He thought of Meg's words . . . asking if he'd ever have enough money to be happy. Did the money in his bank even compare to this moment on the side of a cliff with his lover at his side?

Michael took Ryder's hand and squeezed it. "We both have something to lose."

"Bears some serious thought," Ryder agreed and looked away.

They were silent for a moment, watching the seagulls flying over the waves and picking up their lunch.

"This really is beautiful," he said.

Michael watched Ryder's profile. "Yeah, yeah it is."

Chapter Ten

Mrs. Masini decided a nap in the afternoon was a good idea, leaving Meg to stir the sauce for a half an hour unsupervised.

The woman clearly didn't know how easily Meg could screw up a meal. It probably didn't help that half the bottle of wine was gone.

She filled a pot with water to boil fifteen minutes before the hour, as instructed. According to Mrs. Masini, a late pasta lunch was the perfect meal. Meg was convinced that eating at two was an excuse to soak up the wine.

Meg turned to the sink long enough to wash sauce from her hands and heard the water on the stove boiling over.

"Whoa, there." Of course, Val would walk in the kitchen right as Meg was making a mess.

He twisted down the flame, taming the boiling water. He was once again in a three-piece suit and she was in . . . Meg glanced down about the same time Val swept her frame with his eyes.

The apron around her waist took some of the weight of the flour off her clothing, but there was still a good quarter pound of that crap all over her. She was fairly certain kindergarten kids could make pasta from scratch with less mess.

Val hid a smile behind his hand.

"Oh, go ahead and laugh."

His hand fell away. "You look . . . you look . . ."

She blew a strand of hair from her eyes and walked around him to the stove. She wasn't going to muck up the sauce because he couldn't articulate how ridiculous she looked.

"It took three attempts to make the pasta right." She nodded toward the dried strings of carbohydrates.

"I warned you."

She growled, the sound surprisingly similar to that of Val's mother.

"Where is my mother?"

"Resting. Seems creating culinary greatness takes it out of her. She asked that I wake her when the pasta is done cooking."

Val slid out of his jacket and loosened his tie. "If it's any help, it smells delicious."

"I popped a few gray hairs making this meal, I hope it smells good."

He laughed, rolled up his sleeves, and washed his hands. "I don't think it's gray in the hair. Just flour."

The thought of tossing her pasta-smudged dishtowel at him crossed her mind. But then she'd mess up his linen shirt. Maybe if he wore something more casual . . .

"I told her I didn't cook."

"That was your first mistake." He took the rack of dried pasta over to the boiling water.

Meg stood beside him, managed a whiff of the scent of the man through the garlic and tomatoes. Instead of taking notice, she concentrated on stirring.

Once he placed the pasta into the pot to boil, he stared at her.

She looked through her lashes, didn't turn her head. "What?"

He reached out, brushed at her cheek. "You have a little . . ."

Flour? Sauce? It could have been anything to draw his touch. A zip of crazy energy tingled up her back. "I thought about you last night," he told her.

"Really?" She really wasn't too happy with how charged the man made her feel. His cocky ending to the previous evening tossed her around most of the night. Not that she'd tell him. "I slept like a baby."

"Is that right?"

He moved behind her, reached for the dial on the stove, purposely brushing his body close to hers.

"You know, Masini, I can move."

"Where would the fun be in that?"

He had a point. "You're so cocky."

"You said that last night."

"Still holds."

He laughed and brushed her arm with one of his hands. She started to lean into him when they realized they weren't alone.

Meg tried to hold back her jump, didn't want to be so obvious, but failed. "Hi, Gabi."

Gabi watched the two of them with wide eyes and a smug smile. "Hello, Meg. I knew you were cooking . . . but I had no idea."

Val laughed and Meg placed an elbow into his side. "Your brother's a flirt."

"Is that right? I've never really noticed before."

Meg twisted away from the watchful eyes of Val and dropped her towel on the counter. "I should wake your mom."

"I'll get her," Gabi said. "You two . . . carry on."

Meg waved an accusing finger Val's way the moment they were alone. "I'm supposed to be here with Michael."

"And yet you're not."

"A fact that shouldn't be advertised. Why do you think we're here?"

"You needn't worry about Gabi. She'd never do anything to compromise what happens on this island."

He turned off the heat on the pasta and lifted the heavy pot to the sink. The colander was already in place to drain the pasta. It was obvious that Val knew his way around the kitchen. "I take it your mother taught you how to cook."

He smiled. "My father, actually. Good thing, too. My mother didn't want anything to do with cooking for months after his death."

"You're the good son all the way around." She meant the words as a compliment but they came out a little snarky.

"Family is important."

She wondered if the family loyalty thing skipped her. She loved her parents, but didn't have any undying need to protect and care for them. They'd always seemed to do that for each other just fine, leaving her flapping in a lonely wind.

Gabi jogged down the back stairs and into the kitchen. "She'll be down in a few minutes. Shall I set the table?" She walked over to the eat-in kitchen table and started to lift Meg's purse to set it aside.

Meg thought of the mail from Judy and couldn't remember if Alonzo's name was used. Since the letter was lying in her purse, Meg jumped to take her purse from Gabi's hands. "I'll take that."

Gabi handed it over, and reached back for the papers that fell out.

Meg didn't need to worry, Gabi didn't look at the mail before she swept the table free of everything and started to gather dishes.

Mrs. Masini looked five years younger after her nap. It helped that she didn't wear flour quite like Meg. Val poured wine and Gabi dished up the meal.

Before they forked one spoonful, Val lifted his glass. "To new friends."

Mrs. Masini lifted her glass. "To new cooks."

Gabi joined them. "To the perfect con to obtain stage time with Jim Lewis."

Meg laughed and added her own toast. "To surviving my cooking."

With the taste of wine on her lips, she met Val's gaze as he took his first bite.

"Oh, *cara*. Perfect."

"Better than my first attempt," Gabi said, taking a second bite.

"Really?" Meg lifted her fork, took her first bite. "Mmm." It wasn't bad. In fact, it was pretty damn good.

"Of course it's perfect. I'm a good teacher, no?"

"The best, Mama."

They talked of food, their first attempts at cooking before either of the Masini children got it right. They laughed when Meg described her flour volcano taking on a resemblance to Mount St. Helens.

And they ate.

Meg couldn't remember a better meal. A bit of pride wound inside her head as everyone finished their plates, Val taking on a second helping.

They moved to the outside patio when they were finished, Meg rested a hand on her full stomach. "How do you stay so thin eating like that?" she asked Gabi.

"Lots of swimming."

"Don't let her fool you," Val said across from the two of them. "She eats like a sparrow most of the time."

"I have to fit into my wedding dress."

With the mention of the pending wedding, Mrs. Masini did that growl thing Meg had grown to recognize during their time together.

"A husband should love you heavy or thin."

"I want to be thin for me, Mama."

"I think I'll finish my nap," Mrs. Masini said, excusing herself. She stopped at Meg's side. "Thank you for your company today, Margaret."

Meg stood and hugged her teacher. "Thank you. I really did have fun."

Mrs. Masini kissed her cheek and walked into the house.

Val's cell phone buzzed, taking his attention away. "Looks like I have to get back to work."

"I should wash some of this flour off before it becomes a paste on my skin."

Gabi brushed at her arm. "It's not *that* bad."

The three of them walked back inside and Meg gathered her purse. She removed the note Val had sent her and waved it toward him. "Thanks for the warning."

"She went easy on you."

Meg tucked the note away, determined to keep it, and noticed another envelope beside the other two. Her name adorned the envelope with no return address. She wondered if maybe Val had sent her two notes.

Gabi asked her brother about one of their guests and Meg opened the letter.

Only it wasn't a letter.

It was from the night before . . . a picture.

A picture of her in Val's arms, their intimate embrace leaving little to the imagination of anyone who came upon it. "What the hell?"

"What is it?"

"Is this a joke?" Because if it was, she wasn't laughing.

Val took the folded picture away and grew rigid.

"Oh, my." Gabi's eyes were wide as saucers.

"Where did you get this?" Val asked, his tone accusing, his eyes dark.

"You tell me. It came in my morning mail."

"That's the two of you." Gabi stated the obvious.

"You're just now showing me this?" Val asked.

"I didn't open it until now . . . and why are you talking to me in an accusing tone? I didn't take the picture, Masini . . . I was a little busy at that moment in time."

"No one is accusing you of anything," Gabi told her. "But who . . . and why?"

"Who delivered this?"

"The same guy who brought me your note."

Val said something under his breath in Italian. If Meg could guess, she'd say he was cussing. "This goes nowhere outside of this room," Val hissed.

"I thought you didn't allow cameras on the island? How did this happen?"

"I don't."

"This doesn't look like it was taken from outer space." It looked like it was shot from inside the restaurant with a high-powered lens.

"Someone is taunting me," Val muttered.

"Taunting you? There are two of us in that shot."

"How did this happen, Val?" Gabi asked. "Why would anyone care if you were kissing . . ." Gabi's words dripped to nothing, her face grew red.

Val's eyes narrowed on Meg. "Maybe it has nothing to do with me."

Meg tapped her chest. "I'm not the celebrity. That would be Michael." Oh, wait . . . if someone was on the island with a camera . . . "Oh, no!" She spun on her heel, prepared to run to her villa.

Val took her arm, spun her toward the front of his house. "I'll drive."

They fled to the golf cart, sped out of his drive. Her heart was pumping. What if she was too late? What if Ryder and Michael had already been caught on camera?

She forced a few deep breaths, tried to ward off her lungs closing up.

Chapter Eleven

Val took the corners too fast, slung his arm over Meg's body to keep her from toppling out of the golf cart on the last one. She ran from the cart, stopped at the door. "Wait here."

"Cara."

"Wait." She took a deep breath and walked into the villa calling Michael's name. Seconds later, she emerged and waved him inside. "They're not here."

Val stepped inside, took in the space, and reached for his cell phone.

"Yes, Mr. Masini?" Carol answered on the second ring.

"Miss Rosenthal is looking for Mr. Wolfe. Has he left the island?"

"No, sir. I will make a few calls and call you back with his location."

He disconnected the call. "We'll know where he is in a moment."

She ran a hand through her hair and started to pace the room. "This is bad, Val. Really freaking bad."

"Calm down, Margaret." He could hear a soft wheeze in her lungs and wondered if her medicine was close by.

"Don't tell me to calm down. This shit isn't supposed to go down on this island. Key West was more silent than here." She kept talking, pacing. "I knew this was too good to be true."

"You know, *cara*, kissing me isn't a sin." Unless . . . unless he failed to learn about someone. "Wait . . . is there someone—"

"Oh, good God, no. Are your background checks that limited that you couldn't find a jealous lover?"

"I respect my guests' privacy." He paused and tilted his head. "Wait, how is it your background checks are so thorough?"

She opened her mouth, then closed it promptly.

"Cara?"

"Why are you calling me that? What does it mean anyway?"

"Dear, darling." Seemed fitting since she didn't give him leave to use her desired name.

She grunted, just like his mother. "And you didn't answer my question."

"I'm not going to answer your question. I don't know you well enough."

"I've tasted your molars and you don't know me well enough?"

He wanted to laugh but found the statement unsettling.

"Once. One kiss, Masini. You don't know me, and I don't know you." She looked toward the clock on the wall. "Where the hell are you, Michael?"

She ran a hand over her chest and Val stepped closer. "Please, *cara*. I don't think Michael would want you this worried, worried to the point of not breathing."

Some of the heat in her eyes melted. "We need to find him, Val. Find them both before more pictures can be taken."

Val thought he was starting to see the problem, but didn't dare ask her. If his speculation was correct, *this is really freaking bad* wasn't a strong enough statement.

A click at the front door turned their attention away from each other.

Michael walked in the front door laughing, Ryder at his side.

Meg rushed to Michael, pulled him inside the room, and slammed the door closed. "Thank God you're here."

"What happened?" There was an abrupt end to Michael's laughter and worry marred his face.

"Someone on the island has a camera."

Michael turned white. "What?"

Margaret placed a hand on Michael's chest. "A picture of Val and me was in that stack of mail this morning."

"You and Val?"

Margaret put both hands in the air, looked around the room. She placed a finger over her lips, and waved them all out the sliding door.

"What are we doing out here?" Val asked once they were at the edge of the veranda.

"It pays to be paranoid, Masini." Margaret moved to the outside stereo, turned on a rock station. "That should work."

"Jesus, Meg, you're scaring me."

Val noticed that Ryder had lost the color in his face, but had yet to say a word.

"If someone has a camera, they might have audio."

Michael's jaw clenched.

Val hated that his guests were this concerned about a breach in security. Who was he kidding? Security had already been blown up. The only element missing was a leak to the media.

"I need to notify my security," Val told them.

Meg offered a nod, but didn't look into his eyes.

Once Lou was told of the latest breach, Val returned to the Wolfe party. They were looking at the photograph with rapt attention.

"How did this happen, Mr. Masini?" Michael asked.

"I don't know, but I *will* find out."

Ryder finally spoke. "We should leave."

Michael shook his head. "And appear guilty? I don't think so."

"Mike."

There it was, a look between two people that couldn't be faked or *acted*. Everything became perfectly clear. Michael Wolfe and his lover, who was not Margaret Rosenthal, were afraid their relationship was about to become public knowledge.

Val thought of the first two pictures in his in-box. He hated to worry his guests, then realized the only ethical thing was to open his mouth. Even though it threatened his ability to taste Margaret again.

"Someone is watching you." He directed his comment to Margaret. "I'm not sure if the attention is on Margaret or you, Mr. Wolfe."

"The picture is of me."

"True. And while I hold no issue of it becoming public, it threatens your ploy here. The other one, however, plays into the ploy."

Margaret met his gaze.

Her body went rigid. "Other one?"

Good thing Lou showed up when he did. There was no telling what kind of bodily harm Meg was about to evoke on the man she'd kissed. She'd even cooked for him, for God's sake.

To learn that the first picture had shown up the day after they arrived on the island and she was just now hearing about it ticked her off.

Lou wore a three-piece suit similar to Val's. Only Lou had a shitload of body behind his threads. He looked familiar, too.

Val handed Lou the picture. "I want to know exactly where that was taken."

"Right away, Mr. Masini."

He turned to leave and Meg jumped in front of him. "You're the main guy . . . right? Security?"

"Yes, ma'am."

The man was taller than her, and impossible to look around. Common sense told her to filter her words. "Sweep the villa. Make sure there are no bugs."

Lou looked beyond her.

She waved a hand in front of his eyes. "Now, Mr. Myong. I need to know no one is listening to me pee."

"Yes, ma'am."

Meg followed him into the villa, leaving Michael and Ryder outside. Val followed.

Val had Lou helping him out . . . but Meg had more resources. She'd never been happier about her connections than at that moment.

She picked up the phone.

"Who are you calling?" Val asked.

"Backup."

Rick answered with his usual, "Hey."

"Rick, just the man I need to talk to."

"Hey, Meg. How's paradise?"

She rubbed her forehead. "I need to know if this line is secure."

"What?"

"You heard me."

"Shit."

"Double shit."

"Margaret?" Val said behind her.

"Zip it, Masini." The line clicked a few times. Worry crawled up Meg's spine. "You there?"

"I am. My line is clear. I sent word to Neil. Call him and he'll do a second check," Rick said.

"Got it."

"Call me back if we're clear."

"I will."

She hung up, dialed Neil's number, and went through the same routine. Neil was less than jovial. "You're clear."

"Thanks, Neil."

"Can you talk?"

She looked around the room, worried that ears were hidden behind a clock. "I don't know yet."

"Contact us when you know."

"Oh, don't worry. I will."

She hung up only to start dialing Rick again.

"Why do I have the feeling the secret service has invaded your body?" Val asked.

She thought of the different marriages she'd arranged, the enormity of wealth and power behind those people . . . her friends. Judy, Michael . . . her boss, Samantha. Maybe the loyalty card hadn't skipped her, just bounced away from her blood relatives and moved to her friends.

"The secret service would be lucky to have me," she told him without a thread of humor.

Rick answered on the first ring. "I'm going to hand the phone to Lou. He's Valentino Masini's head of security. Make sure this guy can back up his bulk, won't you?"

"You got it. Judy wants you to know we can be there in four and a half hours."

She smiled. "Have Sam's pilot on standby."

"You got it."

Meg found Lou in her bedroom searching through everything. "Talk to Rick. Give him your name."

"Beg your pardon, Miss Rosenthal but—"

"It's OK, Lou," Val said from the doorway.

Meg eased up her temper. "He's a retired Marine who specializes in security, Lou. Maybe he can help you find anything that might be lurking."

Only when Val nodded did Lou take the phone from her and put it to his ear.

The villa was clear . . . and even if they missed something miniscule, Lou had a jamming device that left a high-pitched feed inside the space that affected any outside feeds. Meg insisted her cell phone return to her purse, and once Rick did another check on that and deemed it empty of covert ears, she took it outside to talk to her friends.

Once she brought them up to date on the situation she encouraged Rick to relay to Sam any and every possible check on Sapore di Amore that hadn't already been done.

"I think I should be there, check for myself where the breach is taking place."

"Let me see what we can do here without you."

"I don't like it," Judy said from a second line in their home.

"I don't like it either. Michael hasn't said much, but he's worried."

"Maybe I should talk to him." As his sister, Judy might be able to help. But Michael and Ryder were strolling along the shore in deep conversation. They were walking yards apart, but she could still see that they weren't paying attention to anything but each other's words. "I'll suggest he call you if he needs to."

She ended the conversation and walked into the living room, where Val was on his phone. "Everyone, Carol. No one leaves or enters the island without talking to *me* first. Our employees know about a lockdown drill. Tell them it's a drill."

Val ended his conversation with his secretary and placed his phone in the inside pocket of his suit.

Meg felt Val's hand on her shoulder.

She jumped and he dropped it to his side. "I will find who is behind this."

"*We* . . . we will find the photographer."

"I'm not convinced they're looking at you, *cara*."

"I'm the link in the pictures. If I were a senator's wife, there'd be hell to pay." She needed to write stuff down to keep it right in her head. She shuffled through the drawers in the kitchen. There was a pad of paper somewhere. She'd seen it when they checked in.

"What are you looking for?"

She pulled the complimentary pad of paper from the drawer and snagged a pen. "Found it. I'm going to need a computer with Internet access."

"Margaret—"

"Don't even think of denying me. We both have something to lose here if we don't figure out who is doing this crap."

"What exactly do *you* have to lose, Margaret?"

She hesitated, not appreciating the position she was in. "Alliance arranges contractual agreements between exclusive clients."

"In English, *cara*."

"We arrange marriages. Temporary marriage contracts between two consenting adults."

"Like a call service?"

She snapped her gaze to his. "Sex is not part of the contract. Ever. It's a business agreement like any other. And the outside world believes the marriages are made out of love."

Val ran a hand over his chin. "And why would someone need this kind of arrangement?"

Meg rolled her eyes. "Look around you, Masini . . . use your imagination."

His eyes lit up when understanding dawned.

She removed three sheets and wrote on the top of them. Michael, Meg, Masini . . .

"Both pictures had me in them." She wrote pictures times two on the paper with her name. Picture times one on each of the others.

Val stepped forward and took the pen from her hand and scribbled out the one on his paper and wrote a two. "A lone shot of me was taken."

Meg scowled. "Anything else you're not telling me, Masini?"

"Nope, I think that's it."

Trusting this man was becoming more and more difficult. She looked at the papers again, grabbed the pen back. "Who is threatened by the actual pictures?"

It wouldn't hurt her reputation if a shot of her and Val circulated . . . nor would it hurt to be found at Michael's side. She shoved her page aside and took Michael's. Of the actual pictures, Michael's rep wasn't compromised. She took Masini's page. "Kissing me isn't the end of the world, but if word got out that pictures were being taken here, your resort might become painfully empty."

She jotted her thoughts on the papers and kept going.

Val watched her in silence.

It was obvious that Michael and Masini had the most to lose if more pictures were taken. Could whoever was taking them have more that they were waiting to reveal?

"The paparazzi would have already circulated the pictures if the media took them. So I think we can rule out that angle. Another guest?"

Val paced the room. "I'll draw a list of names of those here with something to hide. We can rule them out. The others, who knows?"

"Made any enemies getting where you are? Anyone ticked that you made all of this happen?"

"Jealousy? You think someone wants to bring me down out of envy?"

"It's one of the most basic of sins, Masini. I suggest you dig back in your diary and see if you've shoved someone a little hard."

"If I had, wouldn't they have taken pictures of obvious indiscretions? Why snap a photo of me walking on the shore, or kissing a beautiful woman? Wouldn't it be better to find a senator's wife, as you put it?"

"That's a good question." She wrote it on his paper and circled it. "Michael and I are a link . . . why?"

"Ryder's first instinct was to flee. Maybe that's what the photographer wants," Val said.

"Maybe Michael knows someone on the island who doesn't want him to know they're here." Meg wrote the lead down.

"Plausible."

"We haven't spent much time in the common areas of the hotel. Maybe we should."

She flipped over the papers and sat in one of the kitchen chairs. "Now, let's talk blackmail and monetary gain."

Chapter Twelve

Gabi felt her brother's frustration as keenly as if it were her own. The island resort might not be hers, but she was part of it and would do anything to keep what her brother had built on the island intact.

She worked by Carol's side to determine who had arrived on the island, and who might have left and come back during the time the Wolfe party had arrived. Three flights had landed and taken off again. The flight staff never left the building on the tarmac. Most of the guests took the charter to Key West and flew from there.

There were daily deliveries that brought familiar faces to the island. Most never left the dock. Still, Gabi spent her early evening interviewing the staff in charge of taking deliveries and greeting those who serviced the island.

"Thank you for your understanding." Gabi shook the hand of Adam, their head of deliveries. Nothing entered the island without his knowledge. At least in the organic nature.

"I like my job, Miss Masini. If this *drill* will help me keep it, I'm not going to complain."

He was the third person who'd alluded to the drill being something more. Maybe it was because of the intensity of questions, or how Lou brought in everyone on his security team to take part in the "drill."

The first set of employees changing shifts had been interviewed, and slowly filtered onto the off-island charter. Security double-checked their bags and thanked them for their understanding.

Gabi tried desperately hard to smile and thank their staff for their patience as they exited the island. Security interviewed the oncoming staff before they moved to their designated work areas.

When she had a moment to breathe, Gabi took a walk in the warehouse.

She looked at the pallets of food, drinks, cleaning supplies, office supplies . . . any- and everything needed to make the island run. She rounded the corner to find Julio standing over several wine crates. Seeing him placed a smile on her face. "Hello, Julio."

Alonzo's cocaptain of his yacht wasn't a big man. At maybe five foot eleven, he carried an extra thirty pounds for his frame, but he had a nice enough smile. She'd only met the man a couple of times.

"Miss Masini." He seemed shocked to see her there.

"Did Alonzo come early?" His yacht wasn't at the dock and hadn't been all day.

"No, ah . . . he's due tomorrow."

Strange. "How is it you're here?"

"I fell ill last week when we pulled in. Mr. Masini offered me a place to recover. Close quarters of the yacht would have made everyone sick."

That made sense. "You're feeling better, I hope."

"Much. Thank you. Looking forward to getting back to work."

Her gaze fell on the crates of wine. "I really hope that wine hasn't been in here since Alonzo was here." It should have been moved to the cellars, where the wine was kept at the right temperature.

Julio shifted his eyes to the crates.

Gabi looked at the back of the boxes and placed her hand on the sides. They were cool to the touch, as if they'd been placed in the warehouse recently.

"Perhaps Mr. Picano wanted them?"

"That's silly." Gabi walked to the end of the aisle and saw Adam walking away. "Adam?"

The man turned, started her way. Once at her side she pointed at the crates. "Do you know why these are sitting here and not the cellar?"

He shrugged. "I have no idea."

"Someone must have made a mistake. Can you see that they're moved back underground? I'd hate for it to spoil in the heat."

"Yes, ma'am."

"Thank you. I'm going to find my brother and see how much longer we're going to run the drill."

Adam lifted a brow as if unconvinced. "I'll keep the pace here."

Carol interrupted Gabi's path, asking her to intervene with some of the female staff who weren't happy about their purses being searched.

An hour later, and the threat of the ladies' jobs being placed on hold until the drill was completed if they refused a simple search, and Gabi was ready for more than a sparrow's portion of food. And perhaps a tiny cocktail . . . or two.

"I don't like the plan." Val paced his private office, dismissing everything Meg proposed with a flick of his wrist.

"Do you have another one? Because I don't think we're any closer to finding who is behind this now than we were before your investigation."

"Placing anyone in the spotlight for a photographer is a bad idea."

"My God, Val, the man . . . or woman, has a camera, not a gun."

"If pictures of you circulate, each time with a different man . . . that's . . ."

"It's what? My parents are self-proclaimed potheads, not preachers, or deacons of their church."

Val nailed her with a hard stare. "I don't like it and I won't be part of it."

Fine. She stood and grabbed her purse. He didn't have to play kissing games with her, but that wouldn't stop her from playing kissing games with others.

"Where are you going?" he asked when she walked past him.

"I'm getting ready for a late dinner . . . maybe a little dancing."

"Margaret?"

"Stand by and watch, Masini. You do what you have to do, and I'll do what I have to do."

He moved in front of her, blocking the door out. "*Cara*, please. There has to be another way to draw our photographer."

She shoved around him. "When you come up with it, tell me."

She heard him swearing . . . or at least that's what she thought he was doing, hard to tell when he cursed in Italian. Maybe she should pick up the other language to be more socially acceptable with her potty mouth.

Meg patted herself on the back for her brilliance and made her way back to the villa she shared with two gorgeous men. Such a hardship . . .

Later, the three of them entered the dining room, the actor, the singer, and the reluctant costar. She wore the dress she'd arrived on the island with, her hair styled by one of the many spa specialists on the island. Late dinners were the norm and the dining room was packed. Unlike when Michael and she had arrived the first night, for this one they went out of their way to make sure people saw them.

Meg leaned in to hear Ryder talk. "All we did was sit down and everyone is looking," he said under his breath.

"You haven't seen anything yet," she whispered before leaning back and laughing, drawing more attention from the closest tables. She placed a hand on Ryder's and left it there. "Oh, hon . . . you're such a gem."

Michael hid his grin behind the wine menu.

She leaned into Michael's space and pretended to read the list. "Pick something that won't give me a headache, won't you?"

"Italian wines are better for that." He tapped his finger on the menu. "Should we try more of Picano's?"

"You tell me."

"There was something familiar about the bottle we had that first night."

"That's because all wine tastes the same." At least in her humble opinion.

"I'll make you eat those words," Michael said with a laugh.

"Don't you mean, drink?"

"He's ruthless about his wine, Meg," Ryder said.

She knew that already. Michael talked to the waiter about his wine selection while one of the hotel guests made their way to the table. "It's Miss Rosenthal, right?"

"Yes." She didn't recognize the woman asking the question.

"I just wanted to tell you how much we enjoyed your performance last night."

Meg took the compliment gracefully and turned back to Ryder and Michael once the lady returned to her seat.

"Do you know who that was?" Michael asked.

"No idea."

Another couple stopped by their table to express their appreciation of the previous evening's entertainment as they left the restaurant.

"I guess it's not going to be that hard to catch the attention of just about anyone looking," Meg said.

The wine was brought to the table and some fuss was made before Michael approved.

Michael looked into his glass as if it held truth-seeing tea leaves that would tell him his future.

"It tastes like wine," Meg said.

"I've never heard of this label, but the taste is familiar."

"Squished grapes, Mike." Ryder sipped his wine and winked at Meg.

"I don't get it either," Meg said.

They moved through their first course and Michael ordered a second bottle of wine, and pondered it again.

Meg let Ryder and Michael drink the majority of the wine, choosing to keep her brain clear for the rest of the night. They enjoyed their meal without interruption or drama. Meg made sure her laughs were a little larger than life, and once the boys were through half of the second bottle of wine, they were well on their way to being an active part of the evening.

The DJ music was loud and there were several couples on the dance floor. The three of them stood around a tall table and Meg ordered a vodka on the rocks. She hit the dance floor before the drink had a chance to arrive. Once she was there, she turned to Michael and Ryder and waved one finger toward herself.

Ryder nudged Michael and he joined her . . . as planned.

She wasn't that great of a dancer, but Michael knew his way around a dance floor. The music was fast, sexy . . . perfect.

When Ryder cut in there were a few glances their way.

Meg laughed, larger than life.

Ryder put Michael to shame. At one point, she felt his hand on her ass right before he spun her away.

He led her back to their table and waved the waiter over for water and another round of drinks.

After another dance, Michael pulled her outside for a brief moment of fresh air. She took her drink with her and promptly left it on the nearest outside table before he drew her away from the crowd. "This far enough?"

She pretended to stumble. He caught her. "Careful, hon."

He nuzzled her neck as a lover might. "Careful, Michael . . . wouldn't want Ryder to get nervous."

He laughed, grabbed her head with both hands, and laid one on her. It was nice, she had to admit . . . but this was a friend, and other than the physical, she felt nothing. "That should do it," he said before releasing her.

"No wonder you're paid big money."

He wrapped his hand around her and walked back into the club.

All the while, she scanned the bar for one set of eyes and didn't see them. Not until Ryder was whispering in her ear in the ruse of luring her back inside after an innocent kiss.

"Having a good time?" Val asked as he stepped up to the table.

He knew the game, but he still looked at her with a scrutiny that was afforded the father of a teenage daughter.

She leaned into him, kissed his cheek. "I was wondering if you'd show up."

His jaw tightened. "Some of the guests wanted an encore." He motioned toward the stage where one of the employees was uncovering the keyboard.

Meg narrowed her gaze. "You want me to sing for you?"

He pushed her glass away from her when she reached for it. "Before you're unable to."

Seduced by Sunday

Meg tossed her head back and laughed, and then handed her glass to him with a whisper. "Hard to get drunk drinking water, Masini."

Vodka wasn't the evening's drink by accident. Funny how water and vodka looked alike to anyone watching from far away with a camera.

"Well?" he asked after taking a sip of her water and lifting the edge of his lips in a grin.

Meg lifted a hand to the stage. "Someone needs to introduce me, Valentino."

He leaned close so only she could hear him. "Why do I feel like a black widow is crawling over my skin, *cara*?"

She pulled him close with his tie, straightened it. "You worry too much."

Val was the perfect host. He thanked everyone for coming, let the lighting change in the room long enough to invite Meg to the stage.

Once the audience loosened their hold on their applause, Meg made sure she had everyone's attention.

"You'd think I'd have a break on my room rate for all the perks I'm giving you, Masini."

He surprised her with his response. "I've been watching your bar bill, Margaret. I think we're even."

She laughed. "Which reminds me . . . I could use another round." She turned on the keyboard, ran through a couple of chords, and made a downward motion to the tech, making sure the sound didn't push away anyone listening.

"I do my best work after a few drinks."

Michael laughed above the crowd. She pointed a finger in his direction. "Enough from you."

The crowd laughed, and within thirty seconds, a vodka on the rocks was sitting on the keyboard.

"I have to admit, Masini . . . this island is beautiful." She kept talking, the sound of the mic too tinny for her. The sound guy stood in the back of the room and adjusted levels with every word she said. She sipped her drink, added a bit of courage.

The people in the room clapped and she kept talking and adjusting the keyboard. The chords started to sound like an organ, but not something inside a church . . . more like a nightclub. Oh, what she wouldn't do for a few brass players and a guitar.

"However, I might need therapy after so much time away from the Internet."

"Hear, hear!"

The room exploded with laughter and a chorus of praise for her observation.

Val leaned against the bar and crossed his arms over his chest.

Last night . . . last night the song, the experience was for her. The love of singing with Jim Lewis wasn't something she'd ever forget.

Tonight . . .

She started the song . . . waited for the moment the audience realized what she was singing, and stared directly at Val as she gave life to "My Funny Valentine."

Chapter Thirteen

He'd watched as Wolfe pulled her outside and kissed her. Looked convincing enough for him. Ryder did the job with a tiny fumble. Still . . . it killed him to watch. Val could count on zero fingers how many times it bothered him to watch a woman he'd kissed kiss another man. Well, there was Lissa and Philip in fifth grade, but that didn't really count. Besides, he had been friends with Philip much longer than he'd wanted to kiss on Lissa.

Now Margaret stood onstage singing. There was no doubt she meant the song for him. Though he didn't think his looks were laughable, and neither did the snarky crowd, there wasn't any doubt in anyone's head that Valentine stood in place for Valentino.

Every cell in his body fired in unison as Meg finished the song.

"Thank you." She offered a strangely demure bow and left the stage. The DJ cued up a slow song and jumped right in to keep the room alive.

Several people stopped Meg before she wound her way toward her table.

Val cut her off.

More eyes were on them than he would have liked as he took her in hand and dragged her outside.

He walked her around the corner, down a dark hall . . . outside to a location not accessible by many.

She was against the wall, his lips possessing hers before any logical thought could stop him. Good Lord, she was soft and smelled like a breeze off the ocean in spring.

Meg moaned and moved into him. He looked to find her eyes closed, her body lax against his.

This wasn't a kiss for a camera, he told himself . . . this was a kiss for him. The taste of her filled him, made him crave more. He stroked the back of her neck, tilted her, and moved his lips over the beating pulse at her throat and ran his tongue down the length of it.

Nails in his back were his reward.

He found the curve of her hip, traveled lower until he met the hem of her dress.

He was lost . . . knew control wasn't a part of his soul at that moment when he searched her thigh to simply learn her body, learn what she desired.

Meg's head snapped back and hit the wall with a tiny crack. "Crap."

Her expletive stopped the movement of his hand, made him remember how public they were.

Val pulled her away from the wall, ran a hand to the back of her head. "Are you OK?"

She graced him with a lick of her lips. "A little warning, Masini." Her breaths were short pants that lifted her full breasts closer to him with every inhale.

Meg took a slow breath. He didn't hear a wheeze as he had the night before.

Confident that she wasn't in danger of suffocating or needing medical attention for a concussion, he eased his grip and placed a hand to the side of her face. "You sing like an angel, *bella*."

"You liked?"

He placed a quick kiss to her lips, pressed the full length of his body against hers. "You made love to the room with your voice. I was jealous of everyone there."

She lifted her knee against his leg and slowly slid it back down.

They stared into each other's eyes until their breathing eased and a few seconds of time passed.

He knew it wasn't the right time, felt it in his bones . . . but couldn't let the moment go without a confession. "I want you in my bed, *cara*."

Meg lifted her chin with a sharp breath. "Val . . ."

"I know . . ." he placed a soft kiss on her lips and drew back. "I want you there and I'm willing to wait."

A wide-eyed look of surprise filled her eyes before she pulled in her bottom lip. "We have too much at stake right now."

Val smiled and placed a finger over her lips to silence her. "I know."

With reluctance, he placed air between their bodies by moving away. He missed her, every soft curve, instantly.

Meg tugged at her dress, fixed the neckline.

Her fingertips brushed the edges of her breasts . . . a place he had yet to feel himself.

"You're staring, Val."

"*Sei bellissima*."

He moved his gaze to her eyes, felt her smiling at him. "It means, you're beautiful, *cara*."

"I'm sure there have been many beautiful women on this island."

He loved her moment of insecurity, relished in it until she looked away.

With one finger, he lifted her gaze back to his. "None as beautiful as you," he whispered. "None as beautiful as you."

———

Sleep was impossible. Meg, Michael, and Ryder laughed and played all the way back to the villa and closed all the blinds. They'd made more noise than necessary until Michael and Ryder called it a night.

She flipped her pillow over for the fifth time in an hour, couldn't find a cool side or a comfortable position to let her head rest. Thoughts of Val kissing her, the ruse they were all trying to play on whoever was taking the pictures, swirled like tornados inside her brain.

Meg snatched her charging cell phone off the bedside table. She keyed up Val's cell number and let her fingers do the talking. I've been thinking . . . how did this guy print a picture here on the island? She hit *send* without looking at the time.

If her kiss didn't key the man up as much as his did to her, then maybe she shouldn't let him near her again.

She started to think maybe he was asleep. Then three tiny dots at the bottom of her screen let her know that he was texting her back.

I thought about that. Must be one of the printers on the island.

Do you have a lot of them?

I don't know. I'll have Carol check in the morning.

Meg rolled to her side. Not sure how the information will help.

Narrow down the departments to search further. General housekeeping staff would stand out hovering over a printer.

Doesn't housekeeping leave daily? Could they have brought the pictures from home?

The three dots started to blink, hesitated, and blinked again. Do you really believe my housekeepers want pictures of us?

If a letter of extortion comes next, then yes. If not, then no.

If our man needs to print tonight's images . . . Maybe we can catch him.

Meg smiled, felt her eyes growing heavy. Let's hope he does, she replied.

I'm sorry the stress of this is keeping you up.

She considered her reply and decided there wasn't any harm in a little honesty. Seduction is outweighing the stress, Masini.

There wasn't a reply before her phone buzzed in her hand. She answered it with a soft voice.

"Put the phone away and get some sleep, *cara*." His voice was a low purr and the closest she'd come to pillow talk in a long time.

"So demanding," she whispered.

"You've seen nothing . . . yet."

Meg shivered with his intent. "Statements like that aren't going to help me sleep."

His low laugh kept her smiling.

"Good night, *bella*."

"Night, Val."

Her dreams were less of pictures and printers, and more about smoky kisses that stole her breath.

———

"I don't know what's worse, pictures or nothing."

Mike agreed with Meg's words, but kept silent.

Val had called first thing that morning to tell them that nothing had shown up in his in-box. No one delivered any mail.

"Maybe yesterday's interrogation spooked this guy and he didn't risk taking more shots," Ryder said.

They were sitting on the veranda eating breakfast. They'd opted for room service, in hopes of giving an opportunity for their photographer to send another photo. All they ended up with was fresh fruit and muffins.

He and Ryder had stayed up late, talking. Ryder was worried. If word about the two of them circulated, he could kiss his teaching job good-bye. Technically, it wasn't against the rules of the school to teach and be a homosexual . . . but Ryder coached football as well. Someone, somewhere, would hold issue with that. Rural Utah wouldn't stand for it. The scandal wouldn't be worth the stress.

"What do we do now?" Ryder asked.

"I say we carry on as normal." She looked between the two of them. "OK, maybe not completely normal. We don't want to give the photographer anything truly scandalous."

"Unlike last night?" Mike asked.

Meg batted her lashes. "My reputation could stand the boost," she teased. "If all this guy can grab is me swapping spit with a bunch of sexy men . . . then he won't have anything scandalous to pin on you." She waved a finger in the air. "I'm the one who convinced you to come here."

"I'm the one who invited Ryder."

"I didn't have to come," Ryder said last.

"So we all feel responsible. Great. Lotta good that's going to do when Michael's career blows up, you lose your job, Masini's island is no longer Fantasy Island for the rich and famous . . . and Alliance hits the media for what it truly is. Because the reporters chasing this story will dig until they find even more dirt." Meg turned to the sea and muttered, "Shit."

"We should just leave," Ryder said for the tenth time.

"If the pictures are already taken, what good would that do? At least here we can try and corner this person and play them at their own game."

"Pay them off, you mean?"

Meg shook her head. "That would be like negotiating with terrorists. No. Anyone playing dirty *is* dirty. We find their dirt."

Ryder nudged Mike's arm. "Glad she's on our side."

"Let's see what today brings. I don't think this guy is going to stay silent for long."

"We're scheduled to leave on Monday." Only three nights away.

"School starts back on Monday." Mike wanted to take Ryder's hand, but didn't dare out in the open. He offered a sympathetic look instead.

"Business as usual then. Ryder leaves Sunday as planned. We leave on Monday . . . or you leave on Monday," Meg said.

"What about you?"

"We play that by ear. We make sure and take a few photos ourselves. Safe to say since I'm snuggling with Masini I'd want a few shots of us together. If pictures start to circulate of us, we can say we took them."

"I like that idea, Meg. It won't help Val if the person behind this takes pictures of others, but it might help our stake in the matter."

Chapter Fourteen

Gabi waited on the dock as Alonzo's yacht pulled into view.

"There you are." Meg walked onto the dock behind her. "Your brother said you'd be out here."

Gabi accepted her new friend's one-arm hug. "You didn't have to wait with me."

"Completely selfish of me. I wanted to see this yacht I heard you talking about."

"Can you believe I've only sailed on it once?" Gabi asked as they both watched it move closer.

"Why's that?"

She shrugged. Because Alonzo was always coming or going . . . seldom did he stick around, and there wasn't a *good time* for her to join him. "He's very busy."

Gabi turned to find Meg studying her.

"I'm sure that will change once you're married."

"I would think so."

Meg pushed a strand of hair from her face. "Did he do something to tick off your mom, or does she hate the thought of her little girl sleeping with someone?"

Gabi managed a laugh. "I wish it was the latter. Yet Alonzo hasn't done a thing out of line. He even suggested we spend ample time apart to ease my mother's fears of an early grandchild."

"You have no sound idea why she doesn't approve?"

"All she says is she doesn't like him . . . doesn't trust him."

Meg lifted her hand to shield her eyes. "You trust him. That's all that matters."

"That's what I tell her."

Meg opened her mouth and closed it again.

"What?"

"What about your girlfriends . . . what do they say about Alonzo? I've always found my girlfriends clued into the men in my life more than I ever was. If there was a guy I liked and they couldn't stand him, it never worked out."

Gabi shuffled her feet. "Hard to keep girlfriends on an island of employees and holiday guests."

"Oh. There has to be—"

Gabi shook her head, cutting Meg off.

Meg curved her hand around the crook of Gabi's arm. "Good thing I'm here then. I'll give you my honest opinion so long as you don't hate me for it."

"If I don't agree with you?"

"A good friend will offer her opinion and support your decisions. Unless he's violent . . ."

"Lord no!"

Meg grinned. "Good to know."

Gabi wondered if this new friendship could hold up over time. Gabi couldn't remember the last long friendship she'd shared with another woman.

Meg coughed a few times, held a hand to her chest.

"Are you OK?"

"Asthma," Meg offered, as if the one word meant everything. "Been giving me a little trouble since I've been here."

"Please tell me the humidity isn't causing it."

"Stress. Sounds crazy . . ." she coughed again. "But it's worse when things get crazy in my life."

"Is that normal?"

"For me. It might be time for new medication."

Gabi placed a hand on Meg's arm. "Is there anything other than medication that helps?"

Meg looked to the sky as if it held the answer. "I used to target shoot."

Gabi knew her expression showed doubt.

"Seriously . . . the concentration helped. Maybe I should try skeet. Doesn't Val have that here?"

The expression on Meg's face lit up with Val's name on her lips. "He does."

There was a pause before Meg asked, "You approve of me and your brother?"

"I like how he smiles when he sees you. He works too hard and takes everything so seriously. It's nice to see him relax."

Meg nodded a few times before they were interrupted by dock-hands moving toward them.

Alonzo's yacht slowly made its way into their small port. Receiving hands on the dock caught the ropes and tied them up. Gabi searched the deck to find it void of Alonzo. He finally emerged after the crew secured the gangplank.

His gaze moved between her and Meg and back again. "Gabriella."

She opened her arms to his stiff frame. "Darling." His kiss was brief, much more so than the last few times he'd visited the island.

He placed his lips close to her ear. "Public displays in front of a stranger, Gabi."

She laughed off his concern. "You remember Margaret?"

"Of course. I'm surprised to see you still here."

"Good to see you again, too, Mr. Picano. Our visit is scheduled to last a few more days."

"Meg wanted to see the yacht," Gabi told him.

Alonzo attempted to smile, but Gabi could tell he wasn't happy with the thought. "Let me give my crew time to *settle*. Perhaps tomorrow."

"She came all the way out here—"

"I'm sure Margaret understands. Would you want to entertain in a dirty kitchen?"

Alonzo was a bit of a perfectionist. She'd not seen anything he had a part in out of place. The one time she'd sailed on the yacht the staff kept everything immaculate.

"I get it," Meg said with a generous smile. "Another time."

"Yes, another time," Alonzo murmured.

"I should get back," Meg broke the awkward moment of quiet. "I'll see you at dinner."

"Until then," Gabi said before Meg turned and walked away.

"Dinner?"

"We've grown quite close in the past few days. She really is a lovely person."

Alonzo disengaged his arm from her waist and signaled one of his staff over. "I don't know how you can determine that in just a few days. People here tend to pretend they are what they are not."

"What does that mean?"

"It means be careful who you trust, Gabriella." The warning felt odd coming from him.

"She's a friend, Alonzo. Please don't treat her poorly."

He lost his smile. "You have *no* friends."

His words hurt, partly because they were true.

"I do now."

His captain disembarked and walked to their side.

"You're busy. I'll see you once you've *settled*." Anger she wasn't prepared for fueled her quick steps as she walked away.

Alonzo scrambled after her and grasped her arm. "I'm sorry," he said once she looked at him. "I've had a stressful week."

So have I, she wanted to say but didn't. "It's OK."

He pulled her into his arms. It was her turn to feel stiff. The eyes of his staff watched until she noticed them, and they quickly looked away. "Public displays, Alonzo," she tossed his words back.

He kissed the top of her forehead. "I'll see you at the villa."

With a tilt of her head, she walked away. It would be nice to have a friend, especially one as outgoing as Meg.

Why, after only a few days, did the other woman's opinion count? If she wanted Meg's approval of her fiancé, something told Gabi she wasn't going to get it.

Mrs. Masini skipped dinner, a testimony to the company . . . or at least that's what Meg thought.

Val invited two other couples to keep the conversation filtered, which suited Meg perfectly. The thought of bringing up any of the drama in front of Alonzo gave her gut a twist.

Mr. and Mrs. Dray were pure Texan oil. Unless they liked to play dress-up in the bedroom, the only reason they were on the island was for the sunsets and beach. Mrs. Cornwell, a wealthy widow of one of Chicago's celebrated restaurateurs, and her long-time *friend*, Mr. Shipley, filled the seats at the round table.

Meg cringed to see wine set on the table. She really was done with the stuff after so many days.

Mrs. Dray held herself with an air of superiority that reminded Meg of every stuffy neighbor she'd passed, but never met, while living at Michael's home. She was about to write the woman off as someone she didn't want to know until she passed on the wine and told the waiter to bring her a bourbon.

"I think I like you," Meg said from across the table. "Make that two."

"I do apologize, Mr. Picano. I appreciate a nice glass with my meal, but I prefer something a little stronger before supper."

Alonzo offered a smile that Meg could only categorize as fake and shook his head. "Not a problem, Mrs. Dray."

"My fiancé has made me a true wine lover," Gabi boasted.

"Fiancé?" Mrs. Cornwell asked.

"When is the wedding?" Mrs. Dray asked.

"Fall."

"What an exciting time. Congratulations to you both." The comments were homogenized and stale. Meg secretly wished the waiter would hurry with the whiskey.

"Is your gown strapless? So many wedding dresses are these days."

Gabi looked at Alonzo and then to Meg. "I haven't settled on one yet."

Mrs. Dray and Mrs. Cornwell both dropped their smiles. "You're marrying this fall and you haven't chosen a dress yet?"

"That's unheard of. My Millie had her gown six months before her wedding. It took longer to order it than she expected."

"Then there are alterations. Lord knows how that can go wrong."

Seemed the older women at the table had a lot to say about wedding dresses.

The waiter set Meg's drink in front of her. "Bless you," she whispered.

He grinned.

"You really must jump on the dress, darlin'."

Gabi's face had grown pale.

"I know some amazing designers in LA who work on Hollywood's timeline of needing everything yesterday, Gabi. Maybe you can come back with us when we leave."

The color in her friend's face started to return.

"That's ridiculous. There are plenty of dressmakers in South Florida," Alonzo said.

"I like the idea of going to Los Angeles and finding the perfect dress."

When Alonzo patted Gabi's hand, Meg had a desire to kick him under the table. Instead, she nudged Michael and made sure he noticed the subtle gesture.

"I'm sure I can find you someone here you can trust to give you what you need."

Before Meg could chime in, the older women did so for her. "The groom can't see the dress before the big day."

"Certainly not."

Alonzo couldn't get a word in, but he kept his hand over Gabi's until she tugged it away to drink from her wineglass.

Michael diverted the subject. "Mr. Picano."

Alonzo directed his attention away from Gabi.

"I have to tell you, last night we had a bottle of your 2009 merlot. It's one of the best I've tasted," he told him.

"Thank you. I'm surprised there are still bottles available. I thought that was one of the years needing replenishment."

"There was a pallet of wine in the warehouse yesterday. I wonder if the merlot was part of those crates."

"Wine left in a warehouse? That doesn't sound right . . . not in this heat." Mrs. Cornwell would know.

"They were cool, I assure you," Gabi told the lady. "I thought maybe you'd come in early and delivered more wine. Julio seemed surprised they were there."

Meg noticed Val's rapt attention to the conversation.

"I'm sure your guests don't want to hear about wine deliveries," Alonzo said to Gabi.

"Or wedding dresses," Mr. Dray added.

Mrs. Dray nudged him with her elbow. "We did that enough with Millie to last until the grandbabies are married."

"I say we bully Michael into telling us about his next movie." Ryder cut the conversation with his words and the men switched subjects.

Gabi listened without comment, her silence loud as anything Meg had ever heard. Sometime between appetizers and dinner, she stood to excuse herself to the restroom.

"I'll join you." Meg pushed away from the table. "I don't remember where it is."

The men sat back down as they walked away from the table and Gabi led the way out of the dining room.

As Meg expected, once behind the ladies' room door, Gabi collapsed into one of the chairs and fought tears.

Meg grabbed a box of tissues from the vanity. "Don't start that. Your makeup won't hold up."

Gabi grabbed a tissue and dabbed under her eyes. "He's being awful."

"Oh, I don't know . . . Val's quite charming."

The smile Meg was reaching for never emerged from her friend. "He's not like this."

"Controlling, condescending, and difficult?"

"You see it, don't you?"

Meg saw that and a whole lot more. "I think it's important to see all sides of a person before you exchange wedding vows."

Gabi abruptly stood and moved to the mirror. "I'm going with you to LA." She turned. "If that's really an invitation and not something said out of politeness."

Meg stood beside her and adjusted Gabi's dress. "I insist. There's something else I want to do for you."

"Oh?"

"One of my job descriptions is finding every minuscule part of a person's present or past that might impede a contract between two parties."

"You mean between Alonzo and I?"

"Marriage is a big step."

A frown marred Gabi's brow. "Isn't that violating something?"

"It's not illegal to ask around."

"Moral?"

"I'm a Catholic Jew. *Eat the bacon! Don't eat the bacon, it's a sin.* I'm already morally messed up."

Gabi finally laughed. "I'm rather fond of bacon."

Chapter Fifteen

It killed Val to move about the night as if nothing was going on. Nothing appeared in his in-box all day; nothing arrived via mail. Dinner had been tense, but he couldn't put his finger on why.

Seemed Gabi and Margaret were getting along well enough as the evening moved from dinner to drinks at the island's after-hours club.

Surprisingly, Alonzo retired without Gabi at his side. He noticed the two of them talking in rather heated tones outside the restaurant before Alonzo excused himself.

Instead of opening up to him, Gabi moved to Margaret's table and sandwiched herself between the three of them. Before long, his sister's smile returned and Michael took her to the dance floor.

Jim found Val hovering in the corner and slapped a hand to his back.

They shook hands, each of them trying to squeeze harder than the other. "I'm leaving in the morning," Jim told him.

"When will I see you again?"

"Gabi's wedding?" They both looked at the dance floor. "Is there still a wedding?"

Val thought of Michael Wolfe and his "friend," who sat by watching the other man. Then Gabi started dancing with someone else.

"I'll let you know," Val told his friend.

Jim chuckled and walked away.

Val watched Jim tap Margaret on the shoulder and invite her to the dance floor.

He swung her out and pulled her close, whispered something in her ear.

She pushed him away, laughing, and continued to dance.

Val didn't consider himself a jealous man, but damn it, Margaret was changing that.

They were quite the entertainment, the petite, pale blonde and the robust, dark blues singer. Seemed everyone was watching them dance, enjoying Jim's moves and Margaret's demure attention to her dance partner.

Val had to admit, they were engaging.

Then the song ended and Margaret did the unexpected.

She smacked a kiss right on Jim's lips, leaving him stumbling back, holding his chest. Val was too far away to hear the exchange, but several people around them started to laugh as Jim gave her a playful smack on the ass and walked away.

Val moved in, caught her before she could leave the floor. The song was slower than the others, affording him the right to pull her against his frame. "You're killing me, *cara*. Do you know that?"

"Jim is harmless," she said close to his ear.

"The man has been married to five women. Dated women as young as you."

The sway of her hips against his reminded him how much he wanted her. He sucked in a breath of control.

"I won't be his next anything, Masini."

He knew that. Was more secure than that. So why did he release a breath as if he'd just broken the surface of water in need of air? "Are you really leaving on Monday?"

Their quiet dance floor conversation kept him straining to hear her words, except when he felt her breath against the lobe of his ear. That was a torture all on its own.

"And I'm taking your sister with me."

He backed away to see if her eyes lied. "Really?"

She nodded, moved closer to talk to him. "Do you ever leave the island?"

Not often, but he did have people here he could depend on to watch over things in his absence.

"Occasionally."

———

Between Val, Jim, Michael, and Ryder, Meg was having a hard time sitting down. Gabi was dancing just as much and from the look in her eyes, having a great time doing it.

The lack of alcohol the night before made the bourbon Meg had been drinking go straight to her head. She excused herself to the ladies' room between dances. It was when she took a wrong turn and ended up down a service hall that Meg realized she needed to switch to Coke. She rounded two corners before realizing she wasn't walking toward the music, but away from it.

"Whoa. Steady there."

Meg wasn't sure what startled her more. The man stopping her in her path, or his clothing.

"I got turned around."

It was hard to see his features under the hoodie.

Why was he wearing a hoodie? It wasn't cold.

He pointed a finger at her. "You're the one kissing everyone."

"Excuse me?"

The man, who was taller than she was and had a good fifty pounds on her, moved closer.

Meg backed away.

"You shouldn't be back here." His sour breath brushed against her, his tongue licked his lips.

Funny how panic sobered you. The stranger was too close, too shadowed to describe, and much too quiet for Meg's comfort.

The corridor to the left was empty, so was the one to the right. For the life of her she couldn't remember which way she'd come from.

She felt her lungs constrict.

The stranger moved a half foot closer. Any more and she'd scream.

He placed a hand on the wall behind her, pinning her in on one side. "Back off, Margaret."

Isn't that my line?

"Best you leave before you get hurt."

The man placed a finger to the shadow of his hoodie and shushed her. Then he was gone.

There were times in your life when you were given a free pass. Like a run through a red light you simply didn't see and no one smashed into you . . . or a poke into an electronic device that wasn't unplugged, yet you're still standing with straight hair to tell about it.

This was one of those moments.

And Meg knew it.

Her lungs, however, didn't.

And her inhaler was in her purse, sitting on the table.

She took a few steps and found the hall spinning. Instead of fighting it, she slid down the wall and lowered her head.

Slow, deep breaths in, slower breaths out.

"Gabi?" Val motioned his sister to the table. "Margaret's been gone for some time. Can you check on her?"

Though his sister's smile was brilliant, he couldn't remember seeing her eyes so glossed over.

"Meg went to the bathroom without me?"

Val didn't want to tell his sister that it wouldn't be hard with all the attention she was drawing to herself on the dance floor. "Some time ago, *tesoro.*"

Gabi waved him off and headed toward the ladies' room. When his sister returned without Margaret, the itch inside Val's left eye started to twitch.

Michael and Ryder were talking to some of the hotel guests at a stand-up table.

"Stay here," he instructed his intoxicated sister.

Val tapped Michael on the shoulder. "Would Margaret return to the villa alone?"

Michael looked over Val's head. "No. Not without saying something."

"What's going on?" Ryder asked.

"Margaret's missing."

"Seriously?" Ryder's smile fell.

Michael nodded toward the outside. "You check outside," he told Ryder.

"I'll start in the back." Val headed toward the ladies' room, felt Michael close on his heels.

The hall to the restrooms didn't house a petite blonde . . . or at least not the one he was searching for.

He pushed back out into the fray, looked over the heads of the people in the club. He and Michael split up and returned back to the bathroom less than five minutes later.

"She's not in the club," Michael said.

Val stepped back into the hall with the bathrooms, noticed the service door, and walked through it.

"She wouldn't have come this way."

"She's been drinking." Val thought of his sister, the gloss in her eyes. "Margaret!" he yelled. He rounded the corner to the back of the restaurant, knew the corridor well, and started to turn back.

Michael stopped him with a firm hand to the chest.

A soft thump hit a wall, repeatedly.

Both of them ran.

Val felt part of him die when he saw Meg slumped over herself, hitting the wall with a weak hand.

"Cara!"

"Jesus, Meg."

They fell on her in unison.

Val placed a hand on her face, made her focus.

"Purse."

What? "What happened?"

"Inhaler. Purse."

It took Val a moment to process her words. It took Michael half that time. The other man ran from the hall, back the way they came.

Val panicked. Knew he was even when he was doing so. His cell phone was out of his pocket in a nanosecond.

"Good evening, Mr. Masini."

"I need the nurse in the corridor between the lounge and the restaurant . . . now."

"Right away, Mr. Masini."

"Call an air ambulance."

Margaret shook her head.

He didn't listen.

"Right away, Mr. Masini."

He dropped the phone to her side, heard how little air was moving inside her lungs.

Michael burst through the door, her purse in his hand. Ryder, Gabi, and several employees trailed behind.

Michael fished out her medicine, shook it, and placed it to her lips. "Deep breath."

She sucked in a pathetic breath and Michael repeated the process.

"What happened?" Gabi cried behind them.

"Someone call an ambulance."

Val focused on Margaret. Her eyes found his as she sucked in another shot of the inhaler.

He didn't realize he was squeezing her hand until she squeezed it back.

"I'm here, *cara*. You're going to be OK."

"You were lucky, Miss Rosenthal."

She was still wheezing, her lungs not completely right but so much better than when they'd landed at Miami General.

When the second hit of the inhaler didn't do squat, she knew she was in trouble.

Val kept talking. Helped her take slow breaths and control the panic that threatened.

She couldn't remember it ever being this bad.

"When was the last time you saw a pulmonologist?" Doctor Stick Up His Ass asked.

"My general sees me every year."

"You need a lung doctor. You should know that."

She did, but had ignored the need every year she visited her general. The meds she was on controlled her asthma well enough. At least until today.

"Know anyone in LA?"

The ER doctor shook his head. "I have a friend, Dr. Eddy. I'll call him and ask if he knows of anyone close by."

"Thanks."

"In the meantime, there are much better drugs out there." He told her what he was prescribing before she left his hospital. There was a daily pill, a daily inhaler, and a different rescue inhaler she'd not used before. Seemed the meds she'd taken from early high school were obsolete.

Who knew?

The doctor started to leave the room. "Doctor?"

"Yes?"

She sighed, adjusted the tube of oxygen that sat inside her nose. "Thanks."

He pointed directly at her. "Thank me by not coming back. Do you know how many young women like you die every year from an asthma attack by ignoring their symptoms?"

She shook her head.

"Don't be one of them." He glanced at the monitor above her. "You're going to be here for a while, Miss Rosenthal. Might as well try and get some sleep."

She closed her eyes and felt her pulse beating too fast, even her breaths were too short. But at least they worked. Good God, she knew what a fish out of water felt like.

"Miss Rosenthal?" The nurse woke her. How was it possible she'd fallen asleep?

"Yes?"

"There are some very anxious people outside who want to know you're all right."

Meg pushed herself up on the gurney. "Bring them in."

"All of them?"

"Better all together than one at a time."

The nurse smiled and opened the door.

Michael entered the room first, his smile forced. "I knew you liked attention, Meg . . . but this is extreme."

Ryder smacked him, kissed her cheek. "How are you feeling?"

"Better."

Val stood behind his sister and Mrs. Masini. The older woman's painful expression stuck somewhere inside of her.

"You gave us quite a scare," Gabi said from the foot of the bed.

"Sorry."

"What happened? How did you get back there?"

"Took a wrong turn." Her gaze met Val's, his eyes narrowed as if he was searching her words for the truth.

Michael sat on the edge of the bed. "Was the dancing too much?"

That and she had the shit scared out of her. The anxious faces, Mrs. Masini's in particular, kept her from blurting out the encounter with the hooded man. "M-must have been. I'm sorry for all the trouble."

"Don't be ridiculous, Meg," Mrs. Masini said.

Meg glanced at the hospital clock with a frown. "It's after two in the morning. You should go back, get some sleep."

Michael started to shake his head.

"Take Mrs. Masini and Gabi back with you. Make sure they get home OK."

"We can wait for you," Gabi said.

"They want me to have another treatment, make sure I don't have a relapse. It might be a while."

"You can't rest with all of us here, can you?" Mrs. Masini offered the best reason for them to leave. The older woman walked forward and patted Meg's hand.

The jittery reaction to the medication made Meg's hand shake terribly.

"Valentino will stay with you, bring you back when you're ready," Mrs. Masini told her.

Val pushed away from the wall. "I'd have it no other way, Mama."

Michael kissed the back of her hand. "Are you sure?"

"Positive. I'll be back by breakfast." She took another look at the clock. "Maybe lunch."

She accepted hugs and kisses before they all fled the small room.

Val pulled a chair alongside the gurney and took her hand. "What upset you, *cara?*"

His soft, pleading gaze turned hard with her first words. "There was a man . . ."

Chapter Sixteen

The Harrisons' private jet landed on the small island to drop off and pick up.

Val stepped forward to greet Mr. and Mrs. Evans. The retired Marine met his eyes and offered a firm handshake. "Thank you for coming."

"How's Meg?" Judy Evans didn't bother with pleasantries.

"Moaning that I'm making her leave."

Rick Evans had a catchy smile. "Feeling better, then."

"Much." He walked them toward the golf cart that would drive them to the villa. "I'm sorry we're meeting under these circumstances."

"I'm happy someone is using their head. Meg can be difficult when she sets her mind to something."

Val had been told that Judy and Meg were the best of friends and had been since college. Obviously, the woman knew her friend well.

"It's a short drive," Val told them. "It shouldn't take long to have everything ready to go."

Outside Meg's villa, two golf carts were loaded with luggage. After they parked, Judy jumped out and worked her way into the villa.

Rick held back to talk to Val privately. "The reason for my presence here is only between you and me."

"We can trust my security," Val insisted.

"I'm sure you do, Mr. Masini."

"Val, please."

"Trust is earned, not given."

Val conceded with a nod.

They walked in together and overheard Judy arguing with her friend. "You're pale. A vampire has better color."

"I don't want anyone scaring me into changing my life."

Judy placed her hands on her hips. "Are you forgetting who you're talking to?"

"This isn't the same thing, Judy. No one threatened me."

Val would disagree with that. So did the others in the room. "Some guy wearing a hoodie and hiding his face corners you in an empty hall, and no one threatened you? *Before someone gets hurt* sounds like a threat to me." Michael was pissed. "You ended up in the ER, Meg. We're leaving, you're coming with us, and that's it!"

Margaret rubbed her chest and released a few coughs. Something Val had noticed a lot since she returned from the hospital. He stepped in. "Can everyone give us a few minutes, please?"

Ryder and Michael walked out the back door. Rick grabbed the last suitcase in the room and pulled Judy with him.

"Cara." He took her by the hand and sat her on the couch. "What can you really do here?"

"I can help you find who's behind this."

Not without risking your own safety, he wanted to tell her. "You're a beautiful distraction that will keep me from finding him. You heard the doctor, you need to rest and give the medication time to do its job."

"I feel fine." She punctuated her *fineness* with a cough. "Damn it," she mumbled.

He decided to twist her arm to convince her to concede. "Gabi is looking forward to visiting Los Angeles and finding the perfect gown for her wedding. She hasn't been off the island in some time. You can help me trace the e-mails, find their origin easier with the help of your friends. Michael will be safe from prying eyes."

Meg stared at him, seeing through his tactics. "You're playing dirty."

"Do you trust your friend Rick?"

"Of course."

"Then he can help me here. And when we have something, I'll come to you." He kissed the tips of her fingers. "I want more of you," he whispered.

"Now you're really playing dirty."

He leaned forward and kissed her, briefly. He didn't dare risk more and shorten her breath. When he pulled away, he noted her half-closed lids and sighed. No, he wasn't done with her . . . not anywhere close.

He tucked a loose hair behind her ear, waited for her to open her eyes.

"I'll go." She slowly opened her eyes.

Alonzo stood beside Gabi outside the plane. They stood much closer than they had the night before, his sister smiled up at her fiancé before he pulled her in for a tender kiss.

Val looked away, giving them the privacy he could.

"Thank you for everything." Michael shook Val's hand. "We'll be in touch."

Ryder said his good-byes as well before the two men boarded. Judy kissed her husband and followed her brother.

"Call me when you land."

Margaret offered a frown. "If I felt even a tiny bit better, I wouldn't be leaving. I think you should know that."

He smiled for the both of them. "Noted."

"Hey, Meg? Are we going or what?" Judy yelled from the hatch of the airplane.

"I gotta go."

Right.

Val stepped into her space, flattened her body to his, and lowered his lips. The kiss would have to do for a while, so he took it.

———

"The majority of investigative work is anticlimactic and frustrating." Rick Evans looked up from the surveillance cameras and lifted his index finger. "Eventually, however, someone makes a mistake and that's when we find our guy."

"No offense, Rick, but you don't strike me as a kind of guy to sit around frustrated for long."

The phone in Rick's pocket rang, reminding Val that he hadn't yet heard from Margaret.

"Hey, babe."

"No, he's right here."

Val tuned into the conversation when Rick made eye contact.

"No. I'll tell him. Yeah, I will. Love you, too."

Rick put his phone back in his pocket and started tapping on the keyboard again. "That was Judy. They made it back OK. Meg's wiped out and already in bed."

His heart ached at the thought.

Rick hit *enter* with a grand gesture and turned in his seat. "Back to my sitting around? You're right. Sitting sucks. All that data is en route to Russell. My man loves to sit, fiddle, and find. He'll follow the e-mails, watch your feeds, look for anything out of place."

Val felt his left eye twitch. "All my camera feeds are off the island?"

"You can still access them here."

Val wrapped a hand around his own neck.

"Easy, Val. I understand security."

"So does Lou." His main guy was briefing their on-island team on Rick's presence and working on the install of more cameras in the service corridors.

"Good thing about another set of eyes. Russell doesn't know Lou from you. He's going to question everything he sees. Whoever we're dealing with knows the island, knows your rules, procedures, and has your trust . . . or at least that of the staff here."

"No one comes on the island with a private camera."

Rick leaned back in the office chair and cradled his head. "Exactly how can you guarantee that?"

"Guest luggage is screened. Cell phones are placed in holding and the on-island cameras are all accounted for and checked before they leave the island." Val went on to talk about client excursions and how their charters were handled.

"There are watches that have cameras," Rick pointed out.

Val ran a hand through his hair. "The photos taken were with a long lens. While I'm sure the military can take pictures from space, I don't think anyone here can. Besides, my guests covet the privacy of the island as much as I do. It's why they're here. Everyone is contracted to my privacy policy. If there's a breach, they stand the risk of litigation in which I will not lose."

Rick studied the wall behind the computers. "I don't think we're dealing with a guest."

Val didn't either.

"Which leaves my employees."

"Losing their job wouldn't compare to some of the money they could acquire from the pictures they take or the stories they could tell. And what about contracted workers? I'm sure there are repairs needed here all the time."

"I run Sapore di Amore like a cruise ship. Housekeeping has designated areas they are allowed in, my waitstaff is the same way. Maintenance of common areas is taken care of after my guests have left. Emergency situations require the presence of security." Val had gone over everything already.

Rick stood and stretched his back. "Then we start at the lower decks. Those who have the least to lose and work our way up."

Val took his jacket that was lying on the back of a chair.

Rick grinned. "It's still eighty degrees out there. Why the suit?"

Val straightened his tie. "It reminds my employees that I'm the boss."

They started at the dock, where many of the employees never left.

One of the first things that Rick caught was Alonzo's yacht docked along the wharf. "Yours?"

Val shook his head. "Gabi's fiancé."

Rick narrowed his gaze. "All that from the wine business?"

"Wine is big business."

"Even better than moonshine, eh, Val?" Behind them Alonzo walked their way, obviously overhearing their conversation.

"I've had some decent moonshine," Rick offered as he shook the other man's hand.

Alonzo winked. "I have, too, but don't tell anyone."

"Are you pulling out?" Val asked.

Alonzo nodded. "You have enough to worry about without my men here."

Val hadn't really thought about Alonzo's crew.

"Where do your employees sleep when you're on the island?" Rick asked.

Alonzo was slow to smile. "On the yacht, Mr. Evans. Their accommodations are quite comfortable."

"That would make sense."

Alonzo turned his attention back to Val. "Looks like you've had a lot of cabernet drinkers, my friend. I'll be sure and have my assistant send more."

"Thank you." The last thing on Val's mind was wine.

"I know you're preoccupied, but wanted to let you know that once Gabi returns I plan on taking her away for a short trip."

"Does Gabi know about this vacation?"

"Not yet. I'm working on some of the details. I've neglected my fiancée and need to rectify that."

Val couldn't agree more. Having his sister and Alonzo off island for a while was good for all of them.

Val shook Alonzo's hand. "Don't work too hard."

"I'd say the same but know you'll give my words less weight than I'll give yours."

They were both workaholics. It was surprising Alonzo found the time to get to know Gabi, let alone promise to marry her.

Maybe it was sleeping in her own bed, or maybe it was the smoggy air, or maybe it was her neighbor's smelly cooking . . . but Meg slept like the dead and woke up refreshed in a way she hadn't felt in weeks.

Even her shower felt better than she remembered. She sucked in a breath on her peak flow meter to see how her lungs were faring. Her numbers were getting better with the medication the doctor had placed her on. Crazy how oxygen in the bloodstream made her look at the day with bright glasses.

She practically jogged down the stairs to the smell of coffee and breakfast.

"Look who's up."

Meg wrapped an arm around Judy and Gabi, who were huddled over the stove. "Home-cooked food? For me?"

"Don't get used to it. Gabi insisted."

Meg helped herself to a cup of coffee and sat at the kitchen counter. "It's good to be home."

"Vacations are always nice, but coming home can be even better," Judy said.

"Yeah, well . . . that was the least restful vacation I've had in a while."

Gabi offered a frown. "I'm so sorry."

"Don't take offense, hon. The island was beautiful, the food was amazing . . . and the company . . ." She pictured Val with a smile. "Yeah . . . anyway, it's not any of that."

"It's the helicopter ride to the hospital . . . gets ya every time." Judy always had a way to cut to the core of things.

"Worrying about Michael—" Meg cut her words off and glanced at Gabi.

"Please don't. I'm not blind. He's not the first celebrity to go to my brother's island posing as someone he's not. Trust me."

Judy nudged Gabi. "I wanna ask who, but I won't."

"I wouldn't tell." Gabi grinned with a wink.

"Oh no!" Meg thought of Val, and looked around the kitchen for her purse.

"What?"

"I forgot to call Val last night."

"Don't stress it," Judy told her. "I talked to Rick."

Meg sighed, pushed the conversation off for a later time. "I wonder if they're any closer to finding him."

Judy set a plate of scrambled eggs, toast, and bacon in front of Meg. "If the hoodie guy is still there, Rick will find him."

"He didn't do anything."

"He scared the oxygen out of you." Judy dished her own plate and sat beside Meg. "I've known you for a long time, that doesn't happen very often, and I've never had to take you to the ER. So *he didn't do anything* doesn't fly with me. You were scared shitless."

"I'd been dancing all night, running all day . . ."

"Why are you downplaying this? The guy cornered you, said some nasty things, and took off."

Judy had a point.

"I guess I don't want to think a little threat turns me into a melodramatic basket case who ends up in the hospital."

Judy pointed her fork in Meg's direction. "With the exception of that description of yourself, you can't be accused of being melo-dramatic."

The doorbell to the Tarzana house rang and Judy jumped up to answer it.

"Delivery for Miss Rosenthal."

Meg leaned over to see down the short hallway to the front door. Judy was taking a massive bouquet of what looked like two dozen roses.

"Ah, my brother is so sweet," Gabi announced when Judy brought the flowers into the kitchen.

Meg didn't think she was a flower kind of girl, but she was smil-ing despite her own self-perceptions. She took the card and opened it.

She started to giggle.

"What did he say?" Judy asked.

"They're not from Val."

"They're not?"

Meg leaned in and sniffed a fragrant bud. "Nope. They're from Jim Lewis."

Gabi tossed her head with laughter. "Maybe he is trying for his next wife after all."

Judy scratched her head. "Who is Jim Lewis?"

Chapter Seventeen

"You remember Shannon Wentworth." Meg stepped into her client's photography studio with Gabi right behind her.

"Yes, of course. You and your new husband were guests of ours earlier this year."

"Yes . . . I'm sorry but I forgot your name."

"Gabriella Masini. Val's sister."

Shannon shook Gabi's hand and offered a gracious smile. "We had a wonderful time on your island."

"It's my brother's, but thank you. I like to think I help in some way."

"How is the political campaigning?" Meg asked once the introductions were out of the way.

"Exhausting. Not to mention fattening. I swear, there are more dinners than there are days in the week."

Shannon wore her long hair down her back in a slick ponytail. Her tiny waist and petite frame weren't something Meg could easily imagine overweight. "Eat a celery stick, I'm sure that will even things out."

Shannon understood Meg's humor and slapped her arm. "What brings you to my neck of Beverly Hills?"

The studio Shannon had moved to after her contractual marriage ceremony was located in the center of Beverly Hills, just off Rodeo. The high-end real estate was part of the deal. She could shoot candid or even *not so candid* pictures of the exclusive clientele that lunched on Rodeo just to be seen. She also accepted the contracts of others who wanted their children's graduation pictures, baby pictures, or wedding photographs taken by a professional. What was even better, Shannon always wanted to mentor new graduates with talent. Her studio afforded her that effort.

Meg patted Gabi on the back. "My new friend is planning her wedding. She needs a gown, and since you're the photographer of all things weddings, I thought maybe you could point us in a direction. Show us some shots . . . tell us who you know."

Hollywood, LA, the entire scene was all about *who* you knew, not *what* you knew.

Shannon's gaze fell on Gabi with renewed interest. "You're getting married?"

Gabi lifted her left hand and wiggled her fingers. "I am."

"Congratulations . . . wait." Shannon narrowed her eyes and stared at Meg. "Is she a client?"

Meg laughed. There was no way Alonzo would have passed the background check. "Ah, no. Gabi was engaged before we met."

"Oh. Sorry." Shannon turned to Gabi a second time. "Congratulations. When is the big day?"

Gabi looked between the two of them . . . twice. "In the fall. And what do you mean by *am I a client?*"

"I told you I did background checks," Meg offered as a half answer.

"Background checks?"

Shannon jumped in. "I know people. Lots of people. Let's look at some brides and you can tell me what appeals to you. We can go from there."

They sat down to a pile of photo albums, every one of them filled with brides and everything weddings. If there was one thing Meg believed in, it was paying it forward. It helped that Shannon was a kick-ass photographer and a nice person. The nice person part was a plus. Helping her build her business didn't require a second thought.

"Are you getting married on the island? Somewhere cold? Do you know what your bridesmaids are going to wear?"

Gabi pulled her shoulders back and grew silent. Her eyes started to fill with moisture.

"Sweetie, what's wrong?" Meg managed to catch her new friend's gaze.

"I don't have a bridesmaid. How can I get married without a bridesmaid? A maid of honor?"

Shannon jumped up and brought a box of tissues while Meg patted Gabi's back as a few tears fell from her eyes. "Lots of people get married without a big wedding party."

Gabi dabbed her nose. "I have a cousin, but we don't see each other very often. When we announced I was getting married she didn't know if she was going to be able to come." Gabi stood and started to pace. "This is awful."

"It's not awful, and not abnormal," Shannon pointed out.

"I've spent so much time on the island I've forgotten how to foster friendships. How can Alonzo love that? I'm going to be a terrible wife."

"You're not on the island now," Meg reminded her. "And I'm right here. You haven't forgotten how to foster anything. Now unless you're letting something else fester inside of you that's an issue, let's find you the perfect dress." Meg grabbed at one of the photo albums and pointed to the first slim-fitted strapless job she saw. "I think you'd look amazing in something like this."

Gabi still wasn't convinced. She glanced across the room at the picture and offered a pout.

Meg looked back at the photo album. "Didn't your mother tell you that your face would stick that way if you kept it up?"

When Gabi's laugh met Meg's ears, she knew she'd broken through the nervous bride's fears.

The thing was, Meg was still nervous for her new friend. Gabi might have told her that Alonzo made up for his assholiness the last night on the island, but the man had yet to pass her test. Now that she was back home, her test was rapidly moving forward. When Sam's background check, along with her own, didn't cut the man some slack . . . Meg would turn on the anti-Alonzo game full force.

Gabi fell in love with the first designer they visited. His name was Marco and he catered to money. Since Val promised her the wedding of her dreams . . . she wasn't thinking of the price tag on Marco's designs. What Gabi didn't know was that with every gown she put on, Meg was snapping a picture and chatting with Val via text.

Sooooo, how much did you want to spend on your sister's wedding gown?

It's a dress. How much could it possibly cost? Val, the poor guy had no idea.

Marco wore something Bond would be fond of, with the exception of the purple fuzzy tie. "Marco, hon . . . where is the ballpark of that gown?" Gabi was wearing a strapless that had a princess waist and the most spectacular set of pearls along the bodice that even Meg, who didn't know a pearl from a glass bead, was impressed with.

"We're talking price, Margaret?"

The man liked full names. Telling him to call her Meg was like him calling the pope Dad. "Yeah."

"Economical . . . very economical."

Yeah, right. "Economical for Kate Middleton or Honey Boo Boo?"

Marco was in the process of pulling Gabi's breasts into submission, with his full hands, and tossed his head back with laughter. "Oh, dear. What is wrong with a country that let's that . . . *thing* . . . on the television?" Marco placed his hands on Gabi's waist and turned her toward the three-way mirror. "Lovely." He slid his hand down Gabi's waist as if he had the right and fluffed out the train. "I do think we should look at sleeker gowns. Less fussy, but you see how well this style fits the tone of your skin."

"All the dresses are white."

Marco tolerated Meg, but did so with a thin grin. "Bite your tongue. I have nothing white. Every shade is unique."

"I think it's beautiful." Gabi turned in the mirror to admire the beading up the back.

"Marco . . . what are we talking . . . six figures? Five, four?"

"Four? Goodness, I'm not Kmart."

Just what Meg thought. "So, six?"

"No. I did say it was economical."

"Even after taxes?"

Marco held no shame as he moved around Gabi, pulling and tugging. "This would need to be taken in here."

"Marco?"

He waved her off.

Meg sat in a plush white leather couch and watched as Gabi allowed Marco to remove every snap. All zillion of them.

Meg sent the picture of the dress, Gabi in it, to Val. Stab a guess at the cost of this number.

Is that Gabi?

She's stunning. Guess the price, moneybags.

There was a delay with dot dot dot as her response. It doesn't matter. My sister deserves whatever she wants.

So I should tell her that a hundred grand for a dress she will wear once . . . for only part of one day, is good?

Meg found a certain satisfaction in seeing dot dot dot blink on her screen for several seconds. Yes, Val was a giving, considerate person. But she didn't think he was that far gone.

The dot dot dot went on for a while, so Meg sweetened the pot. A veil, shoes, and jewelry are next, moneybags. Choose your words wisely.

Dot dot dot . . .

Divert.

Nice word. "Gabi . . . hon, maybe we should see something with less beading. I can't imagine that will wear well in the heat of the Keys."

Marco removed two gowns from his collection while Gabi slid behind the drape to remove the dress.

"Marco?" Meg waved him over. "I work with a lot of brides, but let's keep this one perfect with less cash, shall we?"

Marco lifted a manicured, and if Meg had to testify the fact, painted, brow in the air. "Shannon said as much."

"Most of my brides can afford that little number with all the trimmings." She pointed to the nearly six-figure dress. "Gabi will be walked down the aisle on her brother's arm, not her father's." Not to mention that she'd be meeting a groom Meg had little faith in her keeping. But she kept that part unsaid.

Marco removed one of the two gowns he had in his hands and found another. "Gabriella . . . we must try this. I think it will be perfect."

Meg tapped into her phone as Gabi walked out for the second sample. You owe me.

Dot dot dot . . .

Meg laughed and tossed her phone aside. "I like that one."

Samantha Harrison was what Meg referred to as a vertically challenged, feisty redhead that oozed poise and money as if she were born to it. In truth she was, but her role as wife, mother, and duchess polished what she'd been born with and made her a tour de force.

Alliance was her baby. She didn't need the money the business earned her any longer, but she kept the machine running for many different reasons. The least of which was she found her own husband through the service and needed two hands to count the successful marriages she or her employees had arranged in the time she'd been in business. If Meg had to guess, Sam enjoyed empowering women, both through the temporary marriages and the wealth it offered said women, and in working for them to push ahead in life. Meg knew her life had done a 180 when she'd gone to work for the lady.

Combating her height with four-inch heels, Sam still had to reach over her head, on her tiptoes, to touch the coffee beans tucked on a top shelf in Meg's kitchen . . . which was where Meg found her boss when she and Gabi returned from Marco's.

"Oh, good Lord, woman. Let me get that for you."

"I don't know why you keep the coffee on the top shelf."

Meg pulled the bag of some of Colombia's best off the top shelf and poured it into her grinder. "If it's on the bottom shelf, I'll make, pour, make more . . . and not sleep all night. Reaching reminds me to stop drinking the stuff."

Sam shook her head, leaned against the counter, and focused on Gabi. "You must be Miss Masini."

Gabi moved forward and shook Sam's hand. "Gabi, please."

Meg made the introductions while she made a pot of coffee.

"I hope you don't mind me invading," Sam told them.

"It's your house," Meg reminded her boss. Not that Sam ever took advantage of the fact that Meg lived there for nearly nothing.

Sam moved from the kitchen into the office off the living room. "I was searching the mainframe for a program I know I used at one point."

Sam sat behind the massive computer that held the data files and contacts of their many clients through the years. The security software included voice recognition and retina mapping.

Meg thought it was overkill until she gripped the magnitude of the information inside the guts of Sam's files.

Standing behind her boss, and aware that Gabi stood close by, she asked, "What program are you trying to find? Maybe I can help."

Sam cleared her throat and kept clicking around. "Income-to-debt program. It helped me crunch numbers for businesses I know very little about."

"I'm pretty good with numbers," Gabi said from the doorway.

Sam kept clicking. "I'm talking gross income from reported profit, to manufacturing cost and client expenditure. Complicated stuff that I'd rather not have my husband's accountant look into."

"Yeah, numbers. My brother called me a mathematical savant growing up. It took me some time to realize he was putting me down. Then he realized it wasn't a bad thing when he went into business."

Sam slowly turned in her chair at the same time Meg realized she was staring at Gabi.

Sam folded one leg over the other and sat back. "OK. Let's say I have an eight million six hundred and fifty thousand dollar loan on a house at an interest rate of four and a half percent . . . what are my monthly payments?"

Gabi tapped her fingers in the air as if it held a calculator. "Fifteen- or thirty-year loan?"

"Fifteen," Meg said.

"Thirty," Sam managed at the same time.

Gabi rolled her eyes. "Sixty-six thousand one hundred seventy two, rounded up for the fifteen and . . ." she paused. "Forty-three eight hundred and twenty-eight per month for thirty years." She pushed away from the wall. "But the national average right now is what? Two and three-quarter percent . . . a little higher, actually. Let's say two point seven nine. That would be about thirty-five thousand five hundred a month. Rounded up."

Meg didn't stop staring. "Is she right?"

Instead of answering, Sam twisted in her chair and started typing numbers into the calculator sitting on the desk. "Holy crap."

A peep from the kitchen diverted Gabi's attention. "How do you like your coffee, Samantha?"

"With cream."

Gabi turned from the room and slid away.

"She was right, wasn't she?"

"Wow."

"I guess she can help you crunch numbers," Meg said.

"On *her* man?"

Meg hadn't considered that. "Keep it generic. Might be best for her to discover what this guy is on her own anyway."

Sam swiveled toward the computer. "I don't like what I'm seeing. I would have passed up his application long before now if he were looking at us to hook him up."

"Anything concrete?"

"That's what I'm working on."

Meg patted Sam on the back. "Thanks. She needs us looking out for her."

Gabi walked in the room with two cups of coffee in her hand and sat beside the desk. "Here you go."

Gabi tipped the cup back and sipped.

"What?" Meg managed. "None for me?"

Gabi laughed. "You said you avoided coffee to sleep at night."

Meg shook her head. "I said I *tried* to avoid it."

The women laughed, and when Meg returned the conversation was already over her head. Sam read off a notepad and scribbled numbers in her margins. "So if the profit potential for the warehouse is twenty thousand per, let's say one thousand square feet of operating space. And the cost to produce the product is four grand, that's labor, supplies, the basics, there's a substantial profit."

"Depending on the space, but yeah. Are you considering mortgage, insurance, taxes?"

Sam shook her head. "That's what I needed the program for. Seems to me this prospective client is spending a lot more than he can possibly make, and I can't find an additional source of income."

"Family money?"

"Can't find it. But maybe I have something wrong. At first glance the income is several million a year, but I feel I'm missing something."

While Sam and Gabi pushed their heads together, Meg did something she rarely did. She left the office and called a boy.

Chapter Eighteen

A charge of excitement fueled Val's energy level when he saw Meg's number light up his cell phone. "Hi," he answered with a smile splashed over his face. He felt like a kid again, even with all the stress in his day.

"Hey, Moneybags."

"Hello, Margaret."

She laughed. "One of these days I'll have to give you permission to use Meg."

Val moved away from the video monitors he was watching and leaned against one of the floor-to-ceiling windows. "Perhaps you will, *cara*, but I might not use it." Her laughter was contagious. "How are you feeling?"

"I'm coughing at night, but other than that, perfect."

"Have you seen your specialist?"

"I don't have one."

Val lost his grin. "The doctor told you to find one."

"I will . . ."

"When?" He wasn't going to let this go. The image of her gasping for air would haunt him for some time.

"Since when did you become my mother hen?"

He sighed, could see the hair rising on the back of her neck if he squinted hard enough. "Please, Margaret. Next time you might not be so lucky."

"I've made a couple of calls, Val. There are channels one has to go through so the insurance company pays the bill."

The thought of her waiting for care because of an insurance company angered him. "Have the specialist bill you."

"Not all of us own an island, Moneybags."

"I'll pay."

"Don't be ridiculous. I can pay my own medical bills."

Correction: she could pay her copayments so long as the insurance company approved of the doctor. He knew the drill. He also knew that waiting for specialists sometimes resulted in delayed care that left people sicker than they should be. His head scrambled for a way to take care of her without pissing her off.

Tightrope, that.

"You'll be happy to know your sister skipped the six-figure dress." Margaret changed the subject with skill.

"Was it really that much?"

"Stupid, huh?"

"Gabi is a practical girl. I doubt she would have said yes."

"A lot you know, women tend to get emotional about the outfit they're getting married in."

"Had I known you were going to introduce her to designers offering hundred-thousand-dollar gowns . . ."

She paused. "Yeah? You would have done what?"

He had to admit, Margaret calling his bluff made him smile. "I would have told her to enjoy and be sensible."

"Then I should tell her to go with her first choice?"

This was a test . . . the kind a woman placed on a man that determined their noble words versus their actions. Somehow, making both work in unison with Margaret was something he needed to do. Though he wouldn't want his sister spending that kind of money on a dress, he wouldn't deny her, either. "My sister deserves the best. She's only going to marry once."

"Well . . ." Margaret released a sigh into the phone as if in disagreement. "Lucky for you, she liked the less expensive gown. You're off the hook, Moneybags. I'll be sure and help her pick out expensive accessories to make up for the dress."

"I'm sure you will."

He heard Margaret cough away from the phone a couple of times, bringing her health into question before she deflected again. "Anything new from the mystery photographer?"

Without any new leads, or any new random photographs making their way into his in-box, frustration sat on the edges of Val's nerves. "What do you know about spam e-mail?"

"It's annoying."

"There's that . . . but do you have any idea how spammers find you, send you e-mail with your name and personal information?"

"The piano is my instrument of choice, not a keyboard."

Val shook his head. "Me either. Rick and his friends have traced the e-mails as far as the Netherlands. Well, one of the e-mails that far, the other diverted to Japan."

"So we know nothing."

"Nothing. And nothing new is showing up on this end." He rubbed the space between his eyes, hoping to ease his tension.

"I know this isn't going to come out right, but that's not what I wanted to hear."

"I hear you, *cara*. If everything is silent . . . how do we know our photographer will keep quiet? What information does he have? How or when will he use it?"

"Blackmail."

Exactly his thoughts. "I hope we're wrong."

"I know Rick and his colleagues, even if the trail is cold, there's still a trail. It might take time, but he'll find the person behind it . . . eventually."

After two days with Rick Evans, Val knew the man was a bloodhound. Rick had nothing to gain by saving Val's ass, but was deeply invested in his wife's family. "Something will break."

"I hate that the person who took the pictures is in control."

Precisely. "If money is the drive, we would have heard something already . . . if in fact the photographer had something."

"What else could a blackmailer want other than money? None of us have a criminal record to uncover and extort."

"Even if one of us did, the end result would be the same."

"Blackmail."

"Yes."

"Which puts us right back at the beginning and the photographer has the control." The conversation was frustrating, even to his ears. "What are you wearing?" The art of distraction took a lot with Margaret. And he didn't want to discuss what neither of them could control any longer.

"W-what? Wearing?"

"Yes, *bella*, the clothes on your back. What are you wearing?" He couldn't imagine her shopping for wedding dresses in her pinup dresses and red lipstick. He knew much of that was for show.

"Jeans and a cotton shirt," she said with a chuckle. "What about you?"

He opened his mouth only to have her cut him off.

"Wait, let me guess. Suit . . . your jacket might be off, depending on where you are on the island."

"You know me well already."

"Do you even own a pair of jeans?"

He hesitated.

"Seriously, Masini? No blue jeans? Everyone has a pair."

Margaret gave him lip about his lacking wardrobe, made a quip or two about his ties, and simply took his mind off his problems for fifteen minutes.

"How is it I miss you already?" he asked when their conversation started to draw to a close.

"I'm a missable kind of girl."

"Humble, too."

"Bite your tongue, Masini. You of all people know it doesn't pay to hide or pretend to be something you're not."

He rolled his eyes to the empty room. "Like the girlfriend of a famous movie star?"

"Ahh, ouch. Points for you. To be fair, that didn't really pay off. Not in this case."

"True. Without your ruse, however, I might not have ever met you."

She sighed into the phone. "Coming from anyone else, that would sound like a line."

He loosened his tie. "But coming from me?"

"You're too controlled to deliver bullshit."

"You'd call me on it if I did."

"You know it."

He liked their easy banter and lack of *bullshit*, as she so eloquently labeled it. "I'll call you tomorrow," he told her. "Sooner if need be."

"Good plan."

"Good night, *cara*." He didn't want to hang up, felt like a teenager with a crush.

"Good night, Val."

He moved the phone away from his ear.

"Val?"

He jumped to put the phone back.

"Yeah?"

"I miss you, too." Then she hung up.

He couldn't stop smiling.

"It's been three days . . . how long does it take to find one dress?"

"Alonzo," Gabi said with a sigh.

"I miss you."

"There are weeks that go by where I don't see you." Gabi snuggled into the guest bed, her cell phone tucked to her ear.

"We fought. I hate when we fight."

How she needed to hear those words. "We spend too much time apart."

"I agree. I need to change that."

Some of the doubt a fight forced into one's head dissipated.

"I know it's not an excuse, but there have been a few miscalculations with the new vineyard that have made me less than agreeable with you. I want it perfect for us."

"I'm not looking for perfection, Alonzo."

"I told your brother to expect me to take you away when you return," he said, changing the subject.

She bit her bottom lip . . . smiled. "Where are you taking me?"

"It's a secret. I will tell you this. It's just us. Only us."

She closed her eyes and tried to imagine just the two of them. Seemed they'd only ever been together with others around them. There were times, intimate times, they managed to carve away from the island, or Alonzo's life . . . but not many. "I'd like that."

"So come home so I can take you away."

"Alonzo . . ." Torn between her new friends and her future life . . . she looked at the ring on her left hand, remembered her promise to her fiancé. "I'll arrange a flight. Meet me in Key West?"

"Yes," he sighed. "Text me the time, I'll be there."

More confident by the minute, she snuggled farther into bed. "Tell me about your day."

"I've been arranging our trip. Making sure everything will go without interruption."

"You're teasing me. Are we going on the yacht?"

"For a time."

"And then?"

Alonzo's voice shifted away from the soft tones he'd been using. "It's not a surprise if I tell you, now is it?"

Her heart skipped a beat. "I suppose not."

"Tomorrow, Gabi. I'll see you tomorrow." His tone was delicate again. Delicate with a trace of sugar. "By morning I will taste your skin."

Michael drove up the coast, his Ferrari taking the curves like she owned them. Past Santa Barbara he headed east, found the 101, and continued north. Vineyards dotted the landscape of Napa and Sonoma Valleys, the green leaves and plump grapes nearly ripe for the perfect harvest. He loved the countryside, the silent insects buzzing around, the lazy way the sun moved over the land. The stark contrast to his daily life didn't go unnoticed.

The walls of his estate in Beverly Hills had closed in on him since his return from the island. He'd managed two conversations with Ryder, both of them sweet and strained.

He was worried. They both were worried. Rick had yet to find anything and no new photos had managed to circulate.

Like a crackhead looking for his next hit, Michael couldn't sleep, couldn't stop moving. Driving up the coast felt right. Like he was doing something.

It might not be the right thing, but it was something.

He wound his way up an oak-studded drive that opened to the Windon Estate. Natalie and Chuck Windon were some of the best people Michael knew in the wine business, not to mention they had a superior product that topped Michael's table more times than not. Instead of pulling into the parking lot for the many wine tours that drove up for tasting, Michael pulled into the private drive of the proprietors.

He took the brown paper bag from the passenger seat and jogged up the steps.

Natalie stepped from inside the house, her smile greeting him. "Michael. Did we know you were coming?"

Michael left the bag on the step and kissed both of her cheeks. "Last-minute decision. I hope it's OK."

Natalie was all of five feet four inches tall, her good cooking evident by her slightly plump frame. She opened the door to the house and welcomed him in. "You're always welcome."

He stepped into the air-conditioned foyer and followed her into the back of the house.

"Chuck is in the field with the foreman. He should be along shortly."

The Windons' kitchen was built for someone who loved to cook. Natalie had been a master chef before she met her husband. Together they decided to buy the winery nearly twenty years ago. Now, with their children grown, one son following in his father's wine-making business, and the other at a university on the East Coast, the house was quiet.

"You're just in time for lunch." Natalie moved to the stove, stirred a massive pot, and dipped a tasting spoon inside. She held it up for Michael to taste.

A broth soup with a hint of spice, a chunk of sausage, and potato. "Mmm, so good. What is it?"

"Portuguese sausage soup. Lovely, yes?"

"Perfect."

Michael pulled out a chair at the kitchen counter and made himself at home. "Can I help with anything?"

Natalie glanced over her shoulder and rolled her eyes. "Wine or tea?"

"Tea."

She moved around the kitchen, collecting bowls, removing bread and fresh butter.

"How does the harvest look?"

"The drought has given us a hit so the quantity will be down."

"But you're doing all right?"

"We'll be fine, Michael."

He sipped his iced tea while they talked grapes, wine, and the weather.

Handshakes and back patting commenced when Chuck entered the house. They caught up during lunch, talked about college kids and future movies.

When Natalie left them on the back veranda, which overlooked the row upon row of grapevines, Chuck kicked back with his feet up on a cushioned chair. "I don't think you drove all the way up here for lunch and a visit."

"Lunch was divine," Michael said.

"No argument there."

Michael reached into the bag at his side and removed a bottle of wine before handing it to Chuck.

"What's this?" Chuck sat forward and peered at the bottle.

"Have you heard of this label?"

Chuck turned the wine around to read the back. "No. Why?"

Michael took the liberty of stepping to the wine cart and grabbing two glasses and a wine opener. If there was a partner in wine crime, Chuck was it. The man knew more than God on the subject.

With practiced ease, Chuck took the offered sample, swirled, swished, sniffed, and finally sipped. An appreciative smile slid over his face. He picked up the bottle again. His smile fell to a puzzled squinting of his eyes.

"You taught me wine by regions. Where is this one from?" Michael asked.

"Umbria. No doubt." Chuck circled the wine bottle again. "But I've been all over that area and don't know this name. Is the winery newly acquired?"

Michael leaned against the outside serving station and poured a splash of Alonzo's wine into a glass. "I'm not sure of the age of the winery, but the man behind the bottle told me this is from Campania."

"No, no . . . unless the grapes were grown in Umbria and processed in Campania."

Like any bum on the street, Michael opened a second bottle of wine and kept the label hidden inside a plain paper bag. He poured a splash of the new vintage in a glass and handed it to Chuck.

Swirl, smell, sip, spit. "It's identical."

Michael offered a short shake of his head while he pulled the second bottle out of the bag and showed it to Chuck.

"How can that be?"

"Wine can taste the same."

"When they're from the same region, maybe. But smell the oak?" Chuck shoved his nose deep in the glass and closed his eyes. "Umbria. I'd stake my reputation on it."

It was nice to have his doubts justified, now the question was why . . . why did Alonzo Picano claim his vineyard, in Campania, grew the grapes used to make the wine in Michael's hands? And how was it the wine tasted identical to a much larger winery, with a solid reputation?

Chapter Nineteen

Val accompanied Rick back to California. His mother took a much-needed extended trip to visit her sister in New York while the weather was still warm. The island was functioning as normal without any new pictures showing up online or off. Security had been doubled, and everything was painfully quiet.

He didn't tell Margaret that he was returning with Rick. If Val needed an excuse, he would use the desire to accompany his sister back to the Keys.

Judy picked them up at the airport. She nudged her husband. "You didn't tell me he was coming with you."

"You didn't ask." Rick kissed his wife and whispered something in her ear. Her gaze fell on Val and didn't shake loose.

"So you flew all the way here to see Meg?" Judy asked as they wove through hoards of people en route to baggage claim.

"I was hoping to surprise her."

Judy started to laugh.

Rick narrowed his eyes. "What's so funny?"

They found the circular baggage drop and waited for the conveyer belt to start emptying the cargo hold of the commercial airline.

"Well," Judy looked at her watch. "You're about an hour late."

"An hour late for what?"

"Meg and Mike flew out an hour ago."

Val stopped looking for his suitcase and stared at Judy. "Where did they go?"

"Italy."

Rick shook his head. "Italy? Why?"

"Mike said he had a lead he wanted to follow up on. The two of them started talking and the next thing I knew Meg was asking me to water her plants . . . again."

Well hell. "Did Gabi go with them?"

"Gabi left early this morning, said she was flying back home and then hooking up with her fiancé. She didn't tell you?"

Val removed his cell from his pocket and released the airplane mode mandated on commercial flights. How could so many people have moved so far and wide in six hours? Sure enough, there was a text from Meg.

Taking a quick trip overseas. I'll call when we land if it isn't too late.

Then there was a voice message from his sister. "I didn't want you to worry. I'm meeting Alonzo in Key West for a romantic weekend. Love you."

Val watched as his suitcase rounded the corner of the rotating belt.

"Where in Italy?"

"They flew into Rome. I'm not sure where they're staying. Sam might know."

Val checked his briefcase, making sure his passport was inside.

They left the arrival level of LAX and he rounded the stairway to the departure and ticketing floor.

"What are you doing?" Rick asked.

"Flying to Rome, apparently." Val waved his cell phone in the air. "Call me when you find out where Margaret is staying."

"But you just got off a plane," Judy argued.

"If Michael and Margaret are following a lead in Italy, it might help if one of them spoke Italian."

"He has a point," Rick said.

"Any idea what kind of lead they have?" Val asked.

Judy shrugged. "Something about Alonzo's wine tasting like someone else's. That's all I heard."

"His wine?"

What do you have, Margaret?

Val moved to the escalator. "Call me," he said, pointing to Rick.

"I hope you know what you're doing," Rick called after him.

"I'm chasing a girl to Italy."

Rick tossed his head back with a healthy laugh. "Meg's going to love that."

Val wove his way through excited travelers, located the international airline he most often used and stood in line. Something told him he was in for a long night.

Her internal clock said it was four in the morning. The clocks in Rome said one in the afternoon.

She and Michael had a two-bedroom suite with a middle great room that overlooked the lights of Rome. They agreed to snag a couple of hours of sleep and then do their best to stay awake as long as possible, grab some food, come up with a plan, and head out first thing in the morning.

They were dragging their eyelids at nine in the evening, doing their best to move past the jet lag as soon as humanly possible.

Meg tossed her purse onto the coffee table when they stumbled into their room.

"I'm dead," Michael managed.

"If you wake me before nine, I might not be responsible for my actions," Meg warned.

Twelve hours of sleep sounded like a slice of heaven.

Michael managed a slight wave and headed to his room.

Meg moved into the bathroom inside her room by braille. She washed, brushed, and flushed before making her way to her bed. While in the process of unbuttoning her shirt, a grunt, or maybe it was a grumble, sounded from the other side of the room.

The room was lit by the lights of the city filtering in from the window. The outline of someone lying on her bed forced her eyes open.

She clicked the closest light and felt her heartbeat slow.

"Val," she whispered.

What the? She'd sent a text when she'd arrived in Rome and hadn't heard from him . . . assuming that he was in bed. In Florida.

In bed . . . but not Florida.

Lying on top of the sheets, he still wore a dress shirt, minus the tie; his slacks hid his long legs. A day's worth of stubble stood out on his chin, his mouth was open a sliver as even breaths told her he was sound asleep. Equal parts sweet and sexy, she contemplated his presence.

Why was he there and why was he in her bed?

With a silly smile on her lips, she quietly turned off the light, retrieved her nightgown from her suitcase she'd yet to unpack, and slid quietly back into the bathroom to prepare for bed.

Meg pushed back the covers and slid under them. "Val?" she whispered his name again, wanted to wake him enough so he knew she was there. "Val?"

He mumbled something in Italian.

"Val?" Her voice was louder this time. She placed a hand on his shoulder.

"Cara?" He rolled toward her.

"What are you doing here, Masini?"

He didn't open his eyes. Truth be told, she wasn't sure he was even aware he spoke. "Airports . . . Italy . . . the rooms were full. So tired."

She understood the last part. Exhaustion threatened her sanity. She moved close enough to reach his shirt and started to unbutton it. "Take this off, Val. You won't sleep well in it."

His hands followed hers even though his eyes were closed.

Half-dead, she admired the view as he sat up and shrugged out of his shirt.

He started to lie back and she kept him upright a little longer. "Pants. The belt in bed might be exciting another time . . . but not tonight."

A smirk managed to cross his lips and one eye cracked open. Val's next words were once again cloaked in Italian.

Val wore boxers was her thought before he moved under the covers beside her.

She started to lie down when he pulled her into the nook of his arm and kissed the top of her head.

"Sleep, *bella*. Thank you for not kicking me out."

"Too tired to kick anything."

He squeezed her closer and she sucked in his scent. Maybe in the morning she could tell him that she didn't do the sleepover thing with men.

Gabi woke to the ocean surrounding her.

She'd fallen asleep in Alonzo's arms after a romantic on-deck dinner the chef had prepared.

She loved being on the sea. The vast open space felt safe on the yacht as gentle waves lulled her to a sense of serenity land couldn't offer.

Alonzo had met her at the airport in Key West and swept her onto his yacht and out to sea within an hour. When she asked where they were headed, he didn't say . . . simply handed her a glass of champagne and told her not to worry. Between the sun, the wine, and the amazing meal, she found herself falling asleep under the stars. They were both tired when they'd crawled into bed, yet Alonzo had made love to her with her eyes half-closed. The act was nearly over before it began but Gabi was too tired to care.

She woke groggy and found a bottle of water and two pills by the bedside. *For your headache* was written on a note next to the bottle.

How did Alonzo know she'd wake with her head cracking from the inside? Maybe it was the wine? Or maybe the sea managed to dig deep.

She took the pills and pushed out of the empty bed. She looked out the starboard and port sides of the ship and could tell they were in the middle of the sea. No land in sight.

The onboard shower was as luxurious as a yacht could offer. The water soothed her headache but didn't completely wake her.

By the time she left the shower, someone had been in their suite and a white sundress, one she didn't own, lay on the bed with another note. *For my bride.*

With a smile, she slid the linen dress over her head and turned to the full-length mirror. The fit was perfect and went to her toes. Even in the heat of the Caribbean Sea, the cloth felt cool against her skin.

She placed her hair in a knot on top of her head and tried to shake the sleep from her head as she left her room in search of her fiancé.

"Miss Masini," the steward greeted her in the living quarters, pulled out a chair at the dining table. "Mr. Picano asked that you eat before your big day. He'll be along shortly."

"Coffee. I'd love some coffee."

"Yes, ma'am."

The young man scurried away and returned with coffee and a bowl of fresh fruit along with a variety of muffins. She was halfway through the coffee and nibbling on a muffin when Alonzo walked into the room.

"There you are," he said, kissing her on the head as he took the seat beside her. "Did you sleep well?"

"Like a rock. Though a rock doesn't sleep, does it?"

Alonzo nudged her nose with a knuckle and waved the steward over. Without asking, the attendant brought a bottle of champagne and two glasses.

"It's a bit early for this, isn't it?" she questioned.

Instead of saying anything, he winked and shooed off the help, leaving them alone.

He lifted his glass and waited for her to pick up hers.

"To us," he said.

How could she say no to the smile that spread over Alonzo's face? "To us." The sweet, fizzling wine tickled her nose and rolled down her throat.

Before she set her glass back down, Alonzo was pouring more into it.

"Are you going to tell me where we're headed?" she asked for the tenth time since he picked her up at the airport.

He moved around the table and sat beside her, pulled her close. "How about a honeymoon?"

The question sounded strange on his lips. "You want to talk about where we'll have our honeymoon?"

He sipped his wine and encouraged her to join him. "Someplace away from everyone. We can make love for hours, come out only to eat . . . or have someone bring in food."

That didn't sound like him at all. The man didn't sit still long enough for lazy fantasies like the one he described. "And what would we do the next day?"

He laughed, kissed the side of her cheek. "You know me so well." He leaned against the back of the seat, placed his head alongside hers. "I've been so busy. I need you to ground me."

Enjoying the feel of his arms around her, she settled beside him and sipped her wine. The thought of being *the someone* he needed in his life to make him complete left a warmth in her chest. In her life, no one truly needed her. Her mother needed Val, especially after their father's death, but Gabi always felt like more of a burden than an asset. "It's nice to be needed," she confessed.

He nuzzled her neck. "I need you, Gabriella. More than you know."

His lips sought hers for a brief kiss. When he pulled away, he lifted his glass. "For needing each other."

She sipped more wine and felt it hit her head. Warmth filled her cheeks as she set the glass down.

"Marry me," Alonzo said at her side.

She giggled. "I already said I would." She waved her left hand in the air.

Alonzo set his glass beside her and knelt on the floor, taking both of her hands in his as he stared up at her. "Marry me now. Today."

She blinked, pushed the fuzz out of her brain. "Today?"

"Yes. Today. I don't want to wait. I want you to take my name today."

"But the wedding—"

"We can do it all again later, dress, flowers, family. Let's do this now, for us. No one even needs to know about it. Just think," he said with a silly smile on his face. "Years from now we will tell our children how we eloped on the open waters on a summer day with a breeze off the ocean."

Are you serious?

The expression on his face told her he was.

She considered the possibility, felt something inside her hesitate.

"Think of the weight lifted if the public wedding isn't filled with emotional stress." He kissed her fingertips. "Please."

She wanted to say yes, was about to utter the words, when she felt her head grow heavy. "How can we? There is no priest."

"My captain has the authority, darling. On the deck, right now. I'll pledge my life to you."

"Oh, Alonzo."

He leaned forward and kissed her, fully. Several seconds passed before he moved away far enough to whisper, "I love you, Gabriella. Make me the happiest man on the ocean and take my name."

Could she? Why should they wait? They could do it all again in a few months . . .

She felt the boat tip, or maybe it was her. The whirlwind Alonzo was pushing her in was a vortex she didn't feel she could avoid. With a giddy heart and a fuzzy head, she found herself nodding.

"Yes?" he asked again.

"Yes."

After another kiss, he handed her the glass again and stood. "I'll tell my captain and arrange everything."

Gabi's hands shook as she tilted the wine to her lips. She looked down to see her glass nearly empty. She glanced at the bottle and realized it, too, was almost gone.

Had she really just agreed to eloping?

She smiled, despite the twist in her gut. Making a decision on her own, without the guidance of her family, felt right. Besides, pushing up the date by a few months meant nothing.

Not really.

Chapter Twenty

On some level, Meg realized she was in a hotel bed . . . but this one was moving. And since she'd graduated from college, hotel beds with magic fingers were no longer part of her circuit. Thank God.

Still, her head moved up and down in a steady motion.

Rome. That's right, I'm in Italy.

Her eyes popped open. *Val.*

Sure enough, it wasn't a dream. Her head was flat against Val's chest, and from her angle, his chest was something to behold. Wavy, firm bits with a small dusting of hair. His Italian color along with living on a tropical island gave him a golden tan many strove for but seldom obtained.

Doing her best to lie still and not wake her bed partner, she took stock of where all of her limbs were and what they were doing. She lay on her left side, her left arm curled between the two of them. Her right arm was shamelessly draped low on his chest, her right leg entwined with both of his. She couldn't resemble a human blanket much more. Even in his sleep, Val hung on. His right hand rested on her hip . . . a hip completely exposed to his touch. Seemed her excuse for a nightgown wanted to ride up in the night. His other hand held her arm that lay over his chest.

I don't do sleepovers.

Yet she was wrapped around him like lips sucking a lime after a tequila shot, and he was hanging on for the ride.

Sleepovers meant commitment. There was nothing about Val that was committed. They hadn't even slept together . . . well, slept, but not . . . she closed her eyes and burrowed a little deeper. *How can he smell good after a full day of traveling and a night of sleep?*

Meg indulged in the feel and smell of him a little longer before forcing her eyes open for good. She attempted to pull her right hand out from under his only to have his fingers wrap around hers and pull her even tighter.

"Don't go," he mumbled.

"You're awake?"

"From the moment you opened your eyes."

She lifted her chin and found him staring at her. Good God, there should be a law against being as sexy as he was first thing in the morning.

She smiled and didn't worry about where her hair was sticking out, or the possibility of morning breath. "What are you doing in my bed, Masini?"

He twisted enough so her leg slipped between his. "Cuddling with a beautiful woman."

"Sneaky of you. How did you manage to get in the room last night anyway?"

"The perks of knowing the language, *cara*. Italy, Rome in particular, is a city of love and romance. A few short words open doors."

"And the greasing of palms?"

He lifted his eyebrows. "That doesn't hurt either."

"So you bribed your way into my bed. I'm impressed."

He released her hand and placed a palm on her cheek.

She spread her fingers and enjoyed the feel of his taut chest against her hand. Her thumb traced the edge of one particularly dominant muscle.

He moved closer, offered a little moan with her touch.

He sighed, his dark gaze held hers. "Now what will it take to make my way inside of you?"

The image of the two of them embraced in passion swam into her head so suddenly she shivered.

Her fingers sank into his flesh. "That's easy."

The smirk on his face was a buck away from priceless. "Oh?"

The tip of her thumb tracked his responding nipple and he hitched his breath. "All you have to do is ask."

He licked his lips over the smile on his face. With an attempt to be serious, he tried to stop grinning. *"Cara . . ."* He ran his hand down the side of her face and placed a feathered touch down her neck. *"Bella*, let me love you." His accent thickened as his voice dropped with his request.

Had anyone ever made love to her with words?

Only Val.

She answered him by placing her lips on his. When mint splashed on her tongue, she pulled away. "You don't play fair. Mouthwash?"

He pulled her back, kissed, tasted, and made all thoughts of morning breath float away. She sighed and let him lead. He held her hostage with his tongue, took his time worshiping her mouth. When he tired of her lips, or maybe he simply needed to breathe, he pushed her onto her back and started a slow dance down her neck, his free hand playing on her leg, her hip, bringing every nerve ending awake with his touch.

Maybe she should rethink sleepovers.

"Waking up with you has its perks," she told him as he pushed her nightgown low and nibbled at the top of her breast. Her nipples tightened and offered themselves to him.

His full hand rounded on her, brushed against her offering. "So does going to bed with me." He nibbled her tip through her clothing. "Showering with me."

How could he suck through fabric? Everything tingled and she pushed her hips closer for some kind of contact. His knee offered some relief to the tight coil of need burning low in her belly.

"Hot tubs," she managed. "I like hot tubs."

A low laugh escaped his lips as he lifted her enough to drag her nightgown over her head.

"Sei bellissima," he said before he dipped his head for a solid taste.

The scrape of the stubble on his chin added to the torment his tongue was delivering to her breasts. The slow, torturous ministration of her body raised her pulse and had her breathing heavier. So far, the tightness in her chest had yet to make itself known, even with her entire being winding like a child's toy ready to spring.

The weight of Val's erection pressed against her stomach, and brought a bolt of lust low between her thighs.

Meg dragged her nails down his back and met with the elastic of his boxers while she pressed her knee closer.

Val murmured something in Italian before taking her lips again. His kiss lingered and he took his time. In the past, Meg would push forward, attempt to move a lover along to the finish line. Not with Val. Kissing half-naked like two young kids in the back of a car brought on its own pleasure she'd forgotten existed.

They kissed, tasted, touched, and learned the places that brought the largest response from the other. He found her soft folds with a string of sensual Italian words.

"You're killing me," she said when he didn't hurry his touch.

"Then we will die together, *cara*."

Using her foot, she helped his boxers make their way to the floor and teased Val as he teased her.

He was hot, ready . . . and she scraped her nails over, under . . . around, but didn't touch fully until Val offered her relief. His first stroke of his fingers against her most sensitive parts brought her off the bed, her heart thundering in her chest.

"Easy. Slowly, *bella*."

Slow was good, her breath caught and she forced a deep breath. He swirled, stroked, brought her to the very edge of release, and backed off. Instead of pounding his chest in frustration, she returned his tease, took hold, and squeezed.

He pushed into her hand, lost the control as she heard him suck in a tight breath.

One minute she was beside him, the next under. She heard a wrapper, felt him move away far enough to cover himself, and knew she was safe. Val took hold of her hands and lifted them over her head.

Bare to him, he shifted beside her open core. *"Sei un dono,"* he whispered as he moved inside.

She stretched, took him, and sighed. "Oh, Val." She closed her eyes for the pleasure of it.

"Perfect. You're so perfect."

Then he began to move. Just like his kiss, he built slow waves of pleasure until sensibility gave way to greedy need. She gripped his hips, wrapped her legs around his waist, and found another place of pleasure deep inside her own body that Meg didn't know was there.

Meg felt the moment Val lost it, the control he held so close was gone as he took and took from her, demanded her body respond. It did.

Her breath tightened and her head grew dizzy as she shattered in her release. Val raced to keep up until they were both panting and limp.

With Val half-dead on top of her, Meg threw her hand to the bedside table and fumbled around for her inhaler.

Val snapped his head up, concern in his gaze.

"I'm OK," she insisted. "Just a tiny hit."

The pressure of his body was instantly gone, and severely missed. But she did find it easier to breathe with his weight off her.

The medicine opened her lungs.

"I'm sorry."

Poor man thought he'd killed her.

She placed the inhaler on the table and pulled him back toward her. "I'm not."

"But your lungs—"

"Are fine." She sighed.

He rolled onto his back and pulled her on top of him right as the sun started to rise over Rome.

Margaret sang in the shower.

Of course she sings in the shower. Did he expect anything different?

He ran a comb through his hair after pulling on a casual shirt and a pair of slacks. He wondered, briefly, if the hotel had a clothing store that sold jeans.

He smirked at himself in the mirror and shook his head. "Time for that later," he told himself before he left Margaret's room.

With her singing . . . well, humming actually, with the water running in the private bathroom, he stepped into the common room of the suite and found the slightly surprised eyes of Michael, who was already enjoying a pot of coffee and a breakfast of fruit, cheese, and biscuits.

"Why am I not surprised to see you walking out of Meg's room?" Michael waved a hand to the seat beside him and lifted the carafe of coffee.

A nod had Michael pouring the strong brew into a cup. "I flew to LA, heard you were both en route here. I was five hours behind you."

Michael pushed the coffee in front of Val once he took his seat. "That will wake you up," he said after his first sip.

"European coffee . . . nothing better."

The second sip sat better on Val's tongue. "Colombian?"

Michael tilted his head. "True. But who spends a lot of time down there?"

"You have a point."

They talked about coffee, travel, and nibbled on a weak breakfast. "So why are we in Rome?" Val finally asked.

Michael lifted his hand in the air, wagged two fingers in Val's direction, and opened his mouth. "I don't know if you want to hear this."

Val felt the smile on his face slip. "Why wouldn't I want to hear it?"

From behind him, Val heard Margaret's voice. "Because we're chasing a lead on your future brother-in-law."

Val wasn't sure what was worse . . . the fact that Michael and Margaret were in Rome . . . in Italy . . . following up on Alonzo, or the fact that Val didn't feel the hair on his neck rise. "Why?"

Margaret and Michael exchanged glances.

"It's the wine," Michael told him. "Something about his wine isn't adding up."

Margaret stood aside, apprehensive about his reaction, if Val was reading her right. The woman he'd just made love to, had loved thoroughly, was nervous.

He waved her over and patted his leg with a smile.

She moved into his space and took his offered spot. Her skin was soap clean, her hair smelled like roses. There wasn't a lick of makeup on her face and she was beautiful. Nervous, but beautiful.

She sipped coffee from his cup and refilled it while Michael talked.

Alonzo's wine tasted familiar, according to Michael. Too familiar, like maybe the wine wasn't made in the region of Italy that Alonzo claimed it to be. When Michael told Val about his time spent with a man who knew wine better than Val knew the business of vacation resorts and meddling Italian mamas, Val found himself questioning why Michael and Margaret flew all the way to Italy on a lead.

"It's all we have," Margaret said as she offered him a buttered biscuit.

"Alonzo's wine tastes like the same brand you're familiar with so you fly overseas to look into it?"

There was another look passed between Michael and Margaret.

"I don't like him," Margaret blurted out. "I don't think he's the right man for your sister. And I think he's hiding something."

"He's hiding something because you don't like him?"

Margaret moved from Val's lap and walked to the drapes closing off the view of Rome. She opened them and ambient light flooded the room. "I don't like him, so I looked into him."

That caused Val to pause. "Looked into him?"

With her back to him . . . a back clothed in slacks and a silk shirt, her feet still bare . . . sexy. "He spends more money than he makes," she told him.

Val realized his finger was tapping against the table. He knew Alonzo lived with extravagance. He took the man's lifestyle into account when he accepted his desire to marry his sister. Gabi deserved a man who could provide for her.

She also deserved her privacy, and that was something that kept Val from doing a complete background check on her fiancé. His eye started to twitch. "How do you know this?"

"Because I've been checking up on him." Margaret turned, leveled her calm gaze Val's way. "The man is hiding something, Masini . . . and we're here to find out what that is."

He gripped the coffee cup tight before setting it down. "Even if he is, what does this have to do with pictures . . . with the two of you?"

Margaret shrugged. "It might have nothing to do with us. Or the man knows we're on to him and he wants leverage to keep us quiet. Hence, the pictures."

"Alonzo wasn't on the island when the pictures were taken." Yet even as the words left his mouth, Val remembered one of Alonzo's shipmates had been. His future brother-in-law, and his crew, didn't go through the rigorous scrutiny that all Val's employees and guests did.

"If we're wrong . . . we leave Italy with a full belly and a case or two of wine. But if we're right . . ." Michael glanced at Margaret.

"We prevent a friend from making a huge mistake."

"You mean Gabi." Val found his smile once again. The fact that Margaret would work hard to make sure his sister wasn't jumping for the wrong man left him pleasantly warm.

"Gabi is too trusting, gullible. Either Alonzo is crazy amazing in bed, or she's—"

"I don't want to hear of my sister's sex life," Val interrupted.

Margaret moved toward him, sat back on his lap, and kissed him soundly. "Let's make sure your sister isn't making the biggest mistake of her life."

Val wove his hands around Margaret's waist, loved the feel and scent of her. "And if Alonzo is legit and we're here searching for his faults?"

"How will they know? Aren't they out messing around on his—"

His back teeth ground together. "Again with my sister's love life."

Margaret took mercy. "She won't know . . . unless we find something. And even if she finds out, I can take the fall. You followed me and had no choice but to follow along. Or you can go home and have nothing to do with this."

"And leave you in Italy without knowledge of the language? What do you expect to find out when you can't tell if someone is telling you the truth or calling you a stupid tourist?"

Michael waved in their direction. "He has a point. You can pretend a lack of knowledge of the language and we can play tourists."

"And when the time is right, you can ask all the right questions to the locals. It's worth a shot. Worse case—"

"We leave with a full belly and a few cases of wine," Val finished her sentence.

Chapter Twenty-One

The man was sexy, confident . . . and completely in his element as he negotiated with the rental car company before they set off from the hotel. Seemed Michael and Val had something in common when it came to cars that moved. Of course that meant Meg was stuck in the backseat of a car that barely had one as Val sped over the highways and byways of Italy. While the road signs weren't completely foreign, they did take a minute or two for her brain to process. Val, on the other hand, shifted gears, veered left and right as if he was right at home.

It didn't take long for the city to fall behind them and the countryside to open to massive space and yes . . . vineyards.

Michael hadn't stopped smiling since they left the hotel.

"It's like midstate California, only better," Meg voiced from the backseat.

Michael nodded. "Optimal grape production. California produces over eighty percent of America's wine. But this is where wine was born . . . well, here and France."

"But no one likes the French." Val's joke made everyone laugh.

Meg didn't know anyone who was uniquely French, and didn't hold an opinion.

"It's the history . . . the years of production that make each region unique. New winemakers study it . . . make it their business to know the subtle differences."

Val liked to drive fast. He made the swift curves of the road his as he guided the sporty coupe to his whims. "You're an actor . . . what do you know of the subtle differences?" Val questioned.

"Hollywood."

Val managed a peek at Michael before returning his eyes to the road.

"Before I was old enough to drink, Hollywood was offering me everything. I was twenty when I shot my first film. When we wrapped up production there were lines of coke and shots of Patrón on the bar."

Meg hadn't heard this story. Knew for a fact her best friend Judy hadn't heard it, either. She leaned in to hear every syllable.

"The coke wasn't an option. Didn't even look at it twice, but the tequila . . . that's another story."

Meg laughed. "Bit you in the ass, did it?"

Michael shook his head as if remembering the pain. "I don't know what people see in that crap. I was sick for a week. After that the after-parties continued and I noticed wine, champagne . . . all lined up with the drugs and hard stuff. I wanted to be grown-up but didn't want to burn for a week after. Hollywood could afford decent wine. I soon learned what I liked and what I didn't."

Meg smiled, liking the fact that Michael shared a personal story with them. "So why do you hide your love for wine? Your wine cellar is stocked yet you drink beer in public."

"My image drinks beer."

Meg snorted. "Maybe it's time to change your image. Beer is a cheap man's drink. Wine . . . and even Patrón, is for people with money."

Michael seemed to consider her words.

"Unless you like beer," Val said.

"Can't stand it."

"Life is too short to drink something you don't like."

Meg agreed. Here she was in wine country, and she didn't like the stuff. A stiff whiskey was just fine, thank you very much . . . wine? *Blah.*

They drove through the countryside until they hit the Umbria region and the winery that produced what Michael insisted tasted exactly like Alonzo's label.

There was no doubt by their stance walking into the tasting room that they were on a mission.

Thankfully, Michael's face was known everywhere. The employees scrambled to help them, asked for autographs, and offered them more attention than anyone else in the room.

It didn't take long for the proprietors of the winery to work their way to Michael's side. His natural charisma and charm opened doors like no one else Meg knew.

"My friends," Michael opened up the conversation to the two of them, "Miss Rosenthal and Mr. Masini."

Val shook the proprietor's hand and spoke in Italian. The incognito understanding of the language was waiting until they reached Alonzo's region. Here, Val had free rein to speak whatever he needed to in order to find the answers they wanted.

"So you want to know more about our wine," their host said.

"I'm afraid our famous friend has us at a disadvantage. He said you were the best. We're here to find out why."

Luciano, who went by Luc, pulled the three of them to the back of the tasting room for a private tour. Meg wondered, briefly, if anyone ever turned Michael away.

The rock-laden walls of the passageway opened to a larger room that housed a few tables and hundreds of bottles of wine. The cool space stood in stark contrast to the room above them where the average taster stood sipping wine.

Luc told them how old the winery was . . . spoke of his ancestors who had owned the winery before him. He would turn every so often and say something in Italian to Val, and then continue as if every one of them understood him.

"O-four was a fabulous year." Luc reached a top shelf in the cool cellar and wiped off the bottle, which was already dust free. "This is the year you told me you enjoyed, yes?"

Michael studied the label briefly before handing it back to their host. "I have several bottles in my collection."

Luc dipped his head as if in appreciation of Michael's patronage. "Tell me what you want to know, *signor*. You already enjoy my wine." He placed his hand over his chest. "Seems you're here to perhaps find a new favorite?"

"I would love to sample more, of course, but I also want to educate my friends on your varieties and learn what sets them apart from other wines here in Italy."

Luc extended a hand to encourage them to sit while he used a simple intercom to request help from his employees. Before Meg could scoot her chair in, three employees walked into the room and started setting up wineglass after glass. Luc pulled bottles from his collection while others were brought from the room above. A tray of crackers, cheese, olives, and a few things Meg couldn't identify was placed on their table.

"The weather in o-four was perfection. We had hoped the next year would do just as well, but as it was, the rain the next season gave us a small yield." While Luc explained weather conditions, he poured a tiny amount of wine into three glasses.

Instead of picking up the glass and following Michael and Val's lead, Meg turned her attention to Luc. "I'd love to fake my way through a tasting, Luc . . . but that seems a shame. Please tell me what I'm looking and smelling for."

"My pleasure, *signorina*." Luc talked about color, and thickness of the wine. She expected the man to dip his nose deep in the glass, but instead he simply hovered the glass under his nose and drew in the scent. Luc spoke of what to be aware of when smelling wine . . . the bad things in any event. "But you won't find any of that here," he said. "Now . . . can you smell the oak?" Meg wasn't sure if it was oak she drew into her nose or not. "We age this vintage in our oldest barrels."

"You reuse them?" Meg asked.

"Yes. Many times over. New barrels have an entirely different scent."

By the time they were ready to sip, Meg was actually anxious to taste the oak-smelling, not too thick, red but not purple wine.

She and Michael both swallowed the pleasing taste, where Val used the spittoon provided for them.

They tasted a few different blends and varieties, each time nibbling on crackers in between. Finally, the question that was burning for all of them was asked.

"What makes this wine unique to this region, Luc?" Michael asked.

"I would love to take all the credit, but the truth is too well known to fake. The unique flavor comes from sagrantino. The grape grows in this region almost exclusively."

"Do all your blends have this grape in it?" Val asked.

"Not all, but during this year of production, we did use more of it."

It was time for Meg to ask the obvious questions. "So we won't find wine that tastes like this in let's say . . . the Campania region?"

Luc offered a placating smile. "It's not possible, *signorina*. Some wines might come close, but they will not match. Not to the educated in any event. For someone like yourself, who doesn't yet know the subtle differences, you may never tell the change in regions."

"I'll bet Michael could tell the difference," she said.

Luc turned his eyes to Michael. "Shall we test your palate?"

"I'm up to the challenge."

Luc tilted his head and spoke in hushed tones to one of his servers, who disappeared only to return with several bottles hidden in sleeves.

Val and Meg sat back and watched as glasses were removed and new ones took their place.

Michael swirled, swished, sipped, and spit without any words. He wrote his answer to the region and placed it facedown in front of the anonymous bottle before moving on to the next.

"He certainly looks like he knows what he's doing," Val whispered in her ear.

Meg shrugged. She could tell the difference in some whiskeys, so it stood to reason that Michael could tell the difference with wine.

Michael hesitated on the last bottle, sipped it twice, letting the vintage down his throat instead of spitting it out. "Nice try," he said to Luc.

"Let's see how you did." Luc uncovered the first bottle, tilted it toward Michael. "Veneto region." He turned over Michael's answer and smiled. "One for one."

The second bottle was Toscana, the third was one of Luc's, the forth from Campania, the fifth Sicilia. "And the last one?" Luc asked with a strange look of pride.

"Napa." Michael laughed.

"I think we can safely say that Michael knows his wine regions," Meg told Val.

With the confirmation of Michael's taste buds, it was truly time to doubt Alonzo's wine.

Luc drew them from the private tasting room and encouraged them to stay for dinner. Considering all the time they'd been given, it would have been an insult to run off.

They stayed for dinner, drank more wine, and when they finally left, Michael and Val had placed large orders of Luc's collection to be sent back to the States.

"Now what?" Meg asked as they drove back to the hotel.

"We drive south tomorrow."

"To Alonzo's winery?" Meg wasn't sure that was a good idea.

"Adjacent properties. Learn what we can from his neighbors," Val suggested.

Worry swam over Val's eyes. Meg placed a hand on his leg as he drove. He kissed her fingers before placing her hand back.

Why was Alonzo passing off someone else's wine as his own?

Meg's thoughts went to Gabi. Something told her that her friend wouldn't be wearing a wedding dress anytime soon. From the look on Val's face, if half of their thoughts were true, he'd toss Gabi in an ivory tower before he'd let a lying man wed his sister.

The ceremony had been brief. Gabi wanted to think it went quickly because often the good things in life passed quickly. Between the sun, the sea, and the enormity of the commitment she was making, her head swam. When the captain told Alonzo to kiss the bride, her husband wrapped her in his arms and engulfed her.

One of the shipmates snapped a few pictures during the brief ceremony and again when they toasted their promise to each other.

Gabi remembered signing a paper and wondering how Alonzo had managed a marriage certificate in the middle of the ocean. Then he had swept her away to his cabin.

Hours later, she woke with a headache and a roll in her stomach. Like before, Alonzo wasn't at her side. The sun was setting with a cool breeze that helped clear her head when she emerged from their bed.

Alonzo was holding on to the rail, overlooking the ocean as the sun set. "There you are," she said as she slid her hands around his waist.

He covered her hand with his and kissed the top of her head. "You were so peaceful, Mrs. Picano. It was my husbandly duty to let you sleep."

"And miss the sunset?"

He pulled her close.

Once in the crook of his arm, she said, "We're really married."

"We are."

"I think that has to be the most spontaneous anything I've ever done," Gabi told him with a sigh.

Alonzo pulled away and his smile fell. "You still have a headache, don't you?"

She squeezed her eyes shut. "A little."

He sat her down and told her to wait for him. When he returned, he had another dose of aspirin and a glass of water.

"You're taking such sweet care of me," she told him.

"I promised I would, didn't I?"

Gabi couldn't really remember if that was part of their wedding vows. She chided herself for forgetting the words so quickly. Maybe when the headache eased off, she'd remember everything clearly.

Alonzo sat beside her and let her drop her head on his shoulder. The lull of the sea and the medication made quick work of her headache. She was starting to wonder if maybe Alonzo's medicine from Italy was a miracle worker. She'd never had such a quick turnaround of pain in all her life. In fact, her head floated a little as the pain drifted away.

"Better already?" Alonzo asked as the sun left their company.

"It must be you," she said.

He stood and reached for her. "Come with me then. I have a meal fit for a new bride ready for you to consume."

She floated, like the pain scattering, while they dined, drank, and even danced. The night was magical. Everything Gabi thought her wedding day and evening should have been.

The next morning, a bottle of medicine stood next to a glass of water.

Alonzo was once again somewhere other than by her side.

Chapter Twenty-Two

"It's our third winery and no one's talking." Margaret nudged her head between the seats. All Val could sense was the smell of her hair. The hotel had a brand that used grapeseed and oil . . . the perfume intoxicated him. Or maybe it was the woman who used it.

"It's almost like they're purposely not talking."

Michael spoke the words already swimming in Val's head. They'd walked into the winery to the east of Alonzo's with Margaret and Michael posing as a couple . . . Val walked in a short time later and stood to the side as they sipped wine and asked questions. As soon as they spoke of the Picano winery, the blinders went on and the smiles shifted off. The second winery to the south was the same. The northern winery held less back, but still said nothing about their neighbor. The property had changed hands a few years past, but nothing more than that. Still, Val thought there was a conversation taking place that he didn't hear. Not even in Italian.

"I say we switch it up," Margaret suggested. "The next stop, you stay in the car," she told Michael. "Val and I can go in . . . I'll be a tad tipsy and my Italian hottie will be working hard to get lucky by getting me into Alonzo's winery."

Alonzo didn't have a tasting room, which in and of itself wasn't completely unheard of . . . but with so many wineries in the region, it wasn't the best business practice.

Margaret unbuttoned the top buttons on her blouse until the creamy expanse of her breasts met the warm Italian air.

"What are you doing?"

"Stacking the deck," she said before applying a fresh layer of lip gloss. She teased her hair and blew Val a kiss.

She was lovely. Even in her attempt to look like a common good time. Val knew the woman beneath. She was more frustrated with the roadblock they'd managed to find than he was. Gabi meant something to her. *We're not going to let her make a massive mistake if Alonzo is playing her.* Her words resonated in Val's ears. He'd been so wrapped up in his own life, his work, that he hadn't done his job protecting his sister. He should have investigated Alonzo more. In the effort to ensure his sister's privacy, he'd taken everything Alonzo presented him as truth.

Val had checked out the fact that Alonzo actually had his name associated with the vineyard. But that was as far as Val checked.

Now, months later, he was traversing the Italian countryside to find fault with his future brother-in-law. The man sleeping with his sister.

Val cringed. His sister was, right at that moment, alone with the man.

A short vacation, Alonzo had called it. *A way to reconnect with his future bride* . . . Why would a fiancé need to reconnect with his future bride?

Michael drove up to the parking lot and Val guided Margaret out of the backseat.

The second they left the car, Margaret started giggling and stumbling into him.

"Are you OK?"

She sent him a sobering look. "Work with me, Val."

He pasted on a smile and led her into the tasting room.

Loud and American was an art form, and Margaret had it down.

"Oh, this one is pretty," she said as they walked into the air-conditioned tasting room.

"The last one was lovely, too."

There were a few patrons standing along the tasting bar, swirling wine and sipping. Most drank, where a few of them spit out their offerings.

Margaret zeroed in on one of the male servers and squinted her eyes at the man. Val didn't consider himself a jealous man, and he knew Margaret was doing her best Hollywood performance, still he didn't care for the attention she was turning on the young man behind the wine counter.

"What wine is this place known for?" This was how she opened the conversation?

The other man passed his eyes to Val.

"We've been all over the region today," Val told the man in English.

"Our whites are award winning," he said in English. "Not that you'll tell the difference with all you've had," he said in Italian.

Val didn't bother pretending he didn't understand the man.

The two of them laughed and smiled sweetly at Margaret.

"What did he say?" she asked as she slipped onto Val's lap like the family dog.

"He said you're lovely, *cara*."

It was the attendant's time to laugh under his smirk.

"Bring us a sample of your award winners," Val told the man in Italian.

The attendant lined up glasses and started to pour.

Margaret swirled the white and grinned. "Am I doing it right?"

Val wanted to bite his lip, but didn't. "Only with red, *bella*. Just smell."

"Oh, OK."

Margaret smelled and gulped.

"Tastes like roses."

Val turned to the attendant, who shook his head with a subtle movement.

Val took his turn, spit out the wine. There wasn't a hint of floral anything in the mix. Not to his palate in any case.

On the third taste, Margaret exclaimed, "Oak . . . I smell oak."

Again, the attendant shook his head. "We don't cask our white in oak."

Margaret tossed out her bottom lip and put out her best blonde moment. "Sucks. I thought I had that one. I bet the winery up the way has oak. What was the name of it?"

"Picano. We'll go there next, *cara*. No worries."

The attendant shook his head. "They don't have tastings," he told them.

Margaret offered an even bigger pout. "Why not? This is Italy, isn't it? Home of wine and love?" She nuzzled Val's neck long enough to make the man behind the bar squirm.

"I'm not sure why they don't host tastings." The attendant removed a red from behind the bar and presented it to Val. "For the lady?"

Val offered a short nod and said, "I know I've sampled their wine in the States. Is there a place to purchase?"

If the discussion about another winery's brand bothered the kid behind the bar, Val couldn't tell. "Not locally. I believe they export exclusively."

Margaret sipped the wine and listened.

"Is that normal?" Val asked.

The attendant lowered his voice to a whisper. "I think they might be intimidated by all the names surrounding them. The new owners are seldom there . . . chances are the quality isn't where it should be."

Margaret slid her glass to Val. "This one is good."

Val tasted and agreed. After buying a few bottles of the red Margaret said she enjoyed, they walked back to the car.

They told Michael what they'd learned as they drove to the final surrounding vineyard to the Picano property.

"Who makes Italian wine and doesn't sell it to Italians?" Margaret asked.

"I've never heard of such a practice." Michael turned up the road to the next winery. "What's the plan with this place?"

"I think you should go into the tasting room and gather a crowd. Val and I can take a little walk in the vineyard . . . maybe get a glimpse of Alonzo's place."

"Trespass?"

"Stumbling out of one vineyard to the next. They all look the same," Margaret told Val with a tiny bat of her eyelashes.

"I knew you were more devious than my background check found on you," Val told her.

"Life is too short to stay on the straight path all the time."

Michael laughed. "You can say that again."

There were several cars parked in the lot. They pulled away from the crowd and found a shade tree in the back. Michael slipped on his glasses before opening the door. "Give me five minutes."

"Go get 'em, Mr. Hollywood." Margaret patted his back and he slid out of the car.

They both watched him walk into the tasting room and disappear from sight. "I like your friends," Val said.

"Michael is good people. The entire family is grounded, genuine . . . it's hard to explain."

"Does his family know about . . . him?" The two of them had yet to vocalize Michael's sexuality, and Val wasn't about to now.

"You mean the Ryder factor?"

Even Margaret skirted around the obvious.

"Yes."

"Most. His parents are still clueless, his youngest sister. It's only a matter of time."

"What makes you say that?"

She shrugged. "Hard to pinpoint why I feel that way. He's changed a lot in the last few years with his brother and two of his sisters knowing. We've talked. He knows his secrets are a burden for his family to keep from each other. None of them want to be the one who slips and screws up . . . ya know?"

"The lies must be difficult."

Margaret settled her eyes on his. "I hate that we live in a society where he feels he needs to *act* like someone he's not."

"Things are changing."

"Not fast enough."

There it was again, the drive and passion about right and wrong that Margaret displayed when it came to the people she loved. Val reached out and placed her cheek in the palm of his hand. "Your friends are lucky to have you," he murmured.

She blushed with the compliment. "None of my friends have *had me* . . . though I'm sure they wanted to."

The woman made him laugh when he least expected it. "So humble, *bella*."

"If you have it, flaunt it, Masini."

He leaned forward and kissed her as if he had every right. When he pulled away, she had a dreamy quality in her eyes. "I'll let you flaunt, and remind anyone trying that they can't *have* you."

"Oh?"

He cocked his head to the side, reached over Margaret, and pushed open her door. "I don't share."

I don't share . . . I don't share . . .

Meg had to concentrate on putting one foot in front of the other, and act like she'd been drinking more than tasting most of the day. Truth was, she had a little buzz going and Val didn't help with all his *I don't share* talk.

Those three words sent an unexpected wave of pleasure through her body. And since when did that happen? Sharing is caring . . . right?

Monogamy is commitment.

And why was commitment such a hard word to swallow?

Something about *I don't share* shook and thrilled her at the same time.

They'd walked a few yards into a vineyard and Val stopped her. "Stand over there," he told her.

Lost in her thoughts, she narrowed her eyes. "What?"

He motioned to their right and she noticed a few employees glimpsing their way.

Val removed his cell phone and pointed it at her as if he were taking a picture. "Smile, *bella*."

That's right, they were on a mission. Sharing, commitment, suits, artists, and all thoughts in between would have to wait. Right now, they needed to make sure Gabi wasn't committing to a criminal, which was exactly where Meg's thoughts were headed.

She posed and the men glancing their way turned away.

"Are they watching?" Val asked.

"Not anymore."

Val took her hand and started up the hill, farther into the thick green fields of grapevines. It didn't take long for them to crest the hill and disappear from sight of the tasting room, parking lot, and farm workers.

"Is that the road to Alonzo's?"

A paved road ran alongside the adjacent winery, they'd seen that on the map.

"I think so," Val said.

They followed the road and zigzagged in and out of the rows of grapevines to keep hidden as much as possible.

"What exactly do you think we'll find?" Val asked her.

"Probably nothing. Sounds like the place isn't swarming with people."

"I wonder how that's possible. Every winery we've visited has had employees everywhere. The closer we are to the harvest, the more hands are needed."

They were slowly climbing again, the road started to curve away from them. The division between the properties was nothing more than a row of olive trees and rosebushes.

"Let's assume Michael is right about the wine Alonzo is passing off as his own belonging to someone else," Meg suggested.

Val led her around the thriving vines. "Still seems like a lot of work. And what does he do with all these grapes if not make wine?"

Alonzo's land was row upon row of vines, just like all the others in the region.

"Maybe it's not enough . . . maybe the wine sucks."

Val seemed to consider her words as the incline increased.

Meg slowed down, pacing herself.

"Time to pass over the boundary," Val said.

"After you."

They crossed into Alonzo's land and moved far from the road but kept it in sight.

"How long has he owned the land?"

"At least five years, maybe more," Val told her. "Most of these properties, the lucrative ones in any event, seldom change hands."

"Could Alonzo have made a bad investment and needs to make himself look good with bootleg wine?"

"At the risk of going to jail? I can't see it."

Maybe Val couldn't, but Meg did. Seemed the man was bitterly cold one minute and sappy sweet the next. Her experience with people like that never ended well.

They heard a vehicle along the road, stopped moving, and ducked into the vines. "Looks like someone is here."

"If workers are milling about the workhouses, we're turning back," Val told her as they stood and started walking again once the truck passed.

"Not if we can learn something."

Val stopped.

Meg walked into him.

"We turn back. I won't risk any problems with you here."

"I'm the one who came up with this crazy idea, now you think my being here is a bad idea?"

"I don't know if I ever thought this was a good idea."

Meg moved around him, chugging up the hill. "It's the only idea."

Val scrambled beside her, caught her hand, and kept them to a slow pace.

There was a massive barn and a small house. Much smaller than the villas they'd frequented all day. Not that the size of the home mattered.

The closer to the barn they drew, the less they talked.

The delivery truck they'd followed up the road was now parked in front of the largest building. Meg called it a barn in her head, but it was probably where the grapes were brought to process.

Their vantage point wasn't great, but she could still see the activity clearly enough. Listening in on the conversation, however, was moot.

There was some kind of heavy equipment brought to the truck, where one of many barrels was lifted from it and onto a lift of some sort. The three men involved in the transfer were careful with the barrel. It was obvious the thing was full.

"Since when does a winery bring *in* barrels of wine?"

Val said nothing, just stared.

The process went through several loads and then the cases started to come. Crates of wine were stacked up on the loader and transferred into the barn.

"Seen enough?" she asked.

Val's jaw visibly tightened before a curt nod answered her.

They inched back until the barn was out of sight, and then they moved quickly down the hill, around the olive trees, and back toward the car.

Val was catching up, figuratively in any event. In an effort to show she understood how hard it must be for him to accept that his future brother-in-law duped him into believing he was something he was clearly not, Meg held on to Val's hand.

He squeezed it.

And she squeezed back.

Chapter Twenty-Three

"I need to know where they are, Lou." Back at the hotel, Val found himself cleaning up a mess.

"Mr. Picano said it was a short trip."

"Where? Do we have any idea where?" Val already knew the answer, but he couldn't help but ask anyway.

"It's a private yacht. There's no saying where they are. Could be a few miles off our shore . . . Cuba."

Val's head started to pound. "Our number one priority right now is Gabi. We need to find her."

"Missing persons report . . . abduction?"

Yes . . . no! "Not yet. Let's learn what we can without the authorities."

"You got it, Boss. Anything else I can do?"

"No. Call, anytime."

Val's employee hung up and all that remained was worry.

Margaret moved behind him, fresh from her shower, and ran her hands over his shoulders. "We'll find her."

A knock on the door indicated room service with their meal.

Val excused himself with a squeeze of Margaret's hand for a quick shower while she answered the door. They had both emerged from the vineyards looking like farmhands.

In any other circumstance, Val would have appreciated the adventure. The fact that he hadn't thought of the day-to-day life on his island since he left was a strange relief. It wasn't until Margaret had informed him of the true nature of Alliance that he understood the stakes at risk.

Only now, he was worried about something, someone, more precious.

Wearing silk pajama pants and a hotel bathrobe, Val joined Michael and Margaret for dinner in their suite.

Michael and Margaret were eating their salads and sipping one of the many bottles of wine they'd purchased during the day.

"Feel better?" Margaret asked him.

"Cleaner."

She offered a half smile in understanding.

Michael poured a glass of something red for Val to drink. "We're talking motive."

Val hesitated when he lifted the glass. "How is it an actor, a hotelier, and the office manager of a matchmaking firm are talking motive?"

"Because we know the players," Margaret told him.

"And when you figure out the motive, you have a chance at catching the bad guy." Michael waved his fork in the air. "I've been in enough movies with the same general theme."

"Movies." Not real life, Val mused.

"Let's not forget Judy," Margaret said to Michael.

Michael's expression sobered.

"What about Judy?" Val asked.

Margaret picked at her salad before pushing it aside and digging into her main course. "A few years past, Judy had a stalker."

Not the answer Val had expected.

"Who eventually kidnapped her."

Val's fork hesitated over his food.

Michael and Margaret exchanged glances. All hints of smiles fled in an instant.

"I met Judy . . . that's Rick's wife, right?"

Margaret nodded. "She survived. But . . . well, that's not important, what's imperative is that we think of this logically. What does Picano have to gain by marrying your sister? What does he have to gain by passing off someone else's wine as his? The man has money, but not enough income to account for every dollar he spends . . . why is that?" Margaret kept rattling. "Is he an American? Is he an Italian national? Could he need Gabi for citizenship? Does she have money he's after? Was he the man behind the pictures? Does he want leverage against you?"

Val saw the pain behind Margaret's eyes and realized she'd been in this position before.

Instead of making her relive her past, Val tried to answer the questions he could. "Alonzo is Italian. Marrying my sister could eventually pave his way to citizenship, but he's never said a thing about wanting that. If anything, he liked that she was an American while he based himself here in Italy."

"But if he doesn't stay at the winery, where does he live when he's here?" Michael asked.

Margaret sighed and picked up her fork again while she listened.

"I couldn't tell you that," Val said between bites.

"I'll call Rick and Judy in the morning with an update," Margaret said. "Maybe Rick can find out."

"As for money . . . I've always provided for Gabi. I started the island with the net worth of my father. In reality, the island and all its proceeds, are a third hers. Though it's not something we discuss. She knows she never has to worry about money."

"Does Alonzo know this?" Michael asked.

"I never discussed it with him . . . I can't speak for Gabi." Which gave another dark mark against the man if Gabi had told Alonzo of their arrangement.

"So money could be a motivator."

The three of them managed to put some food into their systems, and blew through a bottle of wine before giving up on the illusion of eating.

Less than a half hour later, Margaret rested her head in the crook of Val's arm. The only light in the room glistened from the lights of Rome.

"Remind me to come back here," she said as he played with her bare arm. "The city looks beautiful."

"You've never been?"

Margaret offered a chuckle. "I grew up in rain-soaked Washington State. The only travel I've managed has been because of my job . . . well, that and Judy. I've been to her hometown, which makes mine look like New York."

"That small?"

"I've read about small towns . . . but nothing holds a candle to Hilton, Utah. I understand why three of the five Gardner kids moved away."

"Gardner?"

"That's Michael's given last name. Wolfe is for the movies."

Val seemed to remember something about a second name for the actor, but hadn't committed it to memory.

"Rome is beautiful. So rich with history. Architecture . . . Judy would give her left tit to wander the streets."

Val laughed. "Her left tit, really?"

"She's a total geek when it comes to architecture. I can't tell you how many museums she dragged me to in college." Margaret went on to tell about her college experience with Michael's sister. "I made her hit a bunch of dive bars with amazing bands and what does she do? She hustles pool and makes the most of it. Brat." There wasn't an ounce of bite in Margaret's words.

"Sounds like the best of friends."

"We are. I'm lucky. And she wore off on me. I have a crazy desire to visit the Vatican and see Michelangelo's work. And I don't even like that stuff."

Val kissed the top of her head. "Then we'll return. See the city and everything your *I don't like this stuff* heart desires."

Margaret sighed, as if she wanted to say something and held back, then said, "Well, I'm lucky to have Judy. That became acutely evident when Gabi told me she didn't have a close friend. If I knew your sister before she met Alonzo, I would have told her she could do better from day one."

Val closed his eyes against her words. "I should have—"

"No. Val, it's a girl thing. Men don't see things the way women do. You approved a portfolio . . . women approve the person, then ask about if the man is a decent financial match." Margaret groaned. "God that sounded superficial."

"No need to apologize. A man should meet the financial needs of his wife, his family."

She shook her head. "You're such an old-fashioned man. I don't think it matters. What matters is two people working together to make their life work for the right reasons. It wouldn't bode well for Gabi to hook up with a man who sits on the couch and *talks* about getting a job one day."

"Or a man who might be making money illegally."

His words rested between them.

"We'll find them," Margaret said. "We'll find them and question Alonzo until he's within an inch of his life. We have more doubt than Gabi has ever had. Chances are, the questions alone will make her pause and ask if this is truly the man for her."

He hoped so . . . after the questions in his head, Val didn't want Alonzo anywhere near his sister. How could he have been so blind? Gabi was with the man now . . . somewhere . . . alone.

"Hey, stop it!"

Margaret sat up and stared at him.

"What?"

"You're beating yourself up. Stop it."

"You're pushy."

"Says the man who showed up in my bed without an invite last night."

Had it only been one night? Seemed longer with the events of the day.

"Best idea ever."

Margaret seemed to debate his words before leaning over him, hovering an inch above his lips. "It didn't suck."

She kissed him. Pushed her luscious lips against his with purpose and drove all thoughts of dirty vineyards, espionage, and his sister far from his brain.

I'm shallow . . . so shallow. He was instantly hard, his body buzzed with want. He should have been tired, dozing away to la-la land instead of taking the Margaret carpet ride. And since when did he refer to making love as a magic carpet ride? The woman kissing him was seeping into his life by slow degrees, and he liked it.

The woman seduced him. Where he should have been to church, praying to whoever was listening to watch over his sister, he was seduced within a breath of life. All because Margaret wiggled her way into his life and took it over.

She ran her fingertips over his chest, played briefly with his nipples, before moving south. All the while she inspected every molar with her tongue, lapped him up whole. There was nothing timid about her touch, her kiss.

Yet every second he listened for her breath. Was she moving too fast, was her heart beating too fast? Would he have to stop her seduction?

Those thoughts vanished when she moved her talented mouth over his jaw. "Love the shadow, so sexy . . ." she murmured.

"I'll throw away my shaver." Her smooth leg ran between his and against his length. *"Merda!"*

She giggled and ran her nimble fingers under his boxers. "I'm not sure if you're cussing or whispering sweet nothings."

Cussing, but at his own lack of self-control.

Margaret kicked the covers to the end of the bed and carefully peeled away his shorts. The woman was on a mission, he saw her dedication long before she knelt over him.

"This is impressive, Masini."

He clutched the sheets in his hands when she teased him with her fingers. She found a thick vein and traced it until a stream of cussing caught in his throat.

When her mouth replaced her hand, his hips left the bed.

She took him slowly, teasing with her tongue, a gentle scrape of her teeth . . . when she moaned, pleasure shot through him so completely, he felt a cresting wave of release building to the point of explosion.

He told her to hold back, said to stop, while matching her pace with his hips. As his wave shot over, he realized, too late, that he was speaking in Italian.

Margaret's eyes met his and held them when he came.

The room spun until he couldn't keep his lids open. "I'm sorry, *bella* . . . I should have waited."

When he opened his eyes again, she was grinning and running her index finger over her moist lips.

"Apologizing for losing control isn't allowed. I like it."

Without warning, he wrapped his arm around her waist and twisted her under him. "My turn."

"Uh-oh . . ."

He pulled her nightgown over her head, noticed her lack of panties, and thanked whatever god sent her his way. "Be afraid," he teased her, his lips close to her ear.

The back of her ear made her squirm, especially when he dragged his unshaven jaw over her neck.

He took his time, worshiped her with his lips, his tongue, until he was exactly where he wanted to be. She was warm, beautiful, and he told her with words, and showed her with action.

Margaret cussed and opened for him to taste and explore.

He did, every lovely taste until she couldn't talk at all. When she shattered, called his name, he brought her back slowly, only to climb on top to claim her again.

He nestled between her legs, loved the feel of her ankles crossing over his back. "I want you to moan my name again, *cara*."

"Demanding."

He kissed her, tasted himself on her lips, knew his tongue carried her scent. There was nothing easy about how he moved on her. He gripped her hips and took until the brink of his orgasm.

Her nails crawled over his back, squeezed his ass, forced him to where she needed him most, and matched every thrust. She shattered, clenching him deep inside her, forcing him to follow.

"I . . . God," she muttered.

He reached over to the side table, found her inhaler.

She laughed into his shoulder. "I'm good." She flopped her arms to the side in surrender. "So good."

They returned to the universe slowly. He rolled away enough to position her head on his arm to cradle her.

"We're making a habit of this," she said.

"If I have anything to say about it, we are."

"We are really good at this part."

Exhaustion started to set in as they talked themselves to sleep. "We're good at other parts, too. We just haven't explored many of them yet."

"Hmmm . . ." Her breaths were slower now. "I don't do sleepovers."

He closed his eyes. "That's too bad."

"Oh?" She was nearly asleep.

"One of us is going to be deeply disappointed."

"Hmmm . . ."

And it's not going to be me.

The phone ringing in the dead of night never boded well for anyone. Michael reached across the bed and answered his cell.

"Yeah?"

"Holy shit, Michael, where are you?"

Tony! His manager, personal assistant, and whatever Michael could make up for him to do, was yelling into the phone.

"Someplace where it's the middle of the night. What do you need?"

"Are you really in Italy? The e-mail said Italy."

Michael pushed himself up in the bed, twisted on the bedside light, and closed his eyes to the blinding intrusion to his senses. "What e-mail?" He hadn't sent Tony anything. The decision to get on the plane was last-minute.

"This could be bad . . . tell me you're there with a woman."

"What are you blabbing about, Tony? Slow down and start at the beginning."

"Someone sent me an e-mail. Told me to motivate you out of Italy if I wanted your career to continue. They said they had pictures, Michael. Said you, and your friend, would be looking for new jobs if you didn't fly home and keep your nose where it fucking belongs. It even said *fucking belongs*."

Michael woke instantly.

"Jesus. You're with a woman, right?"

"Kinda. Meg's here."

Tony blew out a sigh.

"With her new boyfriend."

"Son of a . . ."

Michael always wondered if Tony suspected something. Neither of them talked about it, didn't try and double date . . . nothing like that. He hinted that if Michael needed media control, he'd work to spin whatever evolved from the tabloids.

"Did you see any pictures?"

"No! Could there be pictures?"

Michael hated that he needed to answer the question. "Never know. The island was crazy."

"OK. We'll handle this. I'll handle this."

Michael kicked off the covers, made his way to the closet, and grabbed his suitcase. "I need to know what you know when it happens . . . no matter what it is."

"Got it. You coming home?"

"Eventually. I need to stop in Utah first." Jesus . . . Ryder didn't sign on for this. And if pictures did circulate . . . Michael's father would see them.

"I gotta go," he told Tony.

"Go. Get on a plane. Is there anyone here I need to call, anyone who can work with us to spin this?"

This isn't happening! "Yeah, call Karen and Zach. Tell them what you told me. Send the e-mail to Rick, see if he can trace it. Don't talk to anyone other than my family . . . and only the family that's in California."

"Got it. All right."

Poor Tony was going to have a heart attack, or a stroke. Or maybe that was him.

Michael clicked off the call and tossed the phone on the bed before shoving his clothes in his bag.

He washed his face, brushed his teeth, and tossed his toiletries in his bag before leaving his room.

Val stood in the living room of their suite, swathed in a bathrobe. "I thought I heard you."

Michael stopped, dropped his suitcase, ran a hand through his hair. "My manager called me." He took a minute to explain the conversation. Watched as Val's eyes grew cold. "I don't know who sent the message. But someone knows we're here, knows we're looking."

Val's brows pinched together. "This is my fault."

Michael shook his head. "This is the fault of the man behind the camera."

"Alonzo."

"We don't know that for certain."

"Doesn't matter. You're at risk because I didn't stand up to my promise."

It would be so easy to blame someone else . . . but Michael wasn't brought up that way, and couldn't let Val take the heat for this one.

"I'm gay. I've hidden that fact from every movie-ticket-buying fan, my parents, my friends . . . I've had a good run. I can survive this. I will survive this." As the words poured out, Michael knew they were true. "It will devastate Ryder, and destroy my trust with my parents. I need twenty-four hours to make this right with the people I love. Then we can spin this to work for all of us."

Val didn't look convinced.

"Go back to bed," Michael told his new friend. "In the morning, find your sister and drag her the hell away from this man. If he is the one behind this, he's willing to take on Hollywood, Florida, and a few spots in the UK to get what he wants."

"Taking me down isn't worth your millions."

"And I'm nothing compared to Alliance."

"Alliance?"

"Meg's boss . . . the man is fucking with a duke. Blake loves his wife, and when someone messes with her . . . God help him."

"Sounds like someone I should meet."

Michael smiled for the first time that night. "Make Meg happy and you will." Michael stuck his hand out, shook Val's. "Call with any news."

"Same to you."

Michael offered a quick nod, picked up his suitcase, and left Italy without a backward glance.

Chapter Twenty-Four

Gabi wanted off the boat . . .

She'd been popping Alonzo's aspirin for four days just to open her eyes. If he noticed how awful she felt, he didn't comment. He fed her, tucked her into bed, and offered to relieve her of the headaches that had been constant since they married.

Maybe she was allergic to marriage?

She wanted to think it was the yacht. Which wasn't good either, but better than the man.

She stood on the deck, dark sunglasses hiding the sun from her eyes, a floppy hat on her head. The island Alonzo deemed their private honeymoon site was on a slow approach. He wanted to give her time off the yacht to see if her headaches would subside. She knew as they drew closer to the island that it wasn't inhabited. Alonzo told her that he'd come across the island on his many trips in the area, and thought it would be the perfect spot to rest overnight, see if her headaches would finally go away.

"Motion sickness isn't always in the form of an upset stomach," he'd told her.

At this point, she was willing to try anything.

The captain maneuvered the yacht into a small cove like he'd done so many times.

"Where are we, exactly?" Gabi asked as Alonzo helped her into the small dinghy that would take them to the shore.

Alonzo hesitated, then said, "South of Cuba." She sat and dipped her hand into the warm water. "I thought we were headed toward the Bahamas."

Alonzo shook his head, offered a placating smile. "This was our destination all along. I wanted to share this with you."

Gabi was fairly certain it didn't take four full days and nights to maneuver around Cuba but didn't question him further.

The small boat carried the two of them and two crew members to the shore.

In a few short minutes, Alonzo was helping her step onto the beach where hot sand and salt water met her toes. Standing up made her dizzy. If not for her husband's shoulder, she would have fallen.

"I feel like I'm still on the yacht."

"Sea legs. It will settle, don't worry. Let's move you to the shade while I have my men set up camp for us."

The small beach wasn't combed like that on her brother's island, and she had to pick her way carefully to avoid cutting her feet on seashells.

They met the edge of the island foliage and Alonzo spread out a blanket. Once she was settled, he went back to the slip to retrieve a small ice chest and brought it to her side. "Here." He opened what looked like an electrolyte drink and handed it to her.

She sipped and winced. "Salty."

"You're probably dehydrated. This should help."

"You're so thoughtful. I'm not normally like this."

He brushed off her concern with a wink and walked away. After an exchange of words with his crew, the other men left the two of them alone on the shore.

"How big is this island?" she asked once Alonzo returned.

"About two miles across, I think."

"How did you find it?"

Alonzo sat back on his elbows and stared at his departing men. "We were diverting around a storm a couple of years ago . . . before I met you."

"You've been back since."

He turned his attention on her. "Once or twice."

"The captain seemed to know exactly where to anchor. I would think that reef would be difficult to maneuver."

Gabi couldn't see Alonzo's eyes, but his smile waned.

"My captain is one of the best." Alonzo's words had an edge to them. As if she doubted him.

"I'm sure he is."

Alonzo stood and reached for her. "Let's take a walk."

She finished her drink and slipped her sandals on.

The brush on the island swallowed them in a few feet. Because the island was small, Gabi didn't worry about getting lost, and let Alonzo lead the way. The throbbing in her head made her wish for more of Alonzo's medicine. Instead of asking for it, she let him lead away from the water's edge.

"I think I found something." Meg was on the phone with Rick the minute she learned of Michael's late-night call and subsequent departure.

"God I hope so," she told Rick.

"Heard of the name Steve Leger?"

"I can't . . . no. No clue. Who is Steve Leger?"

"How about Stephan Léger?" Rick added an accent to the last name, but she still didn't catch the name.

"I have nothing, Rick, who is Stephan Léger?"

Val was half listening to the conversation, his brow shot up in question. "Stephan? What about Stephan?"

Meg held up her hand. "Hold on, Rick. Seems that name means something to Val. I'm going to put you on speaker." Once she was done, she set the phone in the middle of the table and suffered with the delay in the conversation.

"Tell me what you know," Val said louder than his normal tone.

"You know the name Stephan Léger, who has another alias, Steve Leger."

Val gripped the side of the table. "Why would the captain of my off-island charter need an alias?"

"That's a good question. An even better one would be . . . what is the man's real name? Steve Leger died from natural causes in a convalescent home in Milwaukee about twenty years ago. I took the liberty of doing social security checks on your more trusted employees. Stephan's social belongs to a dead man." Rick's voice delayed with a buzz in the line. "I'm working on finding out who he really is. I'm going to have to twist some arms."

"Pull Eliza and Carter's strings," Meg suggested.

"Blake has already done that. I have a few more I can tap into. We'll get to the bottom of this. In the meantime, don't clue Stephan in on anything."

"I trusted Stephan."

"Something tells me the man banked on that. Do you know what you pay him?"

Val shook his head. "Carol will have all that information."

"Clear me for a call. I think his expense account is larger than his income, but I won't know that until I have your numbers."

Val already had his cell out of his pocket.

"You call Carol, I'm going to fill Rick in on what's happened with Michael," Meg told Val.

He offered a curt nod, lifted his cell to his ear, and walked away.

Meg took her phone off speaker and explained what had happened in the last twenty-four hours.

"I know your new boyfriend isn't going to like this, but my gut says this Alonzo guy is just as sketchy as Stephan."

Meg felt her chest tighten. "I know. I wish she wasn't with the man right now. Val's people are looking for her, but it's a big ocean out there. Service isn't available unless you're close to a domestic shore."

"Yeah." Rick paused and then started to laugh.

"It's not funny."

"I just thought of something. Who do we know that understands shipping? If Alonzo is shipping his wine, that isn't his wine, offshore, where is it going? Who is buying it, and why?"

Meg hesitated. "Blake." Blake Harrison, the duke himself, owned and operated one of the largest shipping companies in the US and the UK.

"I'll call him."

"Before you do, call Karen and Zach. Michael wants his brother to know what's going down. It sounds like Michael is coming out. At least with his parents. He's going to need Zach's support."

Rick blew out a sigh. "OK. I'll call."

They talked a few minutes longer about the timeline for staying in Italy, and where they were going from there.

Even though Meg was more pensive than before the call, at least they were learning something.

Not a *good* something . . . but something.

Gabi barely made it back to the small campsite Alonzo's crew had constructed before she emptied her stomach behind a bush.

"I'm not well," she stated the obvious to Alonzo as she dragged her way back to his side.

"Maybe we should get you back on board—"

"No. Please. One night." Just the thought of being on board the ship made her green.

"OK, darling. One night. Maybe Captain Alba can help. He has medic training."

The sun was setting, but her body heat was topping the charts. "Maybe."

Alonzo helped her lie back. "We shouldn't have taken our walk."

"I thought I was better. It's not your fault."

He kissed her forehead before walking away.

When Gabi opened her eyes again, the captain sat over her, his hand rubbing on her arm. "Just a small injection, Mrs. Picano."

She felt the pinprick on her arm and a sudden rush of warmth. The instant nausea brought on by whatever he injected into her quickly faded and much of the pain drifted away.

Then she was floating.

Such a peaceful place, where waves on the side didn't induce a headache, and sun wasn't intense. On some level, Gabi knew medicine to heal her didn't work like what she'd been given. But she didn't care. She felt so much better. Her pulse slowed to a steady pace and her head was dancing in a never-ending yoga class.

Namaste.

Captain Alba watched her closely, then his eyes drifted to Alonzo. "She'll feel better for a few hours."

A harsh voice sounded behind her.

"That's all I need."

Hilton was a small town. It would be impossible for Michael to show up without notice, especially when he was the city's claim to fame. They even had a freeway sign pointing out how proud the town was of his success.

He couldn't help but wonder if the sign would be taken down when and if they all knew the truth about him.

After forcing himself to sleep on the plane, Michael woke with enough energy to rent a car and drive from the airport to his hometown. The streets rolled up before eight on most nights, six on Sunday if the shops opened at all.

It was all quaint now . . . smothering when he was a kid.

Ryder lived outside of town, but not far enough to escape notice if Michael visited him now that he was famous.

He timed his arrival close to dark. Most of the neighbors wouldn't notice a car driving by, or think to walk outside to look unless noise accompanied a lone car.

Ryder's single-story home sat on a few old farm acres that had gone to weeds since Ryder picked up the property. The TV flickered through the front window, the sound of a baseball game played on the speakers.

Michael hesitated, wasn't exactly sure what, or how, he was going to tell Ryder that his life was about to be turned upside down because he picked the wrong lover.

He squared his shoulders and gave a firm knock.

The volume on the set lowered and Michael knocked again.

The moment Ryder opened the door there was an instant smile. A *God I'm happy to see you* smile. The kind a man could grow used to when coming home from work, from a hard day . . . then reality hit.

Ryder's smile made a slow, painful descent. "Oh, no."

"Can I come in?"

Ryder opened the door wide and Michael walked into what would have been his life had he stayed in Hilton.

"I'm sorry."

Ryder clicked off his TV, moved to a minibar, and proceeded to pour liquor into a glass. He downed it, poured another, before adding a second glass for Michael.

"When will it go public?"

Michael took the glass, downed the liquid as quickly as Ryder. "I don't know. But it's safe to say it will . . . eventually. Jesus, Ryder . . . I didn't want—"

"Stop. OK. I'm a big boy. I knew the risk."

"But—"

"Mike. Enough!" Ryder slapped his glass on the bar top and walked away, pulling the blinds closed tight. A small laugh escaped his lips and started to build.

Michael started to worry if maybe Ryder was losing it. The *it* that kept you a step above sanity, and a step below sainthood.

"I'm relieved." Ryder leveled his eyes with Michael. "I can't live here . . . like this anymore."

Not the reaction Michael expected. "Your job?"

"It's almost summer. I'm out. I'll find another job."

The words were easy to digest, but he didn't believe them. "You love Utah."

"Love is a strong word. I'm used to Utah. I didn't leave when I was eighteen. Most of you did, even if only for a little while." Ryder refilled both their glasses and moved to the couch. Michael followed. "Do you know how many states gay marriage is legal?"

"Twenty." The answer came easy. If there was one thing easy to support and follow, it was any topic related to homosexuals.

"Twenty. At least eleven more have appeals in the courts to add those states to the mix, Utah included." Ryder set his glass aside and took Michael's hand. "It's going to take small towns like this forever to catch up even after it's legalized. I don't want to wait for them. I want to live, Mike."

This was that moment Michael knew was coming.

Truth.

"I don't know if I can come out completely." As much as he wanted to say otherwise, Michael didn't think a complete exit from the closet was going to work with him.

"Then don't. I can step into your world. Get a job. What happens in our home is our business. No one else's."

Michael's heart leaped. "Our home?"

Ryder offered a soft smile. "If your invitation still stands . . ."

Michael could count on two fingers the times he'd felt the need to cry like a baby. One was the day he realized women did nothing for him. The second was when he and Karen decided to go forward with their divorce. Didn't matter that Karen wasn't his wife in the true sense, but he knew that relationship, the friendship day in and day out, would be gone for him.

Still, his eyes swelled with the need to shed. "The invitation is paved in gold."

Ryder flashed the smile that undid him the first time Michael had really noticed it.

"We're doing this."

Michael nodded. "Yes. We're doing this." He leaned forward, captured Ryder's lips, and knew the time had come in his life to move on.

Chapter Twenty-Five

"You think I fucking care what you want? You're in this just as deep as I am. Now get in there, and make it look good." Alonzo nodded toward the bed. His wife, for however short their marriage would be, was stoned and squirming on the bed.

Alba ripped his shirt from his shoulders, kicked out of his pants, but left his whites on. *Pussy.*

It sickened him, the look of her like this. Not emotionally, of course, he'd never loved the woman, but how weak she was in such a short time. Day two of mainlining, and she was his bitch. So easy. If he could make a living hooking innocent women on drugs he wouldn't have to prove himself any longer.

Then again, if this worked out, hooking *this* woman would be the first of many.

Alba climbed into the bed, hid his hips with the sheets, and buried his head into Gabi's shoulder.

Alonzo started snapping pictures.

Gabi turned to him, her eyes unfocused, her lips smiling. "Hey, what are you doing over there?"

"Smile, honey."

She did . . . and he snapped a candid that would keep Val quiet forever.

Val wished the never-ending ocean below him would fade away to land. Then he'd know he was closer Gabi.

Closer to ending all of this.

Margaret reached over and grasped his hand for the umpteenth time since the photo had landed in his e-mail.

"He needs her," Margaret whispered.

"She didn't look like her."

Margaret looked away. "I wish it wasn't Gabi. We both know it was."

There were two photographs, one with Gabi holding out her arm for an awaiting needle, and another of her in bed with a man Val didn't recognize. The image left him physically ill, ready to murder. The images were captioned with a simple *if you know what's best for both of you, leave Italy* message.

"How did this happen?" he asked. How would he ever look his sister in the eye again?

"It's not your fault, Val. You didn't know."

The private jet, arranged by Margaret's boss, carried them home. "I'm responsible for her. She's my sister."

"Blame me. Michael and I forced our way on your island . . . then the trouble began."

"That's ridiculous."

Margaret drew her hand away. "Are you giving your sister drugs?"

"No!"

"Did you arrange to take pictures of her in bed with a stranger?"

Val felt his blood boil. "No!"

"Then you didn't do this. Now stop feeling sorry for her, for you, and let's work this out. We're three hours to Miami and we have nearly no plan as to what we're going to do when we get there."

Val pushed out of the plush leather seat of the private six-seater plane, and moved about the cabin.

All the time in an airplane left him with too many stagnant hours with nothing to do but question why he didn't see this coming.

Even with all the pictures, the reconnaissance that Margaret and her friends had provided, there was still little to no proof that Alonzo was involved. Except that the man had his sister. Val had left messages for Gabi on her cell phone to call him. Left a message on Alonzo's that Val didn't expect them to be out so long, that if he didn't hear from him directly in twenty-four hours, he would notify the authorities about a possible downed yacht.

Who was he kidding? Alonzo was the only connection with every dot. The wine, the winery passing off a vintage that wasn't his . . . the crew member left on Sapore di Amore who could have taken pictures. If Captain Stephan was someone Alonzo knew . . . the dots were complete.

"There's a missing link," he vocalized for Margaret's benefit.

"More than one. Let's place our suspect in the role of the bad guy here. Stephan . . . what do we know about him?"

"He moves passengers on and off my island."

"Sounds innocent enough. How long has he worked for you?"

"A few years, I think."

"Longer than Alonzo has been in the picture?"

"Yeah," Val told her. "According to Lou, none of my employees have skipped out of work since the pictures of you and I showed up. Stephan is still shuttling passengers."

"Could he know Alonzo? Be working with him?"

"It's possible. I guess. Why?"

While they talked, Margaret jotted notes down on a pad of paper. "We know Stephan is an alias. That makes him a suspect in something. Not what's happening now with Gabi, since he's not missing from his island duties. But he could have been someone behind the pictures early on."

"That's more probable than a housemaid."

Margaret made a dark line on her notepad and started to question again. "When did Gabi meet Alonzo?"

"A year . . . maybe a little longer. We were at a fundraiser on the mainland. I met Alonzo and introduced them." *I introduced them.*

Val squeezed his eyes at the nausea in his stomach.

"Focus, Masini. How did *you* meet him?"

Val shook the guilt from his limbs. "At the bar, the auction . . . I don't remember. We started to talk. He told me he was in the wine business, and asked who was my lovely wife. I corrected him and Alonzo made my sister blush. I thought it was cute. He sent flowers, wine . . . They started dating. It didn't take long for him to ask me for her hand."

"Archaic."

"Not for me. I expected it. Alonzo knew I'd been the man of our household for many years. I suppose Gabi and I were both honored by his action of asking me permission to marry her."

"But not your mother," Margaret said.

"My mother never liked him. Said he was too smooth, too shady." When did Val stop listening to the ramblings of his mother?

"So Gabi liked him, you liked him, then what?"

Val shrugged. "We fell into a comfortable pace. I asked that he not rush their wedding for my mother's sake. He didn't seem happy about that, but agreed. He drops anchor on the island often. He understands the need for limited access of his crew and has always respected that. In what I believed was an effort to woo my sister, he started delivering crates of wine without charge. My guests enjoyed it, so I added his selections to the menu."

"But the wine isn't his. So he's passing another vineyard's wine off just to schmooze your sister?"

"We won't know that until we find out if there are other vendors buying his brand. The island goes through many bottles a week, but I don't think we take all his stock."

"Aren't there international shipping regulations to jump through to buy direct from Italy?"

Val took the seat across from Margaret. "I hate to sound uninvolved, but I have people for that. In the case of Alonzo, he gifted the wine. I've never paid a dime for any of his bottles. The wine shuffles hands in Italy, then makes it to his yacht . . . or his supplier that sometimes came to port with crates of the stuff."

"Do you know the name of the ships coming in? Their captains?"

Val hated that all he could do was narrow his eyes toward Margaret.

"Let me guess," she said. "You have people for that."

"All good questions, *cara*. Ones I will ask when we get home."

She picked up the pen, scribbled on the paper. "Mislabeled wine travels from Italy, to where? Then it makes it to your island. All to impress a girl? I don't buy it. There has to be more."

"Bootleg wine is big business."

"Not when you're giving it away for free," Margaret reminded him. "No, Alonzo needed you, Gabi . . . the island . . . I'm starting to think the wine is insignificant. Or a decoy for something else."

Val's head went straight to the image forever burned in his head . . . the one with Gabi willingly holding out her arm for a needle.

"The island limits eyes by the nature of it. How do you keep the authorities happy? Who regulates you?"

"The health department passes off on us yearly. Same with the hotel commission and regulating parties. I don't have complaints so I don't have many problems."

Margaret pushed back in her seat and tapped her fingers against the armrest. "So you could be doing nearly anything on the island

and no one would know. You've buttoned down Internet activity, sworn your guests to secrecy, cut out photographs that are an everyday part of every twenty-first-century life . . . you could be trafficking slaves, drugs, sex . . . no one would be the wiser."

Val started to lose feeling in his fingers as he gripped the edge of the armrests. "Jesus."

"Alonzo is trafficking something . . . something better than a few bottles of wine. If he marries your sister, she won't call him out. If he blackmails you, you have to go along with him—"

"The hell I do!"

Margaret offered the first smile of the hour. "Or so he thinks. Bottom line, he thinks he's safe by being *family*. Then before he can marry your sister, Michael and I show up and notice something funny about the wine."

"Alonzo flips," Val suggested. "Sees his plan falling apart." The map of probability started to surface in Val's head.

"He has a plan set to take photographs to compromise your efforts on the island."

Val squeezed his eyes shut, swore in Italian. "One of Alonzo's men said he was ill the week you were on the island. Said he couldn't travel on the yacht until he was better." Val met Margaret's gaze. "He stayed when Alonzo wasn't there."

"The guy that cornered me in the hallway?"

"Maybe."

Val ran his hand over the growing beard on his face. "Then you leave with Gabi."

"After Gabi and Alonzo fought."

News to him. "They were fighting?"

"She was questioning marrying him. Right before we left the island, he kissed and made up. A couple of days later, Alonzo makes a grand gesture to whisk her away for a romantic weekend . . . that is going on a week now. At the same time we chase the wine lead . . .

someone he knows sees us, or maybe a search on Michael shows that he's in Italy . . ."

"Damn, Margaret . . . we're assuming a lot here."

"Are we? What part isn't true?"

"We don't even know if Alonzo has Gabi . . . something else might have happened to both of them."

Margaret laughed . . . a full-throat chuckle with a shake of her head. "I know for a fact that Alonzo spends more money than he makes. I know the winery makes next to nothing. If he makes money legitimately, it's not on any books. What does that sound like to you, Val? And Gabi left with him and now nasty pictures of her follow a threat that we leave Italy immediately. There's only one person who should be threatened by us being there . . . he's guilty until proven innocent in this case."

Val started to shake. "I introduced them, *cara*."

Margaret's voice softened. She moved to the seat beside him and took his hands in hers. "The man played both of you . . . my guess is he knew who you were before you said hello. There are a lot of sick people out there."

If anything happened to his sister . . . if the pictures were any indication, it already had. "I'll kill him."

"Save it, Val. You're not a murderer."

"Watch me."

Margaret shook her head. "They don't offer coed bunking in prison. I'd be an accessory . . . it could get messy."

Val tried to smile and failed. "You don't do sleepovers."

"I really don't do sleepovers with Bertha in the top bunk. So let's put killing talk out of the conversation. Let's find them and pool the resources we have to get Gabi away from him."

"My resources are limited. I can pay ransom . . . pay the help to get her back . . ."

Margaret tilted her head to the side. "*Our* resources, Val. Rick is on this like stink on Alonzo's skin. Why? Because he works with Blake. The pictures of Michael can threaten Samantha's business, which Alonzo knows nothing about . . . he's stepped in something deeper than he's prepared to understand. I don't know if Alonzo is working with anyone else, but I doubt they have hands that reach as far as my boss and her friends. I have serious strings to pull . . . and the best part . . . these are decent people who would be thoroughly pissed that an innocent woman was at risk because of some asshat."

He wanted to believe Gabi would return home unharmed . . . but that was looking less and less likely.

———————

Seemed every time Michael returned, his childhood home shrank. The four-bedroom, two-story house seemed big enough growing up. The quiet street housed the same people since he was born. On occasion, someone would grow old and one of the kids would either take over the house, or move an aging parent in with them in the neighboring town.

Things didn't change in Hilton, Utah.

Which was why Michael had chosen to leave as soon as he could.

He ran from his demons and put the truth on hold.

Now it was time to reveal everything to the two people who above all others deserved to know.

He exited his rental car, made his way to the front door as if he were walking in quicksand.

He waited until after his father had closed up the hardware store for the night to make sure he only had to have this conversation once. Surviving it twice might prove impossible.

CATHERINE BYBEE

Someone inside clicked on the porch light before he made his way to the door. He hesitated, not sure if he should knock or walk right in. His parents were empty nesters now. Hannah, the youngest, was off in college. His oldest sister, Rena, lived across town with her husband and two kids.

The house was virtually empty.

He vacillated on that thought when his mother opened the front door with a surprised gasp. "Mike!" She scrambled out of the door and wrapped her arms around him. "Sawyer," she called into the house. "Look who's here."

"Hey, Mom."

She pulled him inside, her smile genuine and filled with surprise. "I can't believe you're here. Why didn't you tell us you were coming? I could have put fresh sheets on your bed."

They stepped into the living room that hadn't changed since the eighties. The couch with the bad spring still sat in the middle of the room, his father's favorite chair to the side of it. The television Michael had bought, and he and Zach had hung above the fireplace, was one of the only modern pieces in the house.

His parents liked it like that. Comfortable, familiar.

"Last-minute decision," he explained.

Heavy footfalls moved down the stairs. Michael's father had always been a robust man, a real man's man who worked with his hands, liked crawling under cars, and would disapprove beyond any doubt of Michael's sexuality.

The two of them had come to an understanding in the past few years. His father hadn't completely approved of his profession in the beginning, but seemed to come to terms with it after Michael's fake marriage to Karen.

Michael had returned to Utah a few times since his divorce. Holidays and weddings always drove those visits, and there was plenty of family to buffer any adversity.

There was none of that now.

"Hi, Dad."

A greeting that used to be a simple handshake was now a short hug. "What brings my youngest son home unannounced?"

"I can't stop by to visit?"

Sawyer shook his head. "Unannounced? Do movie stars do that?"

"I've been your son longer than I've been on the big screen. I hope it's OK I'm here. I would hate to interrupt poker night."

"That's Wednesday," they both said at the same time.

They laughed, sat, and his mom asked if he wanted something to drink . . . and no he wasn't hungry. The pleasantries of conversation quickly drifted to silence, making the crickets outside fill the sound on the inside.

Janice asked first. "Is everything all right, honey? You look like you have something on your mind."

"There is . . . and I'm not sure how to say it."

His mother reached for her husband's hand. They weren't a touchy couple and the gesture wasn't lost on him.

"You're not sick, are you? Zach? Judy?"

"No. I'm fine . . . we're all good." At least as far as he knew.

Sawyer narrowed his eyes. There was no smile on his face.

"Remember when I told you the reason behind Karen and me getting married?"

They nodded in the silent room.

"I offered you half the reason . . ." Michael reflected on the moment when his father asked if money made through his career was a reason to sell his soul. It was easy to put his father in his place then. Karen didn't deserve his disapproval and Michael was more than willing to offer a buffer for her.

Michael stood, unable to sit during this conversation. He crossed to the mantel, looked at the photographs there. It would only be a matter of time before his siblings added more grandkids to the shelf.

He wouldn't be the one to do that . . . not in the traditional sense, in any event. "I never wanted to disappoint you, either of you."

"You haven't," Janice said.

He didn't look at her as he straightened an askew frame. *I'm about to.*

"Karen and I agreed to a paper marriage because Hollywood likes their leading men on the arm of a beautiful woman. Marriage was a perfect diversion from the truth."

The room grew heavy with the sound of crickets from outside. Did they actually get louder?

"What truth?" Sawyer asked.

Michael turned, met his father's eyes. For better or worse, he needed to see his dad's reaction to his words. "Hollywood wants their leading men to be heterosexual. And I'm not."

It took two seconds for the words to register. Sawyer's nose flared as he sucked in a deep breath. "What are you saying?" he asked, his teeth grinding together.

"I'm gay, Dad. I knew long before I left Utah."

His mom squeezed his father's hand and a strange look of calm washed over her.

She knew . . . all this time.

"Jesus." Sawyer moved from the chair and straight to a liquor closet across the room.

Without asking, his father poured whiskey into two glasses and handed one to Michael without looking at him. "Janice?" he asked.

"I'm fine."

OK . . . they aren't yelling . . . no one is telling me to get out.

The whiskey felt good burning the back of his throat.

Then his mother spoke. "After your divorce, we . . . we wondered."

"You knew?" Michael nearly choked on the liquor.

"We wondered," Sawyer corrected.

"Your father didn't want to discuss it," Janice told him.

Sawyer took a healthy sip of his drink, poured more into his glass, and returned to his wife's side. "Before you look at me like that . . . I didn't want to discuss it not because I thought less of you. I just didn't want that life for you. Maybe when you were a kid I would have tried to beat it out of you . . ."

His father never used his fist so the past threat wasn't real.

"You can't—"

"I know." Sawyer met his eyes. "I know that."

They drank in silence . . . letting the words digest.

On a sigh, Janice patted the space beside her on the couch. "This must have been hard for you to do."

Michael blew out a long breath, parked his ass on the couch. "You have no idea. You're taking it really well."

His mom leaned in. "Your father hasn't touched that bottle since Christmas."

Michael laughed.

Sawyer grunted. "Why now? What prompted this?"

Without many details, Michael told them about Val's island and about pictures that *should never go public* possibly making a debut. He touched on Gabi's fiancé being behind the photographs.

Meg had sent word to Michael that more information regarding Gabi and her fiancé was pending and that she and Val were headed back to Florida. In the meantime, Michael had to deal with his own drama . . . then he'd be back wherever his friends needed him to help.

"So let me get this straight. Someone might have pictures of you and . . . ?"

Ryder . . . but that wasn't his story to tell . . . not yet anyway. "You'll know soon enough," Michael told his mother.

She smiled and patted his hand. "Fine. But the man who has these pictures is trying to blackmail you? Blackmail your friend, Mr. Masini?"

Michael thought of Gabi. He didn't know her well, but couldn't imagine what Meg had described in her brief e-mail. "I think he just wants me to stop looking into him. It's Masini's sister who is in trouble right now."

"You just met this Masini and his family. How is it you're involved?" Sawyer asked.

Michael finished his drink, set it aside. "It started with the threat of being revealed. But it's so much more than that now. Val and his family are good people. This asshole playing them is the ultimate scumbag. The perfect villain for a movie, only it's not a script. And right now Gabi is in danger." Michael spared his parents the details.

"Yet you're here talking to us . . ."

Michael leaned forward, rested his elbows on his knees. "I couldn't have a tabloid telling my parents about my *real* love life. That wouldn't be right."

There were tears in his mother's eyes as she laid a hand to his back and pulled him in for a hug.

Did a mother's love ever grow old? He didn't think so.

"Thank you," she said. "For making us a priority."

There was pride in his father's eyes when Michael met them with his own.

"In the morning," his father started, "you get out of here and help your friends."

Michael smiled.

A massive weight lifted from his life. "We're good?"

Sawyer tilted his drink in Michael's direction. "I might need a new bottle for Thanksgiving. Be sure and bring the good stuff."

"I'll do that."

Chapter Twenty-Six

Val was a wreck, and Meg was close behind. Between desperation, jet lag, and fear, they exited the plane just before dawn and dropped into bed. They acquired three hours' sleep before they forced their eyes open to tackle the day.

Meg finished her shower and padded around Val's home in bare feet.

There was a handwritten note on the coffee pot. *I'm in my office. Rick will be here by noon.* It was signed, *Val.*

Copious amounts of black coffee were in store for the day. Meg poured her first cup and opened the notebook she and Val had taken notes in during their long flight home. She sent a text to Val while she scribbled circles around their notes. Any news?

Nothing.

Not what Meg wanted to hear. Should I meet Rick on the airstrip?

He's coming on the charter from Key West.

The deadline that Val gave Alonzo would pass at three that

afternoon. Unless Rick and his team disagreed, they would be calling port authorities and filling out a missing persons report.

Meg didn't think that would happen. Alonzo was behind all of this, she felt it deep in her gut. The same gut that was sick with worry over Gabi.

Instead of letting her head move to the dark side of what may or may not be happening to Val's sister, Meg dialed Sam's number and listened to the phone ring.

"Hey, Boss," she said when Sam answered.

"Have we heard anything?" Sam asked before saying hello.

"Nothing." Meg glanced at the clock clicking on the kitchen wall. "Three hours until deadline. Have you learned anything?"

"Blake and his team are following up on a strange lead. Looks like Picano is shipping the majority of his wine into Mexico."

"What's strange about that?"

"I have yet to find one retailer buying the wine for their restaurants or stores."

"Why is the wine shipped to Mexico if no one is drinking it there?"

Sam sighed. "That's the strange part. Blake should have an answer from his people in that part of the world by noon. Is Rick there yet?"

"No. Is anyone coming with him?"

"Neil is. He's staying on Key West and chartering a boat to follow Alonzo, should he show up."

It sounded like something was happening, but still, without word about Gabi, none of it mattered. "Have you heard from Michael?"

"Roundabout. Karen called to let me know the conversation with his parents went well. He has a PR team ready to spin whatever might happen."

The thought of Michael's life falling apart sliced inside of her. "What about Alliance?"

"Stop, Meg. I'm fine, we're all going to get through this. Concentrate on Gabi."

"That makes me even more crazy. I can't get to her, Sam. It's like watching someone drown a mile offshore and my feet are knee-deep in sand."

"It's awful, I know. Stay strong and don't worry about anything here. Call if you need me."

"I owe you so much already." Private planes all over the world, endless hours of security, not to mention all the investigating Sam and Blake were doing privately on Meg's behalf.

"Don't be ridiculous. I'll be in touch."

"Thanks, Sam."

———

Weakness, Alonzo despised weakness.

Yet his hands shook as he answered the phone. There were only two men who sickened him, and the one calling him now had a thick Latino accent and enough money and power to wipe the planet free of everyone Alonzo knew.

"Señor Diaz. How nice of you to call."

"Is it?"

Alonzo's head started to heat and sweat formed on his brow. "I was going to contact you today."

The deep-throated laugh of the man on the other side of the line made Alonzo squirm. "Why do I not believe you? My shipment, Picano. Where is it?"

"Safe." But that wasn't what Diaz wanted to hear. "I'm arranging transport."

"I have heard this before." There was no laughter in the man's voice now. "You have twelve hours. From then on, a series of unfortunate events will begin and continue on the hour until I have what I need. Do you understand, Picano?"

Alonzo bit back bile. "I-I need more time."

"Eleven hours and fifty-five minutes." Without another word, Diaz hung up.

———

Meg took Val's position at his phone in his office while he met Rick on the dock. Because Stephan was the man behind the bow of the charter and none of them wanted to tip the man off, Val insisted on greeting his new guests.

Val observed the charter with different eyes. It was larger than most passenger charters. There were times that the ship had been used to pick up last-minute supplies, so there was a loading ramp on the port side. Today, the ramp was elevated, the passengers hung off the side, getting their first glimpses of the island.

The charter arrived like it always did. Three parties departed the craft and Val's staff stood by to deliver the newcomers to the island. Val greeted them by name with Rick last.

Acting unaffected by Rick's presence, Val left him with one of his staff and stepped onto the charter for a brief moment with Stephan.

With hands in his pockets to avoid wrapping his fingers around the captain's neck to squeeze any information out of the man, Val forced a smile as he moved on deck. "Captain Léger," Val called the man's attention his way.

A smile followed a brief look of confusion. "Mr. Masini, to what do I owe the pleasure of your company?"

Acting as a confidant, and not an adversary, Val nodded away from the other staff. "A moment, Captain."

Léger offered an instruction to one of his mates and joined Val at the bow of the craft. "How can I help you?"

Val kept a low voice. "Seems we have had yet another security breach."

Concern passed the captain's face. "What kind of breach?"

Val waved a hand in the air. "Nothing from your end, I don't think. I want to keep it silent, but want you aware of my concern for stowaways."

"Not on my end, I assure you."

Val forced a hand from his pocket and patted Léger on the back. "Just keep your eyes open. Report to me directly if you see anything suspicious."

"Of course."

Val stepped off the charter as other passengers from the island stepped on.

Rick was already out of eyesight.

Val found Lou and Rick in the warehouse. Adam walked them around and pointed out the space designed to accept food and beverages that needed to be kept cool.

"Who delivers the wine?" Rick was asking when Val walked up to the group of men.

Adam told him the name of the company in charge of delivering the wine. "Mr. Picano himself will often bring in cases. But the crates started to come in between his personal deliveries. We have quite the stockpile."

Rick removed his phone and sent off a text. "How long does it sit in the warehouse?"

"As little as possible."

The four of them followed Adam as he led them to the wine vault. An entire ten-by-twenty-foot space was stacked with Picano's label.

Val knew the system of taking deliveries, but hadn't realized that Alonzo's wine had started to arrive in such large quantities.

Rick shrugged off his coat, even though the vault was just below fifty degrees. "This is going to take some time."

Val narrowed his eyes. "What is going to take time?"

Rick pointed to the pallets. "We're opening every crate."

Lou took a box cutter and started slicing into the plastic wrap that sealed in the crates of wine.

"What do you hope to find?" Val asked.

"Answers."

Without anything else to do, Val removed his jacket and pulled off his tie. "Adam, bring in a pallet to transfer what we've already gone through. Don't mention what we're doing to anyone in passing."

"Yes, sir."

An hour and a half later, they were on the last pallet, each crate was opened, the wine and packing removed, then placed back in to return to the stacked pile. They worked in silence, each crate a disappointment as they found nothing but mislabeled wine.

The hour grew near when Val needed to go to his office and make the call to the authorities about his missing sister. The last text from Meg stated that the phone had yet to ring.

Val yanked open one of the last crates and carelessly removed every bottle. One broke but he kept digging through the box, removing the straw as he went. When all he found was a wooden end to the dig, he lifted the empty crate in both hands and yelled at the object, "Nothing. We have nothing." He hurled it at the crates they'd already gone through and watched it splinter. "Damn it!" He closed his eyes in frustration, pushed his palm into his forehead to ease the pounding.

Gabi is out there, suffering, and I have nothing.

"Holy shit!" Rick said in a low, rumbling roar.

"What?" Val turned away from the mess he'd made to find Rick and Lou staring at the broken crate.

He swiveled and stared.

The crate had taken the force on the bottom. The wooden box had a deep pocket between the bottom of the bottles and the actual base of the crate. In between was a space not larger than an inch. But that inch held something other than air.

The three of them approached the broken crate.

Rick reached it first and lifted a hammer they'd used to open the boxes to pry the unbroken wood away. The box shattered and displayed a false bottom. In it was a tightly bound substance. Using a pocketknife, Rick poked into the wrap and removed something black. He brought it to his nose and sniffed. "Jesus."

"What is it?"

"I need a test kit to be sure . . ."

"What do you *think* it is?" Val asked.

Lou answered, "Heroin . . . in its early stage."

The image of Gabi holding out her arm for a needle smothered Val.

Lou and Rick sprang into action. They moved to different pallets, removed a random crate, ripped open lids, dumped the wine, stuffing, and anything inside into a garbage bin, then smashed the boxes to find more of the same.

"Looks like we found out why Picano is giving away his wine."

The three of them looked at all the pallets. "Someone is going to want this back," Lou said. "There's enough here to kill for."

"Drug lord quantities if you ask me," Rick added.

"Gabi," Val whispered.

Rick rested his hand on Val's shoulder. "As long as we have this, he'll keep her alive. It's his only real leverage."

Val grabbed those words and pulled them deep inside. He couldn't lose hope, not now . . . not when they were close to all the answers.

Chapter Twenty-Seven

After hours of staring at Val's phone and willing it to ring, when Meg's phone buzzed, she jumped. Without looking at the screen, she answered, fully intending to blow off whoever it was to pine by a phone that wasn't ringing. "Yeah," she answered . . . short and clipped.

There was a pause, a little static, then laughter.

"Hello?"

When her greeting met with silence, she pulled the phone away from her ear and glanced at the screen. *Number unknown.*

Meg heard a moan . . . a female moan. "Gabi?" The skin on Meg's arms prickled and her heart thumped in her chest.

The weak voice was impossible to hear. "M-Meg?"

On the landline for Val's phone, there was a device ready to record, but not on Meg's cell. She had no recourse to trace or record. All she could do was talk. "Gabi, dear God. Are you OK?"

"It hurts, Meg. He won't make it stop." Gabi's voice cracked and she started to weep.

"Where are you?"

"Please . . ." There was a shifting of the phone and Gabi's voice drifted farther away. "Please, Alonzo. I need it."

"Gabi, where are you?" Meg heard the frantic tone of her own voice.

"Yes . . . yes . . ." Gabi's tone shifted from crazed to relief.

"No!" Meg yelled into the phone. "Don't, Gabi. It's poison. Stop it!" She was screaming now. "You bastard. Stop!"

Gabi was still there, in the distance. "Thank you . . ." She repeated the words over and over.

"You sick bastard. Pick up the phone you ball-less prick."

Carol ran into Val's office with one of the security team right behind her. Meg lifted a hand, noticed how much it shook. "What do you want? I know you're still there."

Meg turned away from Val's employees and plugged her open ear.

Alonzo's voice was stone cold, his words held a threat. "Step out onto the veranda, Miss Rosenthal."

Wasting little time, Meg ran to the French doors of Val's outdoor office space. She stayed to the shadows, in case someone was close enough to take target practice. "Where is Gabi?"

He paused. "Red suits you."

Meg looked at her red silk shirt, then stepped a little farther outside. The ocean was steps away, but free of any large vessels. A few sailboats drifted a good mile from the shore, but she couldn't rule out if Alonzo and Gabi were on board one.

People were gathering behind her and talking, rushing around. Meg ignored all of them and kept the monster holding Gabi hostage talking. "I think an orange jumpsuit will work fine with your complexion."

"Tsk, Miss Rosenthal. No need to be hostile. Tell your boyfriend I need my shipments onto his charter within the hour."

"Shipments, what are you talking about?" *The wine? Was he talking about his stupid wine?*

"You don't have the right to ask questions. One hour. You will accompany the captain when he leaves."

"So you can hold two of us hostage? I don't think so."

The phone shifted again. "What's that, sweetheart . . . you want more? Anything for my bride."

"Stop! You'll kill her."

Behind Meg, someone gasped.

"Why would I kill my wife? She's much more valuable to me alive than dead."

Wife? Bride?

"One hour, Miss Rosenthal. I have eyes everywhere on Masini's pathetic attempt at a private island. You and you alone with my shipments. Or poor Gabriella will have an unfortunate accident. I don't think she can tread water for long in her current state."

"You're sick," Meg cried.

A hand grasped Meg's shoulder. She turned to find Val staring at her.

"One hour."

Val yanked the phone from her hand, a string of Italian spewed from his lips, his eyes narrowed as he repeated Alonzo's name. He drew short of throwing the phone against the wall and pulled Meg close.

"She's alive," Meg said with a whimper. *Barely.*

"You spoke with her?"

Meg nodded, looked beyond Val to the employees who had gathered. "Make them all leave," she whispered.

Rick pushed through as Val dispersed the crowd.

When only the three of them were left, she told them about the call, about Gabi. "Alonzo said his shipments need to be on your charter within the hour. What shipments? Is he talking about the wine?"

Val and Rick exchanged glances.

"What?"

"Heroin, raw heroin is lining the crates," Rick informed her.

"Drugs? Seriously? Alonzo is running drugs?" Meg asked.

"Afraid so."

"Well, he wants them back. If we don't start moving that wine onto your boat, someone is going to clue him in. Gabi didn't sound like she could take another hit without it killing her." Meg stood and started for the door.

"Wait, we need a plan. Following Alonzo's orders is playing into his hands."

"He had me step outside and proceeded to tell me the color of my shirt. Either the man can see us or has someone close by watching for him. Come up with a plan as we pack your charter with wine. We're already ten minutes into the hour."

Rick held up his hand and stopped her. "The minute we load that boat, we become drug runners."

"What choice do we have?" Val asked. "He has my sister."

Meg watched as Val and Rick argued. She didn't add that Alonzo had mandated that she be on board.

"When you boys finish arguing, you can find me at the warehouse." Without more, Meg left the office and went out of the building.

Val caught up with her two minutes later. He left Rick back long enough for him to call Neil and put into action some sort of plan.

Margaret was right, however, sitting around and acting as if they weren't compliant wasn't going to ensure Gabi's safe return.

Val darted around Margaret and pulled her along a shortcut to the warehouse. One that wouldn't be littered with guests. "This way."

She followed, held his hand tight, and shifted her eyes behind them. "I hate to think someone is watching us."

"I will fire everyone. Start over."

"This is crazy. He is crazy. His words were even and practiced, but I could hear the panic between his words."

"I wish we knew if he was the dealer, or the delivery man. If he's only transporting, then the dealer is looking for his drugs."

Margaret slowed and met his eyes. "And how is it you know the ins and outs of drug dealing?"

Val offered a dry grin. "I grew up in New York. Everyone knew someone. Small dealers become big dealers if they don't take their own crap. If Alonzo is the delivery man, then someone is probably threatening him."

"That makes him desperate," she said.

"Desperate men are dangerous."

They rounded the corner to the warehouse and slowed their pace.

"Something else Alonzo said has me puzzled. He kept calling Gabi his wife, his bride. Not in the sense that she was his future bride, but as if they were already married."

Val stopped walking altogether.

Margaret moved beside him.

"Gabi wouldn't—"

"Gabi is higher than the moon. There's no telling what she's done."

Val ran a hand through his thick hair. "Why?"

"I don't know. Maybe if she's tied to him, and he gets his shit back, then he can keep her, you . . . all of us quiet? Who knows the thoughts of a psycho?"

"We need more time, *cara*. Time to learn his plan."

Margaret glanced at the watch on her wrist. "We have forty minutes. Think fast."

Val pulled her along, shouting orders the minute he reached the ears of his employees in the warehouse.

The off-island charter was pulled along his dock. Captain Stephan stood to the side of the ramps that allowed passengers on and off the ship. Only passengers weren't coming or going. In fact, the charter didn't normally sit on the dock at this hour.

"Stay here," he told Margaret as he released her hand.

She looked at the boat and lost color in her cheeks.

It took divine intervention not to throw Stephan into the turquoise waters of the Keys.

Stephan tracked Val's approach with his eyes . . . a smug smile on his face.

Without thought, Val reached a hand up to Stephan's throat the moment he stopped in front of the man, and squeezed. "I don't know what he promised you, but I will promise you this. I will find you and you will pay."

Something hard bit into Val's side. Instead of looking, he eased his grip. Of course, the captain would have a gun. Drugs and guns were synonymous, weren't they?

"Good choice, Valentino." Stephan rolled his head on his shoulders once Val let him go. "Now, don't you have some packing to do?"

Val's fists itched to fly.

They didn't. Maintaining control was paramount. He knew that.

Shifting his focus, he moved back to Margaret's side. Her skin hadn't recovered her normal color and she stared at the boat as if it had grown horns.

The two of them moved back into the warehouse and down into the wine vault. Rick was there, coordinating the packing effort.

Rick was shouting orders, and Val's men fell in place.

Margaret sat on the far end of the cellar, her phone in her hand.

Signaling Rick over, Val said in hushed tones, "If we give this over, there's no need for him to keep Gabi alive."

Rick leaned forward and whispered. "Look closer."

The staff stacked the pallets, but as they did, they pulled crates of wine that didn't belong to Alonzo in the center surrounded by the crates holding the drugs. The ratio of missing drugs would be a third.

"Leverage?"

Rick nodded. "Neil is assembling backup. He's offshore."

Val clenched his fist. "Feels like a trap. I don't like any of this."

"Have a better idea?"

"Call the police?"

Rick offered a smile and a wink. "Neil has done one better."

Val hoped to hell that Rick and his friends were more than just talk.

Margaret caught his attention again. She shivered. Reluctant to let her out of his sight, he removed his jacket from one of the wine racks he'd carelessly tossed it on hours before, and placed it over her shoulders.

"Thanks," she managed.

Val kissed her forehead. She was a strong woman, but it was obvious that everything was taking its toll on her. "Do you need your inhaler?"

She shook her head. "My new daily meds have made big changes. Don't worry about me."

That wouldn't be possible. Val knelt in front of her and captured her cold hands in his.

"I'm sorry this happened, Val."

"None of this is your fault."

She didn't look convinced.

The last of the crates were packed onto a pallet and wrapped before a mini forklift removed them.

Val leaned forward and met Margaret's cold lips for a brief kiss. "You should stay here."

Her eyes grew wide. "No. I can't."

He understood the need to witness whatever was going to happen with his own eyes, but he didn't want Margaret anywhere near Stephan. Then again, he didn't want her roaming the wine vault still filled with illegal drugs either. If someone who had helped them pack up the wine in record time was in with Alonzo, they'd be called out before Stephan left the dock.

Sandwiched between Rick and Val, Margaret walked with them to the charter. The heat outside was close to ninety, but Margaret still shivered. When Val moved away from the two of them to talk to Stephan, Margaret stumbled and Rick caught her.

"I'm OK. Sorry."

She looked positively sick and there was nothing Val could do about it.

Val halted the driver of the forklift before he placed the last pallet on the overloaded boat.

"C'mon, Masini . . . get it in there." Stephan kept a hand in his pocket, the same one Val knew held a gun.

"Only when I know Gabi is safe."

"You don't hold any bargaining chips."

"Pick up your phone and call your boss. Or you can leave with a partial shipment, and once Gabi is safe, you can have the rest."

From the expression crossing Stephan's face, he wasn't prepared for conflict.

"For all I know Gabi is already gone."

A phone started to ring.

Everyone turned and stared at Margaret. She answered . . . "Gabi?"

"Move the crates onto the ship, Masini," Stephan yelled.

Val tried to hear Margaret's conversation and looked at Rick for a hint of what he should do.

"Where are you?" Margaret yelled into the phone.

"Time is ticking . . ." Stephan said with a laugh.

"You see the island? Can you see people?" Margaret was turning away from Rick, looking out over the ocean.

Stephan moved from where he stood, kept his back to the ship, and removed the gun from his pocket. He waved it at the forklift driver. "Move!"

The men on the dock ducked away from the swinging barrel of the gun.

Margaret moved closer to the edge of the dock. "She says she's on a small boat and can see lots of people on a beach," she told them. "No! Don't. We'll find you. You can't swim that far."

Val's heart sank. He'd save his sister only for her to jump into the water, high on God knew what, and drown.

The forklift started to move.

Val's phone rang from his back pocket.

Rick was inching his way closer to Margaret, who didn't seem to notice any of the unfolding drama on the dock.

"You might want to take that call, Masini," Stephan suggested.

The last thing Val needed was an interruption.

Without taking his eyes off Stephan and the gun that was rotating between them, Val answered his phone without looking. "Yes?"

"Your hour was up ten minutes ago. I expected you to take my demand seriously."

The man who he'd once let into his home, allowed the privilege of courting his sister, now sounded deadly.

"Where is Gabi?"

"Bobbing along. Close enough to see her blow up if you don't move faster."

The last pallet was loaded, the driver pulled the forklift away, and the men loading the wine ran.

"Meg?" Rick called her name.

Before Val could tell Alonzo the crates were loaded, Stephan lunged between Margaret and Rick.

Rick had his gun out and pointed at Stephan's head. "Back off."

Stephan shook his head, slow and easy. "Not part of the deal. She goes with me."

All the blood in Val's brain drained to his feet. "No!"

The phone in Margaret's hand hung loose in her fingers. The breeze off the ocean whipped her short hair into her eyes, smoky amber eyes that expressed more than any words spoken.

"Drop the gun," Rick ordered.

"Shoot me, and Gabi is dead."

Val hadn't realized that Alonzo was still yelling into the phone. He lifted it to his ear. "You're wasting my time, Masini," he said. "Pay close attention . . . the next one will blow in five minutes if my shipment hasn't left . . . with your woman."

"Andare all'inferno!"

"I'm going to hell anyway, Val." The words left Alonzo's lips when an explosion drew all their attention to the ocean.

"Gabi?" Margaret screamed into the phone. "Gabi?"

Rick cocked his gun, took a step closer.

Val was sick, felt his life slipping away.

Margaret gasped, her knees buckled. "No, baby . . . hold on. We're coming." There were tears in her eyes. Her lips trembled.

"Do you get my message, Val?" Alonzo asked.

"Four minutes, thirty seconds . . ." Stephan reminded him. "Let's go, Blondie." He nodded toward the boat.

"Christ."

Margaret's feet were in motion, only she was walking onto the boat, not away.

"Margaret, no!"

"He's going to kill her if I don't." She glanced at Rick, briefly. "Ask Judy what sport I excelled in when we were in college."

When her foot stepped up to the boat, Val knew he wouldn't see her alive again. His sister . . . or the woman who had stolen his heart?

Rick uncocked his gun, lowered it.

"Anyone follows us," Stephan said as he backed into the boat behind Margaret, "and this one's dead."

Left without choices, Val stood beside Rick as Stephan released the rope holding his ship to the dock and jumped onto the vessel.

Stephan took hold of Margaret's arm, pulled her phone from her fingers, and tossed it onto the dock. "Wouldn't want you to trace a phone."

He shoved her inside, where he maneuvered the ship away. It didn't take long for him to clear the dock and find speed.

Rick slipped away and all Val could do was stare.

Alonzo was still on the phone.

Frustrated rage built and boiled. Once again, Val was yelling into a phone. "Harm her, and you're a dead man."

"Murder is messy, Masini. Not that I mind it. Now go find my wife and keep her safe. I'll be in touch."

Chapter Twenty-Eight

So hot . . . escaping the sun wasn't possible. And how did she end up on a two-person dinghy?

Her head hurt, but it wasn't bad . . . not as bad as it would be.

Gabi grabbed her head with both hands and started to rock. If only she could sleep. That would be better than waiting for the pain to worsen.

She stood, and felt the boat tip under her bare feet. The white dress she wore at her wedding was hanging off her shoulders. When was the last time she changed clothes?

And a shower . . . she wanted a shower.

The boat tipped again. She slid to the floor, curled into a ball, and closed her eyes.

"Do we have a trace?" Rick asked into the phone.

Val rushed beside Rick as he jumped into a golf cart and released the emergency break.

They were speeding toward the island airport.

Lou stayed behind with orders to lock all employees down. It was obvious there was more than one accomplice on the island. Who they were and what they could tell them might be the difference between life and death for Margaret.

Rick spoke quickly, most of the conversation lost on Val. When he hung up, he relayed their plan.

"I placed a tracking device on your charter when I came over. There's another one on the inside of one of the crates. If the boat and drugs divorce, we'll trace them both."

Some of the tension in Val's head started to relax. "How will we know where Margaret is?"

Rick, who always seemed to have a smile, didn't have a hint of one now. "She's my wife's best friend. Losing her isn't an option."

Val could beat that . . . "She's my future."

Rick offered a nod. "How well do you shoot, Masini?"

"Well enough. I wouldn't take a shot with someone I cared about close by."

They skidded to a halt in front of the airstrip and jumped out. Rick reached behind his back and stopped short. He patted his belt line, removed his jacket to reveal the holster he had strapped to his shoulders. "Son of a bitch." Rick was smiling now.

"What?"

He held up a finger and removed his cell phone. "Hey, babe. No time to explain. Tell me, what sport did Meg excel in during college?"

Val shuffled his feet as he watched Rick listen to his wife. He started to laugh, the sound in complete contrast to the emotions inside Val's stomach.

The sound of a helicopter on approach drowned out the call.

"Love you, too." Rick hung up, smiled. "Learn something new every day."

"What?"

The wind kicked up as the helicopter spun around to land. Val moved back, found himself turning away to avoid the blowing sand.

"Meg was part of a marksmanship team her sophomore and junior years," he yelled. "I had no idea."

"What good is that without a gun?"

Rick kept smiling, reached around his back, and removed an empty holster. "Decent pickpocket skills."

For the first time in hours, Val felt his heart lift.

The pilot waved outside the window for them to jump in.

It wasn't until they clicked their seat belts and were in the air that Val realized they were in a military helicopter.

Neil sat next to the pilot and handed earphones to Val.

Once the earphones muffled the sound of the chopper, and the voices of the men on board could be heard without yelling, Val said, "I thought you were both *retired* Marines."

It was the pilot who answered, "Once a Marine, always a Marine."

"Let's find your sister," Neil said.

Val looked in the direction Margaret sailed. "What about Margaret?"

Rick tapped on a device that sat in the center of the helicopter. It reminded Val of a submarine gauge, or maybe something air traffic control used to keep track of what was in the air. There were blips and dots . . . "The red one is Meg."

"The others?"

"These two are Blake's, positioned to avoid detection . . . and these three"—Rick winked—"friends."

"Looks like a small army."

"Close enough," Neil said.

Rick shoved a pair of binoculars into Val's hands and they all peered out over the ocean.

Time ticked slowly.

Val scoured the ocean, glancing into every boat, every personal watercraft. The only redemption was not finding an empty boat. Even though frustration made his foot tap, he kept looking. Gabi was out there.

An hour into their search, Neil called out and pointed. "There."

The pilot circled around and moved with purpose.

All Val saw was a small boat and a pool of white resting on the bottom of it. The closer they approached, the more hopeful he became.

Dressed in a dirty white dress, her limbs bright red with the sun, Gabi lay with her arm over her head. She wasn't moving.

"How low can we get?"

The pilot moved away from the small craft, but even then, the waves rocked the vessel enough to worry Val that it would tip. Without thought, Val removed the earphones and stripped his shirt over his head.

Understanding transferred from Rick with a look.

Val kicked off his shoes and removed his seat belt.

Rick handed him a chunky radio. Val assumed it was waterproof and held on.

Val felt the wind kick when Rick opened the sliding door.

"We'll move closer," Rick yelled.

Val estimated the height, knew his limits. If there was one thing living his life on an island had taught him, it was cliff diving. With his feet on the skids, Val pushed off, and sliced into the water seconds later.

Once he bobbed over the surface, he gave a thumbs-up, held the radio in his teeth, and swam to his sister's side.

He was winded when he peered over the side of the boat. "Gabi? *Tesoro?*"

She moaned.

He hoisted himself on board, nearly pulling her into the ocean twice before he managed to climb in.

Seawater dripped on her as he leaned close to get a better look.

Her face was drawn, red, with dark spots under her eyes. She'd aged ten years in the week she'd been out of his sight.

Her lips were cracked and bleeding, her hair matted. "What has he done to you?"

Val lifted her arm, felt for her pulse, and noticed all the bruises. Some were angry and swollen. Others were yellow and fading.

She moaned again, but didn't open her eyes.

"What do we have down there?" Val heard Rick through the radio.

He lifted the device, pressed the button. "Alive. Barely. She needs a hospital."

"Do you see any explosives?"

Merda, he'd forgotten about that. He looked under the one seat and noticed a device stuck to the underside. He knew nothing about bombs, but assumed it was. "Yeah. About three inches in diameter, a few wires . . . a light."

Val stroked Gabi's brow as he spoke.

"I'm coming down."

An eternity later, Rick was lowered in a harness. The boat barely handled the three of them, but Val countered wherever Rick stood to keep the vessel upright.

"You've got to be kidding me." Rick laughed when he saw the explosive. He reached for it.

Val stopped him. "Careful."

Rick pushed his hand away. "I built better shit in my teenage backyard." He pulled two wires and the light went out. "Amateur. Alonzo might run drugs, but he knows squat about bombs."

Val didn't realize how fast he was breathing until that moment. "Let's get her out of here."

Val followed Rick's instructions and helped secure his unconscious sister to Rick's frame.

Once they were ready to go, Val said, "Don't come back for me. Get her to a hospital."

"One step ahead of you, Masini. There's a boat on its way to you now." Rick reached into a pocket and handed Val his cell phone. "In case Alonzo calls you directly."

"Got it." Val kissed the top of his sister's head. "Keep her alive."

Rick winked, shot his thumb in the air, and was gone.

———

To say she was scared shitless would be an understatement.

Meg watched Val's island sink away without any trace of anyone following. She considered her options. She could jump overboard and swim away, but outrunning a bullet was impossible. And swimming more than a few hundred yards wouldn't be smart, not with her set of lungs. Then there was the fact that she had no idea if Gabi was safe.

Meg trusted Rick and Neil, knew of their abilities to track and to find. She had to bank on the fact that Alonzo and his shit-pot of men knew nothing about her friends.

How would Alonzo take a two-thirds shipment of goods? Would he shoot her on the spot, or negotiate a swap? Rick had alluded to the cost of each pallet. Close to a million dollars in its current state, triple that after it was refined.

"Where are you taking me?" she finally asked after the sight of Val's island disappeared completely. Jumping overboard now would be suicide.

Could she shoot the captain and take over the boat?

Maybe if he was threatening her with more than a look. Cold-blooded killer, she wasn't.

"You'll find out soon enough."

Asshole.

"How does it feel to know your friends abuse women?"

Stephan didn't comment and continued to man his boat.

The quiet was killing her, so she kept talking. "Alonzo seemed like a complete putz to me. Too stupid to pull all this off."

The captain shifted on the balls of his feet.

"I bet there's someone else waiting to take delivery. Maybe even cut you out of the pie."

Stephan's eyes swung her way, then back to the horizon.

"How well do you know Alonzo anyway? I bet he's not even Italian."

"You talk too much."

And you're fidgeting.

"I'm new at this *held against my will* thing. Am I supposed to sit here and be scared? Is that what Gabi did?"

"Gabi wasn't smart enough to be scared."

That burned.

Sweet, innocent Gabi would never be the same. "You fixed her, didn't you? No chance she'll trust anyone ever again. You must be proud." Meg bit out her last words.

"I never touched Gabi."

"And that makes it OK in your head? Men can justify anything." It was strange how anger took away the fear. With that anger came clarity and the ability to think.

A radio on the control panel offered static and then she heard a male voice. "Alpha to Beta, you there?"

Stephan picked up the simple radio and answered. "I'm here. On target with cargo."

"Any trails?"

"None in my visibility. Yours?"

"We're clear. Continue to target and hold your position once in sight."

Stephan discontinued the call.

Meg found herself squirming. "Alpha and Beta? That makes them the boss and you their bitch."

She didn't see his fist coming until it was on her. She went with the punch as best she could. Pain exploded in her jaw, her teeth cut a nice gouge in her cheek.

"Shut your mouth."

Yeah . . . that sounded good to her.

Chapter Twenty-Nine

Val pulled on the dry clothes offered, slipped into ill-fitting shoes, and made his way to the bridge of the ship that picked him up. He wasn't sure what kind of vessel it was. It moved with the pace of a speedboat but housed a dozen crew members with the capacity of carrying passengers and cargo. The only other similar ships he'd seen were those used by the port authority. This ship, however, didn't have the markings of the ocean police.

Someone handed him a bottle of water. "Thank you."

"Glad we can help."

"Any word on my sister?"

"In the hands of Miami General's finest." The captain stopped him before he could ask. "I don't know more than that. Neil and Rick are back in the sky."

One down, one to go.

The captain pointed at a map similar to what Val had seen on the helicopter. "She's here, we're here." Some of the dots on the map were lit up. Others were just blips.

"What are these?"

"New players? Someone out on a pleasure cruise? Hard to say without a visual."

"How do we get a visual without being seen?"

The captain flipped a few switches, a monitor to his left flickered to life. "Bigger toys."

Val peered closer, realized he was seeing the ocean from thousands of miles above. "Satellite image?"

"Big brother. We just need to narrow our location and focus."

Val stood back. "Who the hell are you?"

"Brenson, Coast Guard DEA division. I worked with Neil, briefly, in the Marines."

"You just happen to work in Florida?"

The captain shook his head. "California, actually. He said there was trouble here and I pulled a few strings."

One of the captain's men stood on the other side of Val, his binoculars in front of his eyes as he scanned the horizon. "We've been on the trail of one of Mexico's finest, or sleaziest, of pushers. His name is Diaz. We captured some of his men, but none brought us close to how the drugs were making it into the country."

"Packed in wine crates."

Brenson shook his head. "Who would have known?"

"I sure as hell didn't. Alonzo has been shuttling wine to my island for six months. God only knows how much was trafficked right under my face."

"These guys are good about making innocent people accomplices. The fear of jail keeps them silent once they learn what's happening."

Didn't that sound just like him and Gabi? Not that Val feared jail. It might be worth it to end Alonzo's miserable life. Val thought of his sister, how she looked as Rick hoisted her limp body into the sky.

And how was Margaret doing? Had she used the gun? Did the man holding her know about it? Had someone injected her with poison?

He shivered.

Jail . . . he could do a little time if it meant Margaret would survive.

Val couldn't decide if he was making a deal with God or the devil.

Probably both.

———

Meg tried not to panic when Alonzo's yacht moved into view.

It had taken over two hours for them to meet, and while she would have liked never to see the man again, she held some satisfaction to know she'd have the opportunity to spit in the man's face.

The two vessels bumped sides, and Alonzo with three of his men boarded.

"Why isn't she tied up?" Alonzo asked, his arms swinging in her direction.

"What am I going to do, fucktard? Jump overboard?"

Her head snapped back with the slap of Alonzo's palm. At least she'd have equal swelling on each side of her face. "I knew you were trouble the minute you opened your smart mouth on the island. Poking your head into someone else's business is bad for your health, Miss Rosenthal."

Meg didn't give him a reason to tie her hands. Keeping them gripped to the railing, she used her words. "Gabi *is* my business."

"Because you're screwing her brother? Or do you consider her a sister?"

He thought calling out what was happening between her and Val would shake her. It didn't. "Yes, and yes," she replied.

He laughed. "That would make me your future brother-in-law by marriage, then, wouldn't it?"

"Why marry her, drug her, then leave her for dead?"

He shrugged, moved away from her to inspect the crates of wine. "Running drugs through the island, making sure Val and Gabriella were tied to me . . . that would keep them silent. Gabi wouldn't last a day in jail and Val knows it."

"She's stronger than you know."

He moved around the crates and Meg tried to move around the railing to distract him. She didn't want him noticing the missing portion of drugs yet. Stephan along with one of Alonzo's men made a show of pointing their guns in her direction.

She held her ground and lifted her hands to her sides. The last thing she wanted was for them to decide frisking her was a good idea.

"My plan would have worked if you hadn't taken a trip to my vineyard. Gabi might still be alive if not for you."

For the first time in hours, Meg felt her lungs constrict.

No, please no. Gabi can't be dead. Not after everything, every risk she'd taken.

"Don't cry, Miss Rosenthal. She was so high she probably didn't feel a thing."

"You bastard." She lunged at the man, only to have two men hold her back. This time, when Alonzo moved alongside her, she did spit in his face.

His deadly stare unnerved her as he took a handkerchief from his back pocket and wiped his face. "I should blow a hole in your leg and toss you overboard right here . . . watch the sharks come and feast."

Meg had to force her breathing to slow. A slight wheeze started to build.

Alonzo ran a hand down her face and gripped her chin with his thumb and forefinger. "But you're my gift. Diaz likes blondes."

The men holding her laughed as if Alonzo had made a joke.

He pushed away from her and boarded his yacht.

Stephan took the helm again, followed Alonzo's yacht.

Within ten minutes, they were narrowing in on an island. From her vantage point, there weren't any inhabitants.

Once in the cove, Stephan dropped anchor and Alonzo shouted orders for her to be dragged on board his ship. There were too many of them to fight, and struggling made her wheeze.

Alonzo pushed her across his deck and over the side to a smaller boat. Under gunpoint, she followed and watched. Stephan and all Alonzo's men moved onto the pleasure ship, and it pulled away from the one filled with drugs.

They were leaving it there.

Which meant someone was going to come and pick it up.

Diaz? The Alpha behind this Beta? And when would the pickup happen? A day, an hour?

Could she swim out to the charter and call for help? She had no idea if Rick and Neil knew where she was. Her mind scrambled for a way out.

One of Alonzo's bigger men pulled her from the boat the second it hit the shore. Before she could scramble to her feet, he placed his foot onto her ass and pulled out a knife.

She screamed as he gashed the back of her right calf.

He pushed her to the sand and jumped back in the small boat.

Blind with pain, she rolled onto her back and cradled her leg.

"Take a long look before you dive in, Miss Rosenthal," Alonzo said as he motioned toward the water. "Those fins aren't dolphins. And they love fresh blood."

"Burn in hell!"

Alonzo laughed, looked at his men as they maneuvered the boat back to his yacht. "People keep damning me today. Must be a full moon."

Meg found her footing and ran behind the safety of the trees.

For the first time since she'd lifted Rick's backup gun from the back of his pants, she checked the weapon. A 1911 with a twelve-round magazine. Perfect, reliable, accurate as all hell.

Ignoring the pain in her leg, she kept her eyes on the receding boat. Once the dinghy full of shitheads inched closer to the fins in the cove, and was too far away for the passengers to make it back to shore, Meg took aim. Three consecutive rounds splintered the wood, startled the passengers, and water started to fill the boat.

A bullet whizzed past, not close enough to do anything but tell her they had ammunition in their guns.

She moved position and located the cap to the fuel tank of the charter.

While Alonzo and his men were scrambling to stay afloat, those on the yacht were trying to move closer to their boss. One man went overboard and started swimming to the larger boat. Meg ignored their efforts and concentrated on her own. It had been a while since she held a gun. And the charter was probably outside of range, but she had to try.

If the charter blew up, someone would see it.

Or so she prayed.

She squeezed one eye shut and forced her breath to slow. It came back, all the training . . . the reason she picked shooting as a sport.

The wheezing in her lungs slowly went away as she counted down.

Squeeze.

Missed.

She lifted the barrel, felt the wind on her face, and lifted a little higher.

Squeeze.

Wood splintered. Nothing exploded.

"For Gabi."

Squeeze.

They were closing in, finally.

Val saw enough on the satellite feed to know there were two vessels next to each other, and a third was following close behind. Just when he started to catch his breath, the blip on the radar disappeared.

"Damn it!" Brenson yelled.

"Where did it go?"

Val swiveled toward the satellite view, the delay a good thirty seconds behind the other monitor.

The charter became a flash of white, and even from miles away, Val heard the explosion.

Brenson picked up his radio. "Move in, all units, move in."

The men on board the ship scrambled. "Full speed."

Val looked up to see a helicopter overhead. He heard Rick's voice on the radio shouting orders.

They stopped the engines cold when they found the wreckage.

His charter was still in flames, much of the hull already becoming an artificial reef.

There were at least two bodies floating in the rubble. Val looked for his jacket or Margaret's red shirt and found neither.

Alonzo's yacht had attempted to flee. The helicopter buzzed over the vessel, letting those on board know they weren't going to outrun them.

It didn't take long for a marked Coast Guard ship to position itself in a way to keep Alonzo from escaping . . . if in fact he was on board. Val had yet to locate him on the deck.

Instead of searching for his enemy, Val scanned the ships and the shore.

A booming voice filled the air. "United States Coast Guard, drop your weapons."

The air was filled with the sound of more air support, the ocean dotted with ships filled with backup. None of it mattered without Margaret.

Val gripped the side of the ship, wanted to swim to the yacht to find her.

The men on Alonzo's deck slowly dropped their weapons . . . one at a time until six men held their hands in the air.

They moved close enough to board the yacht. Val let the guard with guns go first, but wouldn't let them hold him back once the guns of Alonzo's men were taken away.

Alonzo's captain, the man in the pictures with his sister, and Stephan were among those on deck.

Val clenched his fist and pushed his way through the armed guards. "Where is Margaret?"

Stephan offered a smug smile and Val's fist flew.

Something crunched, he wasn't sure if it was his knuckles or Stephan's face.

"Which one is Picano?" Brenson asked.

Val looked again. "None."

"What about out there?"

The two men bobbing dead in the water Val recognized as Julio, Alonzo's cocaptain, and one of the waiters Val employed. "Not him."

They executed a search of the yacht within a few minutes. They brought up the cook from below in handcuffs. No sign of Margaret.

Val's eyes moved to the burning charter.

He wasn't ready to believe she was on board. "Margaret!" His voice carried over the ship, drawing the attention of everyone who could hear him. "Margaret!"

A flash of red limped out onto the sandy beach.

Val's heart wept.

Margaret waved her hands in the air. "I'm here."

Brenson pointed toward her while men moved to dislodge a Jet Ski.

Val blinked, twice, and heard a gunshot.

Everyone froze, ducked. When Val looked again, Margaret was holding a gun and pointing it toward the rocky point of the cove.

Alonzo stood there, taking aim, then a series of shots fell from above.

Val couldn't tell if Alonzo jumped, or was wounded and fell. He bobbed in the water and the Coast Guard launched a boat to go after him.

Dead . . . alive . . . it didn't matter. What mattered was Margaret was alive, safe, and whole.

He rode on the back of a Jet Ski, hit the sand, and ran to her.

Her arms wrapped around him, the gun in her hand fell away. "Oh, *bella*. I thought I lost you. Thank God." Val stroked her hair, heard her sniffling against his chest. "Don't cry, *cara*, I have you."

"Lousy shot."

He inched away to see her face . . . her bruised and swollen face. "What?"

"Lousy shot. Alonzo was a lousy shot." She smiled and winced.

The tension in Val's body dropped, making his knees buckle.

Margaret kept hold.

"*Ti amo, cara.* I thought I lost you." He placed his lips on her forehead, the only part of her face that didn't appear hurt.

New tears formed in Margaret's eyes. "What about Gabi?"

Val placed his palm on her cheek. "In the hospital. Alive."

It was Margaret's turn to slump against him.

"Let's get you out of here," Val said.

When Margaret took a few steps, he noticed the cut on her leg. Without words, he lifted her in his arms and carried her.

Margaret let him.

Chapter Thirty

Meg sat at Gabi's bedside the week she was in the ICU, and pestered every nurse and doctor taking care of her for the entire time she was in the hospital.

Mrs. Masini brought food daily and stayed when she could. But seeing her daughter broken took its toll on the woman. Seemed everyone blamed themselves for Alonzo's deception.

It was hardest on Val. He couldn't stop apologizing to Gabi, no matter how often she told him it wasn't his fault. At night, when Meg returned to the hotel room she'd called home for two weeks, she would often find Val in her bed, waiting for her.

The day before Gabi's discharge, she sat in a chair overlooking Miami. Her silence was a direct contrast to her previous personality. The therapists said it would take some time for her to trust again, some time for her heart to heal.

Meg forced a smile on her face when she walked into the private room and shut the door. The tray of uneaten food sat to the side. Gabi had lost ten pounds and wasn't putting them back on.

She survived Alonzo only to become an empty shell.

Meg placed a designer duffle bag on the bed and focused on the positive. "It looks like you're going home tomorrow."

Gabi moved her gaze from the window to the hands resting in her lap. "That's what the doctor said."

"I brought a bag to help you pack your things."

"Thank you," she mumbled.

Meg pulled a chair closer and lowered her voice. "How are you feeling today?"

It took a full minute before Gabi answered. "Old." She met Meg's eyes, the hurt so deep in her gaze it felt like a knife in Meg's heart. "I feel old, Meg."

In the two weeks it took for Gabi to kick her brief addiction, none of them had actually discussed what had happened. Papers had arrived on the island confirming that Alonzo did in fact marry Gabi while at sea. When Val and Meg asked the doctors about her physical condition, they said she was stable, or improving . . . no details were given. When asked, the doctors told them Gabi didn't want her condition announced to her family. In an effort to give her the privacy she obviously needed, Meg didn't ask, and Gabi didn't tell.

"I can't go back to the island," she said without preamble.

Meg's head scrambled. If not the island . . . to her family . . .

"I can't have everyone staring at me, wondering . . . asking questions."

"That would suck."

Was that a smile on Gabi's lips? Good God, Meg hoped so.

"Where do you want to go?"

"Someplace to start over." She stood, the nightgown she'd worn for a week engulfed her tiny frame. "Someplace where I can scrub his image from my head. Where I can learn to respect myself again."

Meg wanted desperately to tell Gabi that she didn't need to prove anything. Yet, apparently, she did . . . if only to herself.

"A place where you can grab hold of your life and take charge."

Gabi nodded. "Yes."

Meg thought of the strong women in her life. Sam had built her business in the ashes of her torn-up family. Eliza lost her parents when she was young, survived it. Each of them had a crossroads in their lives and rose above adversity to come out on top.

"Come with me."

Gabi blinked.

"To California. We'll have to check with Sam about a job. We can always use help with Alliance."

Some of the pain in Gabi's eyes faded. "A job?"

"An occupation. Supporting yourself is empowering. You'll be so busy you won't have time to look out the window and dwell."

"The social worker said I needed to face what happened in order to overcome it."

Meg nodded. "And you will. In the meantime, you need to take control."

"A job."

Meg stood and took her friend's hand. "A new life."

Gabi took hold of Meg's hand and squeezed.

And smiled.

———

That night, Meg packed her bags and found it was her time to stare out a high-rise window and debate her life.

What did her life even look like anymore? She'd spent over a month of her life buried in Val and his family. Kidnapping, drugs . . . bootleg wine. Everything had changed, and outside of the obvious, Meg couldn't completely tell why.

Watching the light slowly fill Gabi's eyes again reminded Meg that life was meant to be lived. The entire situation with Alonzo, Stephan . . . the drugs, could have had a fatal turn. As it was, the

DEA seized the rest of the drugs in Val's cellars. Two additional staff members had been flushed out and charges were brought against them. Stephan would spend a significant time in jail, and if he ever managed to get out, he'd most likely be a target for the Mexican drug runner who was still out there.

Then there was Alonzo. The man was barely conscious and half-dead when the Coast Guard fished him from the water. Meg held some satisfaction to know that Val shoved a fist into the man's wounds, made him hurt just a little more. He'd made it into surgery, but the amount of holes from Rick, Neil, and at least two others from aboard one of the Coast Guard's ships were simply too much for the ass to handle. He still clung to life, with little chance of breathing off a ventilator.

There weren't many people that Meg truly wanted dead . . . but Alonzo was one of them.

He'd shattered Gabi, and it was going to take a long time to bring her back to the smiling, happy woman she was only a month ago.

The door to her room clicked and Val walked inside. His jacket was on his arm, his tie loose around his neck. He'd been burning daylight hours with rehiring staff, building his virtual defensive walls, and balancing his sister, mother . . . and even Meg.

"Hey," she managed.

"Hey." Val dropped his jacket on the bed and crossed the room. He pulled her into his arms and held her. He did that a lot, just held her as if she were the most precious thing in the world.

"I-I packed."

"I don't want to think of you leaving."

"My flight is at noon." The lump in her throat made her choke. She wasn't an emotional sap, so why was she on the verge of crying?

He drew away and kissed her forehead. *"Ti amo, bella.* We'll figure this out."

A sad smile emerged with his soft words. She never asked what they meant, just thought they were endearing, and from the tone, she felt it, too.

"Gabi is coming with me."

At first, Val held his breath . . . then he sighed and pulled her onto the loveseat. "Is that smart? Shouldn't she be with her mother?"

Meg held his hand, saw the pain in his eyes. "She needs to heal, Val. The island will be a reminder of him . . . of everything. In time, maybe that will change. A change of scenery, people. She needs to control her destiny and not be dependent on anyone other than herself now."

Val didn't appear convinced.

"She smiled today. After she made the decision to move away. She'll stay with me. Sam already offered her a job. I think it's the right move."

"I want to argue, but think you might be right."

"She can always come back, if I'm not," Meg said.

He tilted his head, ran a hand over the five o'clock shadow that never seemed to completely go away since she'd told him she liked the look. He really was one of the most beautiful men she'd ever feasted her eyes on. Not seeing him daily was truly going to suck. Her heart broke a little more as the hours ticked down to her departure.

"Damn it, Val. I'm going to miss you." She slapped a playful hand on his chest.

He captured it and kissed her fingers. "We might be apart by miles, but not here." He tapped their joined hands to his chest.

"I don't do long-distance relationships." She swiped the moisture under her eyes. Damn mascara was going to make her look like a zombie.

Val chuckled. "You don't do sleepovers either."

She rolled her eyes. Her bed hadn't been lonely since Italy.

"Come here," he said, drawing her close. His head dipped to hers and his lips chased away her tears.

He tasted her, slowly, burning the memory of his kiss deep in her soul. Meg opened to him, familiar with the dance of their tongues, and languished in his kiss until he stole her breath.

The soft scrape of his beard left a path of want down her chin, her neck. After only a few weeks, the man knew her body better than any other man cared to explore. The spot behind her ear, the space between her collarbone, the brush of his fingers over her breasts right before he sucked one into his mouth.

He made love to her slowly, drawing her to the bed and laying her down and starting all over again. Head to toe, with plenty of stops in between. When he moved into her, with her, and pushed them both to the point where passion met the stars and flew on past, Meg realized one thing . . . she loved him.

Desperately.

Completely.

Telling him would just make it harder to leave. Instead, she felt the tears gather again, listened to Val say beautiful things in a language she didn't understand, and made love to him until the early morning hours.

They kept quiet the next morning, made love in the shower one last time, dressed, and went to the hospital to gather Gabi and say good-bye.

Val held her hand, kept telling her they were going to be fine . . .

Meg didn't see it. His life was in Florida, and hers was an entire country away.

Gabi woke before the sun. The nurse made her rounds and removed all the needles and medications from Gabi's room.

She showered, dressed, and waited for the doctor's last visit. She hurt, still. Two weeks and her body had aged ten years.

Alonzo had drugged her. The pills he told her were aspirin weren't. The strong opiates left her with headaches. The alcohol he'd given her made it worse. Then the pain had gotten better. She remembered her wedding . . . how Alonzo had constructed the whole thing. She'd been high, even then, but she couldn't say she didn't know what she was doing. And that was the biggest betrayal of all. After that, everything was a blur. The first time the needle had pierced her skin the euphoria had been instant. She remembered, briefly, that it wasn't right. Nothing worked against pain like that. Nothing legal, in any event. He had her out on the ocean for a week. She remembered two days of it.

Once she arrived in the hospital, all she did was beg for more drugs. The staff had to restrain her, give her weaker drugs until she could be pulled off them completely. She was humiliated, damaged.

Gabi shook the thoughts from her head, realized she wasn't alone in the room. "Dr. Hoyt. I'm sorry . . ." she waved a hand in the air.

"Distracted. It's OK, Gabi. I wanted to check on you before you left."

They talked about how she was feeling, cravings for the drug she'd held a brief addiction to. She told him of her move to California and he found a list of doctors to follow up with when she got there.

Dr. Hoyt studied the floor, or maybe his shoes, but he stopped meeting her eyes when he cleared his throat. "I-I ah, I know you've been through hell. But I need your permission about something."

Doctors seldom stuttered, and Dr. Hoyt, who had to be in his late sixties, seemed seasoned enough to speak in complete sentences.

"My permission?"

"It's about your husband."

She shuddered. "Don't call him that."

"Sorry. It's about Mr. Picano."

His image, the one of him smiling as the needle slid in . . . "What about him?"

"His brainwaves are nil, the ventilator is keeping his vital organs moving . . . without it, he will die."

Good. The world would be a better place without him. "What do you want of me?"

"Permission to remove him from the ventilator. The family in Italy has refused to speak to us. We can obtain a court order, but it would be better if you'd allow us to remove the breathing tube."

You need to work through this to get over it, Gabriella. The therapist's words sounded in her head.

Closure . . .

Finding her backbone, Gabi stood. "Take me to him."

Dr. Hoyt's eyes grew wide. "I don't think that's a good idea."

"You want me to pull the plug, that's what it is, right?"

"Essentially."

"Then take me to him."

It was clear by Dr. Hoyt's stance that he wasn't sure what to do.

Gabriella followed alongside Dr. Hoyt, up the elevator, back into the ICU where she herself recovered the first week she was in the hospital. She'd been too disoriented at the time to realize the man who put her there was feet away . . . that the same staff caring for her was taking care of him.

The bastard didn't deserve it.

A hush went over the staff when they saw her enter the unit. Another doctor stood behind a nursing desk, and moved quickly to follow them into the private room surrounded by windows.

She braced herself, wasn't sure what to expect when she lifted her eyes to the man who had nearly killed her.

He was hooked up to more machines than she knew existed.

His face was swollen, nearly unrecognizable; the pasty color of his skin was slick with sweat. The smell of the room was a mixture of the powerful cleaners they used on every floor and death.

She stepped closer, noticed the staff gathering behind her, watching her.

Any connection to the man she'd wanted as her husband, as the father of her children, was gone. How could that be? She thought she'd loved him, at one time. The feeling had never been mutual, she knew that now . . . but it had been real for her.

Or maybe that, too, was an illusion.

He deserved this. Living in a state of not alive and not dead.

The vindictive part of her wanted him to be aware, even if a little bit, of the state he was in.

"Can he hear me?"

One of the nurses answered, "They say that hearing is the last to go."

She moved close, leaned over the bed, and felt her skin prickle. He couldn't hurt her now, but she still shuddered.

"Can you hear me, Alonzo?"

Nothing.

"May God have mercy on your soul." She paused and said what she truly felt. "Because if it were up to me, you'd burn in hell."

She twisted on a heel, grasped the paper a nurse handed her, and signed her name. "Pull the plug, Doctor."

The words left her lips and someone behind her shut down the machine.

The room grew silent, and Gabi walked away.

Alonzo died, officially, twenty minutes later.

Chapter Thirty-One

Gabi was a natural . . . once she remembered where she'd put her smile.

Who knew a woman who'd been sheltered, pampered, and cared for all her life would jump into a full-time job as easily as she did.

Meg knew it was all about distraction, but it seemed to be working. Watching her new friend come back to life was a slow, sometimes agonizing process.

Their first few weeks in the Tarzana house together met with daily phone calls from Val or Mrs. Masini. If Meg wasn't there to talk with Val, he would text her . . . remind her he was thinking about her.

He'd offered to fly out and visit, but Meg kept putting him off. "Gabi needs a complete break. She'll let you know when to visit."

"I want to see you."

"I don't do long distance," she reminded him, not really feeling the words that left her mouth.

"Is that why you sent three text messages yesterday, one with a picture of Michael and Ryder sipping wine?"

"I just thought you'd like to know that everything is working out," she defended herself. Ryder had moved in with Michael, though with the "friends" angle. Meg had never seen Michael happier.

"You want to share your day with me, *cara*. I know the feeling. By the way, Jim sends his love."

Meg found herself smiling into the phone. "Did he offer marriage again?"

Val grumbled. *He's so easy.*

"He did, didn't he?"

"You're taken."

"I am, am I?"

"Yes."

She wanted to see him, desperately. But was afraid walking away again would be impossible. Her life was in California, she kept telling herself. His was not.

Meg heard Carol talking in the background before Val said, "There's trouble in the kitchen I have to take care of."

"Go. I have some last-minute touches on Eliza's baby shower I need to attend to."

"*Ti amo, bella.* Think of me when you close your eyes tonight."

The brat, now she would only think of him . . . his lips . . . his touch. "Good night, Val."

———

Having a home without tiny feet running around made it easy to decorate and prepare for a baby shower. Sam and Eliza insisted on having the shower in the Tarzana home. Between Gabi's and Meg's efforts, they'd prepared a massive pot of homemade pasta, and the sauce was simmering on the stove long before the first guest arrived.

Blue and pink balloons filled the corners of the room, and flowers, candy, and cakes sat on top of every table. Spiked and unspiked punch sat in two different crystal bowls. It was silly and sweet, and perfect for an expectant mom. The guest list for this shower was limited to immediate friends and family. Not that Eliza had any of her own, but her mother-in-law, Abigail, arrived with Eliza and Sam. Behind them, Karen and Judy shuffled in with Gwen. The small Tarzana house was overflowing with less than a dozen guests.

Everyone talked at the same time, made a great show of patting Eliza's expectant belly, and laughed, even Gabi.

The two most likely to fall into the baby world were Judy and Karen, who were doing their best to avoid the questions of when. Meg knew Judy wasn't quite there yet, but Karen seemed to be eyeing Eliza's stomach with longing.

"How do you like California, Gabi?" Gwen asked.

"Dry. I like it."

"The East Coast is sticky," Eliza agreed.

"But green," Meg offered. Not to mention that was where Val lived. What was he doing at that moment?

"Hmm . . ."

"What?" Meg asked Judy.

"Nothing," she replied.

Meg shook her head and glanced at Gabi. Only she was watching Karen stroke Eliza's belly as the baby kicked. *Longing?* Had Gabi wanted children with Alonzo? Had he destroyed those dreams, too?

Meg took Gabi's arm. "Let's see if I've screwed up your mother's recipe."

The distraction worked. When they set out the food, Gabi was smiling again.

They ate, played silly games, and gathered to watch Eliza open dozens of gifts for her unborn child.

Meg watched with interest, but her head . . . her heart wasn't there. It had been over a month since she'd seen Val. Getting over him wasn't happening. Maybe she should tell him to come. Maybe she should jump on a plane. As she sat in a room full of happy women, most of which were married to loving, wonderful men . . . Meg wanted to join them.

"Earth to Meg?" Judy said with a wave in front of her eyes.

The room had grown silent and everyone stared at her.

"Where are you?" Sam asked with a smile.

Her eyes started to sting with moisture. "I-I think I'm in Florida."

Gabi reached over, took her hand. "Then why are you here?"

She offered a sad smile. "For you . . . for Alliance. This is where I live."

"But your heart is somewhere else." Sam was as wise as she was beautiful.

"I'm trying to stop thinking about him. Long-distance relationships don't work."

Sam laughed. "Blake is in Europe right now. Won't be home for two weeks."

"You're married, it's different."

The air in the room thickened and the attention moved off the expectant mom to Meg. "You won't know if Val is marriage material if you don't spend more time together," Judy said.

Only Meg did know he was the right material. She loved the man, but was afraid to tell him. Sadly, she fell into the group of women that wanted to hear the words come from him first. Maybe then she would believe they could do this long distance . . . or make a different arrangement.

Gabi squeezed her hand. "You've given me plenty of sound advice I needed to hear from the moment we met, so let me give you some. My brother loves you."

Meg scoffed.

"And you love him."

She snorted, tried to deny it. The women in the room shook their heads, rolled their eyes.

"Nothing else matters."

"You matter. My job."

Gabi's sad smile made Meg pause. "I'm OK, Meg. I appreciate your desire to help me survive the summer, but how do you think it would make me feel to know I destroyed your chance of holding on to love?"

Oh, God . . . she was right.

"As for your job . . . Eliza has successfully found clients and helped manage the business from Sacramento. Gwen continues to scout clients when we're in Europe and during social events."

Karen tipped back her spiked punch. "I managed the phones and assisted clients the entire time you were in Florida."

"The point is," Sam said, "Alliance might have a home base here, but we're everywhere. A second office in the Keys sounds good to me. I love that part of the country."

Judy nudged Meg's arm. "So, do you have another excuse or hurdle to jump over, or should I call the airlines?"

Her fingers tingled, her heart knocked a few times in her chest. "I-I need to pack."

Gwen sat back, crossed her legs as if she'd just signed a multi-million-dollar deal. "Not really. Lingerie maybe."

"And condoms . . . unless you want this." Eliza patted her stomach.

Meg stood, felt doubt creep in. "What if it's a mistake?"

"What if it is? You won't know if you don't try. Since when are you a quitter?" Judy's challenging tone made Meg's feet move.

Twenty minutes later, Eliza's driver was tossing her suitcase into the back of a limousine and she hugged her friends good-bye.

———

Gabi watched Meg leave and was the last to return inside the house.

Her new friends gathered to help Eliza unwrap her gifts and eat cake. They laughed, shared stories, and gave Gabi advice about the neighborhood. More importantly, over the last few hours, she didn't think of Alonzo once.

They were cleaning dishes when a knock sounded on the front door.

Gabi heard the door open and someone say, "Oh, my."

"Sorry to interrupt."

Gabi dropped the soapy dish and grabbed a towel. She rounded the corner and smiled. "Val!"

The women started to laugh.

Gabi opened her arms and hugged her brother, his movements hampered by the roses he held in his hand. "You look lovely, *tesoro*." He kissed both her cheeks.

"What are you doing here?" As if she didn't know.

He looked over her head and frowned. "Looking for Margaret."

Judy started laughing first, then the infectious sound spread until the room filled with joy.

"Stop," Eliza giggled. "You're going to make me pee."

They laughed harder.

Sam glanced out the front window. "Is that your cab?"

"Yeah."

"You might want to stop them," Gwen told him.

Judy pushed past the crush of people standing at the front door and outside to hail the cab.

"What's going on? Where's Margaret?"

"En route to you, actually," Sam said.

"Excuse me?"

Gabi glanced at the clock on the wall. "Her flight leaves in an hour. You might make it in time if you leave now."

Judy stepped back into the house, patted Val on the back. "You know, Romeo, you might try calling before flying in. This is becoming a habit."

Val slapped the flowers against his leg, turned around to leave. "Nice to meet you all."

When the door shut, Sam said, "That's your brother?"

"Yes."

Eliza lifted one brow. "Go, Meg!"

———

The last-minute flight was delayed. Still, Meg couldn't stop smiling. She probably looked like she was on drugs, but she couldn't help it. She picked up her cell phone and considered calling Val to tell him she was coming.

Her screen blinked with a text she didn't hear ring in.

Don't get on the plane. The text was from Val.

"Now boarding, flight fifteen sixty-eight to Miami."

Meg glanced at the hordes of people lining up with their boarding passes in hand.

Her hands shook. How do you know I'm at the airport?

Gabi told me.

She swallowed, hard. You don't want me to come? Her heart started to crumble.

No, bella. I want you to walk out of the terminal so I can hold you right now.

She stood, dropped her purse, spilling its contents. You're here?

Yes.

Meg scrambled to fill her purse, shoved the unused boarding pass into her pocket, and sprinted through the airport.

He stood in a suit, of course, jacket wrinkled, tie loose around his neck. His ruffled hair evidence of his fingers running through it. The scruff on his chin made her mouth water, the flowers in his hand made her sigh.

Their eyes caught and she slowed her pace as she walked closer.

There were no words, just a hungry embrace and an indecent kiss that lasted much too long for a busy airport.

When he let her up for air, she asked, "What are you doing here, Masini?"

"Claiming you, *mi amore*."

"We almost passed in the air again."

He nipped at her lips, kissed her again as if he couldn't help it.

"I missed you," he managed between kisses.

"I missed you too, damn it."

His blistering smile lit the terminal.

Val pushed the flowers he held into her hands. "These are for you."

They were battered, a little wilted, but the most precious flowers she'd ever seen. *You're a sap, Meg!*

"Thank you."

He lifted a finger, then patted his jacket pocket. "I have something else for you."

The smile on her face froze as he removed a small box from his pocket and dropped to his knee.

Her heart kicked hard in her chest, her lungs squeezed.

Breathe!

Meg was vaguely aware that people around them stopped moving and started to stare. Was this really happening?

Val locked his eyes on hers. "I met you on a Monday, you enchanted me by Wednesday, and seduced me by Sunday. You've stolen my heart, Margaret. For that, I want to selfishly steal yours. But I know I can't take what you won't give me, so I'm going to ask for it. *Ti amo, bella*." He paused. "Do you know what that means?"

She shook her head.

"It means I love you."

Ti amo . . . an endearment that sounded beautiful, but held little meaning, now said so many things.

Happy drops of sunshine fell from her eyes.

"Marry me, *cara*. Give me your heart." He opened the box. It held a vintage engagement ring, the round diamond sitting in a cluster of smaller stones that tapered down the side of the setting.

She moved her gaze from the box to Val's eyes.

He held his breath, waiting.

She dropped her purse, heard change rattle across the floor of the airport, and held out her left hand.

Val smiled, removed the ring.

She clenched her fist at the last second, made him look at her. "Fair warning, Masini. That goes on, it doesn't come off."

He tossed the tiny black box over his shoulder and slid the ring home.

Meg fell to her knees, stared at her future. "I love you."

The sound of clapping didn't stop her from kissing him over and over again.

Epilogue

The simple silk dress for an island wedding proved perfect for the warm winter day. Sapore di Amore held only family and friends.

Meg's parents flew in the day before and were all too happy to welcome a son-in-law to their family. However, in the words of her mother, "You don't have to marry him to stay committed."

That was when Meg learned that her parents, the throwbacks from the sixties flower children that they were, apparently never signed on the dotted line. Crazy how weddings and funerals brought out family secrets. Not that it mattered. Her parents adored each other.

Val and Meg spoke their vows overlooking the Caribbean, Judy stood beside her, and Lou stood beside Val.

A nondenominational minister performed the ceremony, because what else could it be and keep all sides of the family happy?

When he pronounced them husband and wife, Meg heard her grandmother say mazel tov, and Mrs. Masini say amen. When Val kissed her, she sang her own praises.

Hand in hand, Val led her into the reception, where the party was in full swing. The first to intercept them was Jim. He pulled her away from her husband and sighed. "I guess this means I have to look for a new woman," he teased.

Meg flashed her ring and a smile. "'Fraid so. I'm taken."

Then Jim kissed her. Full-on kiss on the lips.

"Hey!" Val said from the side.

"Just kissing the bride, Val." Jim winked and walked away, his eyes already on wife number six.

Meg stopped Val from going after the man. "You have nothing to worry about, Masini."

He removed two flute glasses filled with champagne from a passing waiter's tray and moved to the mic, pulling her alongside him.

He tapped a spoon on the side of his glass, captured the attention of their guests.

"Thank you all for coming."

Some of the guests mumbled, lifted their glasses in the air, and drank.

"I've heard it said that a man takes a wife . . . but those of you who know Margaret, know that it's she who has taken me."

A collective sigh went over the crowd.

"I built Sapore di Amore without realizing exactly why. Over the past few months, I figured it out. I built it for my family, yes, but I built it for you." Val stared into Meg's eyes, lowered his voice. "The short time we were apart, I knew Sapore di Amore meant nothing without you here." He kissed her fingertips. "Thank you for saying yes, *bella*."

"Thank you for asking."

Val lifted his glass in a toast. "To my beautiful wife, Margaret Masini."

She sipped from her glass and took his lips.

When cheers ensued, she pulled away and whispered, "I think you can call me Meg now."

Acknowledgments

Thousands of preventable asthma-related deaths happen every year. Having seen some of those tragic moments with my own eyes, I wanted to create a heroine who suffered with the disease. While Meg is fictional, her lack of care for her health is not. Many ignore their symptoms until it is too late. If you have asthma, don't disregard your symptoms. Changes in medicine happen every day. Stay on top of your medication and see your doctor.

Now, it's time for me to line up all the handshakes and heartfelt thanks.

Sandra aka Angel Martinez aka my amazing critique partner. You've put up with Michael's story dragging through many books . . . but as you can see, he does get his HEA. Know that you inspire my every Michael. Thanks for pushing me.

Jane Dystel, for always having my back.

Again, Kelli Martin, for getting just as excited about another Bybee book as I do.

For JoVon Sotak, who doesn't force a synopsis, aka suck-nopsis, of my books . . . believing I can deliver something readers will want to read is an awesome thing.

For the Montlake team and everything you do to help my work sing. Thank you all.

Now let's get back to Meg . . . when I told you I wanted to write a character with short blonde hair and a sassy mouth, I asked you to come up with a name. When you failed to deliver one, I used yours. And why not? You sing like an angel, cuss like a sailor, and are married to an Italian. Now if only you had a Jewish grandmother and lived on a private island in the Keys . . .

Love ya, darlin'.
Catherine

About the Author

Photo © 2012 Lindsey Meyer

New York Times bestselling author Catherine Bybee was raised in Washington State, but after graduating high school, she moved to Southern California in hopes of becoming a movie star. After growing bored with waiting tables, she returned to school and became a registered nurse, spending most of her career in urban emergency rooms. She now writes full time and has penned the novels *Wife by Wednesday, Married by Monday, Fiancé by Friday, Single by Saturday,* and *Taken by Tuesday* in her Weekday Brides series and *Not Quite Dating, Not Quite Mine, Not Quite Enough,* and *Not Quite Forever* in her Not Quite series. Bybee lives in Southern California.